The Artist's Missing Muse

Miss Hayward and the Detective series

By Helen Goltz

Atlas Productions

A catalogue record for this book is available from the National Library of Australia

Proofreader: Heather Thompson.
Cover images: Harsanyi Andras, Kathy SG, Shutterstock.
Cover design by Atlas Productions.

Dedicated to a woman ahead of her time, my mum,
Merle Frances Goltz (nee Watson),
I miss you.

Also in the Miss Hayward and the Detective series:

Murder at the Freak Show
The Artist's Missing Muse
Mystery at the Asylum
The Mortician's Clue
Murder in Bridal Lane

Chapter 1

Miss Matilda Hayward inclined her head to the side and studied the painting in front of her. She was no artist or art critic, nor did she take a great interest in art – writing was her passion and since securing a position with the *Women's Journal* and working with the respected editor, Mrs Dora Lawson, she felt rather pleased with herself. She was a woman with a career path despite the less than enthusiastic acceptance of her new role by her family matriarch, Aunt Audrey, and Matilda's new beau, Detective Thomas Ashdown. In all fairness, he didn't discourage it but didn't encourage it either. Looking at the painting Matilda tried to keep a neutral countenance but, truth be told, the painting was awful and it shouldn't be – it was a Marlon Dominey original.

'Well then,' her friend and fellow writer, Alice, said as she joined her.

Matilda looked to Alice for her thoughts.

Alice lowered her voice. 'It's rather awful, don't you think?'

Matilda stifled a laugh. 'Thank goodness. Yes, awful is kind. I thought it might have been brilliant and I was too ill-advised of the art world to know the difference.'

Alice studied it some more. 'I too am no art expert, but my father has a fine collection. This is not nearly as good as Marlon Dominey's past collections – I saw one of his exhibitions in Sydney before I arrived here.'

'I wonder if he has lost his inspiration?' Matilda whispered.

'Hmm, he's lost something,' Alice agreed, and the ladies moved on to the next of his paintings hanging in the exhibition. Matilda glanced around for their dates. Her eyes easily found Thomas Ashdown, Detective, in the room. Tall, dark, lightly bearded and handsome. His eyes met hers for just a moment and softened. Her brother Daniel broke their gaze, distracting Thomas with a nudge as he passed him two filled flute glasses of champagne – one for Thomas and the other to give to Matilda. Daniel picked up another two for himself and his date, Alice, on this, their first outing together. Matilda watched two of her favourite men walking towards them bearing the flutes.

'Champagne for you, Miss Doran,' Daniel said, offering the glass to the young English beauty who had escaped a less than desirable partnering in England to spend some time in the colonies – Australia. Having taken a job at the *Women's Journal* as well, she had become firm friends with Matilda. As a consequence, she was warmly welcomed into the breast of the Hayward family, to Daniel's great delight.

'Cheers,' Thomas said, raising his glass. 'This might help us discern if the art is any good or not,' he said in a low voice.

'It's not something I would want hanging in the drawing-room,' Daniel responded in an equally low voice. 'Have we seen enough? Shall we depart and find somewhere to dine?'

'Best idea you have had tonight,' Thomas agreed.

'Daniel and Thomas, before the speeches?' Matilda scolded them, and Alice laughed.

'No, you are right of course, Matilda,' Thomas said with a wry look to Daniel, his childhood friend whose sister he had just officially asked to court after years of friendship. 'Let's make our way around and enjoy the exhibition… we might find one we like,' he muttered.

'Thank the Lord they're serving alcohol,' Daniel said, swallowing half his glass in two easy gulps. His comment earned him another stern look from his sister Matilda. He gave her a wink.

'It was so good of your brother, Gideon, to get us tickets for tonight,' Alice said in her British accent. 'Everyone is talking about the exhibition.'

'God knows why,' Daniel continued, and earned a glare from a fellow guest. 'Poor Gideon has a disaster on his hands.'

'I feared as much,' Matilda agreed, 'and the showing does not seem to be overrun with patrons. Gideon has sold very few of the paintings.'

Matilda dropped her programme and Daniel and Thomas both reached to claim it for her. Her brother rose, leaving Thomas to be chivalrous. Thomas dusted off the program and returned it to Matilda. Her small, slim hand touched his for a moment, the warmth of his skin, the strength of his hand. Her eyes rose from the programme to look at him.

'Thank you, Thomas,' she said, holding his gaze as if no one else was in the surrounding room. Daniel noticed, cleared his throat, and Matilda dropped her gaze. Thomas stepped back slightly, giving his best friend a smirk – Daniel was hardly one to lecture on impropriety.

With a little colour rising on her cheeks, Matilda turned to Alice. 'Mrs Lawson is quite happy for us to co-author a small article on the exhibition for the *Women's Journal*.'

'Let's do so!' Alice exclaimed. 'It can be our second co-authored piece.' She lowered her voice. 'However, it might be difficult to write the piece, when I can't, in all honesty, say I like any of the works.'

'Hear, hear,' Daniel agreed and raised his glass.

'There's your brother, Gideon, now,' Alice said, looking across the room to a young man who looked like her date, Daniel.

'Yes, he doesn't look happy,' Matilda said. 'He's only managed the gallery for a short while,' she explained to Alice, 'but he's attracted some big names for showings.'

'He does look a lot like you, Daniel,' Alice said, looking from one brother to the other.

'He is devilishly handsome,' Daniel agreed, and Thomas smiled and shook his head.

'If you ask me, he looks somewhat agitated,' Thomas added, studying Gideon's expression and movements.

Matilda nodded. 'I think you are right, Thomas. I imagine the response to this showing hasn't been all he hoped.' She bit her lower lip as she watched her brother from afar.

'But Marlon Dominey is still a big name in the art world

regardless of what we think,' Alice said, looking at the nearest painting hanging on the wall.

'They are saying he's the most talented artist of his generation,' Thomas agreed, and Matilda gave him a surprised look.

'I do my homework,' Thomas told her.

'I can't see it,' Daniel said.

Thomas gave a small shrug. 'Me either. The art world is in trouble if this is our best offering.'

'Oh, and what was the last thing you painted?' Matilda teased Thomas as she turned and looked up at him.

'My house,' he retorted and made the group laugh.

'A fine job you did of that too,' Daniel said. 'You're good with a brush.'

'Thank you, it's been said before,' Thomas agreed.

Matilda laughed again and shook her head at their antics. 'But what did the critics say of your house painting?'

'A masterpiece in white,' Daniel quipped. He turned his attention to his date. 'Speaking of masterpieces, did I mention you looked beautiful tonight, Miss Doran?' He admired her red evening gown, which set off her blue eyes.

'Why, I think you might have, Mr Hayward, but thank you again,' Alice said coyly.

The matchmaker in Matilda couldn't help but smile; they looked most handsome together and Daniel was smitten. Thomas cleared his throat. Daniel's ease at complimenting put him in the awkward position of now having to compliment Matilda again. But Matilda stepped in before he formulated a sincere response.

'I think we all look rather splendid, even if I say so myself,' she said and then nodded towards the front of the room. 'Gideon's coming our way.'

They turned to see the youngest male of the Hayward family coming towards them. It intrigued Matilda – it wasn't every day she got to see the rascal of the family, one year her senior, looking so mature and sensible. He shook hands with a few gentlemen and bowed to the ladies as he made his way to her group.

'Miss Doran, Matilda, Thomas, brother, glad you could make it,' he said.

'Thank you, Mr Hayward, for the tickets, it's very exciting,' Alice said, all manners. 'But where is the artist?'

'Where indeed? Gideon asked under his breath. 'He was due here some time ago and we are late for speeches.'

Just as the words left his lips, there were noises from across the room, and spontaneous applause broke out. The group looked to the entrance where a confident man had walked in with a beautiful woman on his arm.

'That's him, is it not?' Matilda asked, 'Marlon Dominey?'

'It is, excuse me,' Gideon said and left the party to go greet and organise the guest of honour.

Matilda's eyes widened. Marlon Dominey was the most handsome man she had ever laid eyes on. His dark hair brushed back from his face highlighted a square jaw, deep brown eyes, and a smile that could best be described as seductive. She felt herself blush. The woman on his arm was a match for his beauty – dark-haired, full red lips and tawny eyes. She sashayed in, her hand looped through his arm. Her figure was a perfect hourglass, and her red gown showed it to perfection. She did not leave his side as they made their way to the front of the gallery, accepting greetings and applause on their way. They made a handsome couple with an air of mystery. Matilda was mesmerised; they appeared so glamorous and worldly, so European, perhaps. She felt like a young girl in their presence.

'Oh my, isn't she glamorous,' Alice said, eyeing the woman on Marlon's arm.

Thomas did the gentlemanly thing and feigned disinterest, and Daniel took the question figuratively.

'She's a little too showy for my liking,' he said.

'If only the paintings had as much presence as the artist,' Thomas said for Daniel's ears, but Matilda overhead.

She agreed, her thoughts interrupted by Gideon introducing the guest of honour for the evening. A robust round of applause welcomed him, and Marlon gave a small bow before speaking.

'Ladies and gentlemen, I apologise for our tardiness,' Marlon began and the guests all appeared to have forgiven him immediately as they watched him, enamoured. He continued, 'the dusk light on the beautiful river of your city inspired me, and Sapphire and I had to admire it.'

A small murmur of appreciation rose from the audience, and spontaneous applause broke out. Matilda glanced to Thomas, who gave her a raised eyebrow and restrained himself from rolling his eyes. She gave a small smile and returned her attention to studying Marlon's muse. Sapphire, so exotic and womanly – full-figured and glamorous. Matilda could not imagine what it must be like to be someone's muse, to inspire their work and creativity. It did not occur to her that beside her, Detective Thomas Ashdown, who had known her since they were children, stared at his own muse: Matilda, his first thought every morning and last thought at night. The woman he wanted to keep safe from harm, provide for, and make happy. She looked at him again to find him staring at her. Thomas righted himself and returned his attention to the speeches.

'I am glad to be here, to extend my stay in your beautiful country for another season and my thanks to the owner of this fine establishment, Mr Steinman and the Fine Art Gallery Manager, Mr Hayward for the opportunity to display my art for you,' he began. 'I cannot with a clear conscious say that I have sacrificed everything on the sacred altar of art, for I have not.'

'That would appear obvious,' Daniel muttered.

Marlon continued. 'My muse, Sapphire, and I have enjoyed ourselves too much to call our visit and my creations suffering. To gaze upon the beauty of your city—'

Matilda tuned out as she looked around the room. The audience was in the palm of Marlon's hand as he charmed with his words and beautiful face. But a glance at Thomas, Daniel, and some other young men showed the men dragged along to the event under sufferance were not quite as enamoured.

Thomas leaned towards her and she whispered, 'His inspiration and creativity from our city does not seem to have met the canvas. I wonder if all is well between Marlon and his muse.'

'Will you be writing that in your article?' he whispered.

'Heavens no!' She returned her attention to the speaker.

Marlon was finishing his speech: 'My enduring creative partner reminds me that the best part of any speech is brevity and so be it. Thank you again.'

There was much applause as the artist and his muse gave small bows and then began to meet the guests.

'Can we get out of here now?' Daniel asked.

'Yes,' Matilda said, 'your duty is done.' She took one more look at Mr Dominey's beautiful muse, never imagining for a moment what might befall Miss Reubens in the very near future.

Chapter 2

Detective Harry Dart arrived at the office not long after his younger partner, Thomas. The pair had a comfortable routine – Harry, a few years short of hanging up his badge and enjoying his retirement – had been teamed up with the young gun. Thomas's ambitions sat well with Harry who could mentor and not feel the need to be in the limelight or line of fire. He also recognised the young gun's talent and wasn't averse to rising on the success of their crime-solving rate to see out his career.

'The Mrs made you a sandwich,' Harry said, entering and passing over a wax-wrapped bundle. 'I told her your nephew, Teddy, was a chef and living with you now, but she appears to have this soft spot for you.'

'She's a saint is Mrs Dart.' Thomas said, gratefully reaching for the sandwich. 'Thanks, I'm starving,' he muttered and took no time unwrapping it and taking a large bite.

'So, did you buy a painting?'

Thomas snorted and tapped the small headline on the bottom of the newspaper front page. Swallowing his bite, he exclaimed, 'God no, I could have done better myself after a few stiff drinks.'

'I'd like to see that then. Let me know when you'll be taking up the brush,' Harry joked. He leaned over the edge of Thomas's desk and read the headline aloud: 'Artist's work unredeemable.'

'That's being kind,' Thomas said.

'Oh dear,' Harry said and proceeded to read the review: '*The last time I saw work as deluded as Mr Marlon Dominey's recent collection, I was in a children's playground and could excuse it. Scrambled and wasteful, it may be time to rinse out the brush.* Harsh!' Harry said.

'But close to the truth,' Thomas said. 'There was little to admire amongst the lot except for the ladies in our company, of course.'

'Ah, the delightful Miss Hayward and her writing friend. And to think you got to spend the entire evening together uninterrupted with not one dead body or a good mugging to interrupt you,' Harry joked.

'Good of the city,' Thomas agreed and started on the second half of the sandwich.

A knock at the door made both men turn sharply to the intruder.

'Ah, don't bother taking off your coat, Harry, you've got a body, a dead one,' the crusty desk sergeant clarified and handed him a slip of paper. 'That's the address. The coroner said he'd meet you there.'

'Thanks, John,' Harry said, taking the paper as Thomas rose and wrapped his sandwich.

'I'll finish this on the way.' He grabbed his hat and coat and followed his partner down the hallway.

'Well, that was a short-lived reprieve from crime,' Harry sighed.

'Where's the body?' Thomas asked as he caught up and they descended the office stairs into Roma Street to fetch a hansom cab.

Harry looked at the note with the victim's name, address, and a few scribblings of explanation on it. 'Just across the river. Oh, there's a coincidence,' Harry said. 'The deceased is an artist. Maybe your artist?'

'His works weren't good but not bad enough to bump him off, surely,' Thomas said and Harry chuckled.

A hansom cab pulled to a stop in front of them and Harry gave the driver the address.

'What was your artist's name again?' Harry asked.

'Marlon Dominey.'

'Hmm.' Harry shook his head as they stepped into the carriage and seated themselves. 'He couldn't have a normal name like Fred, could he?'

'That would be most unartistic,' Thomas agreed. 'So, is it him then?'

'No, we're off to the studio of Benjamin Bannon,' Harry said, pocketing the slip of paper. 'I wonder what the poor bloke did to deserve a visit from the grim reaper.'

'A disgruntled customer, an unhappy lover, a muse misrepresented,' Thomas guessed, and finished the last bite of his sandwich, pronouncing it excellent as he balled the waxed paper.

'A jealous rival with a critical review in today's paper,' Harry added, and got a look of interest from his partner.

The hansom took the Victoria Bridge across the river to South Brisbane and, exiting at their destination, Harry settled the fee with the driver. 'Not short of a dollar then,' Harry said, taking in the area. 'This is the studio and residence, I believe.'

Two young police officers stood at the entrance to the small terrace house and already neighbours and interested parties were hovering around outside.

'No reporters yet,' Thomas said, relieved.

'That'll be short-lived,' Harry agreed. 'What do we have, lads?' he asked the constables.

The senior of the two policemen spoke up.

'Sirs, the dead man is an artist who lives on the right of the terrace house. His studio is on the left. The housekeeper, who comes early every morning to prepare his breakfast, could not find him when she went to announce his breakfast was ready. She did not enter his room when she saw his bathroom door closed but called us immediately after not being able to get a response.'

'How did she even know he was home?' Thomas asked.

'They had a system, Sir,' the younger constable answered. 'He left his keys and hat at the entrance when he was in, but she was not to disturb him until breakfast was ready. If she arrived and they were not there, she cleaned and left.'

'Righto.' Harry nodded. 'Where is she?'

'She's next door with a neighbour, Sir, having a cup of tea.'

'Where's the body?' Thomas asked, cutting to the chase. His partner always looked after the matters of the heart where others were concerned.

'We found it in the bathroom, Sir, in a most unusual pose, but we have touched nothing,' he assured the detectives.

'Good work, men, thank you,' Thomas said and, with a nod to the two constables, he entered the building with Harry on his heels. They took the stairs to the top floor, as advised. The building was beautifully outfitted, with rooms to the right of the staircase, and a large room that appeared to be the studio to the left.

'Strange,' Harry muttered at first sight from the doorway. The room was pristine, not their usual death scene. The white and cream embossed wallpaper was amplified by the light streaming in through the windows.

'Good light for an artist, I imagine,' Harry said.

The body was not in sight from the living area, and Harry entered tentatively while Thomas remained in the doorway, studying the room. Nothing was out of place – the desk was neat, the paintings were straight, the curtains tied back, the ornaments and lamps upright and intact, and not a mark on the flooring.

'Ready?' Harry asked after a few minutes, and Thomas nodded. They made their way to the bathroom and Harry pushed the door open wider. The room was large, adorned with glossy white bricks and gold fittings.

Both men's eyes widened with surprise. Sitting in a large green enamel claw-footed bathtub was the victim, the artist Benjamin Bannon. He sat as if alive, perfectly still and looking forward, his hands placed on either side of the bathtub. The detectives moved closer to find there was no water in the bathtub and the artist was naked or appeared to be from the waist up. His lower body was buried under leaves – autumn leaves of every colour that filled the bathtub to a quarter full.

'Well, that's one of our better death scenes. Perhaps you'd expect that from an artist or his murderer,' Harry said, thinking aloud. 'No obvious sign of death unless we burrow through those leaves,' he added reluctantly.

Thomas studied the tub, sniffed, and moved a few handfuls of leaves.

'There's no obvious wound or blood evident. He has got a strange tint to his skin, don't you think? He might have been poisoned,' Thomas suggested, studying the stiff, pale body of the victim.

'Detectives?' A voice called from the other room and Thomas stuck his head out of the bathroom to find the coroner had arrived. Dr Patrick Nevins entered, his cane tapping lightly on the parquetry flooring.

The men greeted each other.

'The stairs give you hell, Patrick?' Harry asked the coroner, ten years younger than Harry, but looked the same vintage with his grey mop of hair, glasses and a limp courtesy of a childhood accident.

'Always,' he sighed, 'I just wish they'd all die on the ground floor.'

The men chuckled.

'Well,' Dr Nevins said, pausing in the bathroom doorway. 'A most considerate death scene, so clean.'

'Indeed, even artistic, one might say,' Thomas agreed.

Dr Nevins tapped his way over to the bathtub and looked in. He nodded and smiled.

'What? What does that expression mean?' Harry asked him.

'I understand this is the artist Bannon… Benjamin Bannon?'

'Correct,' Thomas said.

'I think you will find this is a self-portrait, emulated.'

Thomas snapped to look at the doctor, his breath hitching. 'Where is it now, the portrait?'

'I don't know,' Dr Nevins said with a shrug, 'but Bannon's manager or agent may know.'

Harry spoke up. 'The Hayward brother who manages the gallery…'

'Yes, Gideon Hayward,' Thomas said. 'He could find it for us. One moment, Doctor, please.'

Dr Nevins nodded and stepped back. Thomas explained: 'I just need to take in the scene now that it has a different interpretation.'

Harry and the doctor exchanged looks, well used to Thomas's quirky traits. After a few moments, Thomas stood straighter, exhaled, and looked at the two men.

'Thank you, I'm done if you are Harry?'

'I'm finished,' Harry agreed.

Dr Nevins began his observation of the body. 'The portrait, it's called something like *An Artist Bathing in the Season* or similar. Quite lovely, I saw it and some of his other work when he was on tour last year.'

Thomas paced. 'An artist killed in a style emulating his own successful work.'

'I'll have a time and cause of death to you later this afternoon,' Dr Nevins said as he moved the leaves from the body. A small, red puncture wound in the lower leg was barely visible, and he made a knowing sound. 'Looks like he might have been injected with a substance.'

The two men glanced over the edge of the tub at the mark and then left the coroner to his work and went to question the housekeeper and neighbours.

'I wish all our death scenes were as gentle,' Harry said.

'It's odd,' Thomas said. 'No clothes lying around, perfectly positioned, no evidence of a struggle, and someone knew his work. Why that painting?' He continued to mutter as he went down the stairs.

'The timing on the back of Marlon Dominey's exhibition and bad reviews is interesting,' Harry added.

'Indeed,' Thomas agreed. 'I just hope Matilda and the ladies of the *Women's Journal* don't feel the need to report this crime.'

His eyes scanned the small group waiting outside and, on this occasion, it relieved him not to see the woman who filled his thoughts every waking moment.

Chapter 3

Nearly every desk at the office of the *Women's Journal* was occupied when Matilda entered that morning, and a relaxed and happy atmosphere filled the room. It was to be expected, after all, the fortnightly newspaper had gone to print yesterday and the pressure was off for another week before the next deadline approached.

Matilda greeted some of her fellow writers, the illustrators, and typeset ladies as she made her way to her desk and removed her hat and placed her bag nearby. She glanced to Mrs Lawson's office hoping to get an audience with her mentor, but several other ladies were already in there with their notebooks in hand, most likely planning next fortnight's major features. Matilda only worked several days a week and was assigned stories, unless she had an idea that was accepted. She saw Alice making a pot of tea in the office kitchen area and gave her a wave.

'I hear the artist's showing was a disaster,' Georgina Urry said, approaching Matilda. She dropped in the seat opposite Matilda's desk, wiping her hands on a small discoloured cloth to remove the smudges from her pencil.

Georgina was what Matilda's housekeeper, Harriet, would call a rough diamond; a heart of gold, but needed some buffing.

Matilda sighed. 'Sadly, yes. The gallery itself was beautiful, the guests most glamorous, the champagne delicious, but the paintings…'

'Tea?' Alice asked, carrying a small try with a pot, milk jug and several cups.

'Please,' Matilda said.

'Ooh, I'd love one, thanks,' Georgina said. 'My mother says I drink far too much tea, which encourages me to eat more biscuits and thus I am putting on weight and will never find a husband.'

Matilda groaned. 'Ah yes, we must all maintain our figures for the purposes of finding a husband.'

Georgina gave a small, throaty laugh. 'Apparently so. It does not matter that I've got a good job, I'm good at what I do—'

'—You are great at what you do,' Matilda cut in and Alice nodded with firm conviction.

'Thank you,' Georgina said, looking delighted at their praise. 'So I told my mother that I am perfectly capable of looking after myself and do not need a husband unless I desire the company.'

'Bravo,' Alice said, 'I couldn't agree more. Fortunately, I had a very handsome date last night whose company I would like to enjoy again,' she said with a cheeky smile in Matilda's direction.

'One of my brothers,' Matilda informed Georgina.

'How many are there?' Georgina asked, reaching for a biscuit from the plate on Alice's tea tray.

'Four, but some days it seems like more, especially when Daniel and Gideon are so boisterous.'

'And which one do you like?' Georgina asked Alice.

'Boisterous Daniel,' Alice teased, 'and Gideon is the owner of the gallery that staged Marlon Dominey's exhibition last night.'

Matilda nodded. 'The paintings were awful, Georgina. You are an artist with an eye for good work; you must see them for yourself and let us know what you think.'

'I have read two critic's reviews in this morning's papers and I wondered if the exhibition might close earlier than the promoted date – although the reviews might attract an audience who want to see for themselves just how awful they are,' Georgina said.

'That is a possibility and could be good for business, I guess,' Matilda agreed.

Georgina continued: 'I'm partial to landscapes. I am not keen on this fine art focus on beauty for beauty's sake.'

'Fear not,' Alice added, 'there was little beauty in last night's offerings.'

The ladies shared a quiet laugh and talked as they sipped their tea. Before Alice could offer seconds, Mrs Lawson's office door opened and the editorial ladies filed out. Mrs Lawson came to the door and, on seeing Matilda and Alice, invited them in when they were finished with their tea.

'Best not to keep the boss lady waiting. Thanks for the cuppa, Alice,' Georgina said and, rising, took her cup and a second biscuit and departed.

Matilda and Alice armed themselves with their notebooks and pencils. Alice juggled the tea tray with several cups of freshly brewed tea still in the pot, and the ladies headed to Mrs Lawson's office.

'Will you take tea with our meeting, Mrs Lawson?' Alice asked, standing in the doorway with the tray.

'Delightful, yes please.' Mrs Lawson rose from behind her desk and returned to the small meeting table in the corner of the room where Matilda and Alice set themselves up.

Alice poured.

'Well, a minor dilemma for you if you were hoping to write a positive review of Marlon Dominey's exhibition,' Mrs Lawson said. 'Do you think it is as bad as the critics' state?' she asked of the young ladies.

Matilda nodded, and Alice invited her to explain.

'Mrs Lawson, it truly was awful, although I would value Georgina's opinion. The critic who said it was a clash of colours and an affront to nature perhaps sums it up best. Alice has a better appreciation of art than myself, but there was little to find beautiful or skilled in the collection.'

Alice handed Mrs Lawson her tea and placed the remaining biscuits close by.

'Yes, I'm sorry for the artist and for the gallery owner and Matilda's brother who manages the gallery,' Alice agreed.

'Most unfortunate,' Mrs Lawson agreed. 'So do you have a thought on the angle of your article?'

Matilda knew Mrs Lawson would have several thoughts, but she was in the practice of not offering those until she heard what her writers came up with. She liked to challenge them, and it was wonderful for her employees to find their voice and not be just the voice of the editor. She was greatly admired.

Alice spoke first on Matilda's invitation.

'I would still like to do the piece but thought maybe we could focus on the women in his art,' she said.

'Go on,' Mrs Lawson encouraged Alice.

'Well, many of the paintings on display last evening featured women, or a woman – his muse, Miss Sapphire Reubens – embedded in the environment. Some were quite violent. I would like to interview Mr Dominey about his representation and interpretation of women and nature.'

Mrs Lawson smiled and nodded. 'Alice, I think that is an excellent topic.'

Alice blushed with the praise and Matilda smiled at her friend happily.

'If you wished to work in a comment from Mr Dominey about his reaction to the critics' reviews, I am sure our readers would welcome that,' Mrs Lawson added. 'Deadline midday of Monday next week?'

Alice beamed. 'Thank you, Mrs Lawson, yes that's perfect.'

Mrs Lawson turned to Matilda.

'Would you like to work with Alice on that piece? I like to partner my writers if I require them to call on men. Or do you have another idea you would like to explore?'

Matilda nodded. 'I love Alice's idea and I would like to suggest another piece to run with it, at your discretion.'

'Go ahead,' Mrs Lawson encouraged her.

'I would like to do a piece on the influence of an artist's muse and, in particular, Mr Dominey's muse.'

Matilda watched for Mrs Lawson's reactions, and her eyes widened with interest. Matilda continued.

'Last night, Miss Sapphire Reubens was very confident and comfortable in the limelight on the arm of Mr Dominey. I would like to know how they met, how she inspires him, what other muses, if any, he has had. And I would like Miss Reubens' views on being a muse as well.'

'Yes, I love it,' Mrs Lawson said. 'I am happy to commission both articles. Same deadline but be sure to do the interviews together or see me if you need a chaperone. Agreed?'

'Thank you, Mrs Lawson, that's very exciting,' Matilda said.

Rising, the two ladies took their notepads, pencils and tea tray and were departing when outside they could see a stirring amongst the ladies. There was much excitement as ladies gathered around their deputy editor, Mrs Betsy Purcell.

Mrs Purcell waved to Mrs Lawson and headed towards her office, but stopped as Mrs Lawson, Matilda and Alice headed to meet out in the open office area.

'What has happened?' Mrs Lawson asked.

'An artist has been murdered and posed in the fashion of one of his portraits,' Mrs Purcell said.

Matilda gasped and looked over at a shocked Alice, who promptly put the tea tray down before she dropped it.

'It is most shocking and the police are interviewing people on his street now,' Mrs Purcell continued.

'Do you know his name?' Mrs Lawson asked.

'Not Marlon Dominey?' Matilda spoke up.

'No, an artist by the name of Benjamin Bannon,' Mrs Purcell said. 'He had the showing last year featuring the change of seasons.'

'I do recall, it was quite beautiful,' Mrs Lawson said. 'Well, that is distressing news.' Then she clapped loudly to get everyone's attention.

'Ladies, there is a murderer in our town. Any appointments or interviews that you have in the future while undertaking work for the *Women's Journal* must be done in pairs. That applies to our advertising ladies as well, even if you know your clients. Understood?'

A murmur of agreement went up from the ladies on the floor.

'Until further notice,' Mrs Lawson added, and then turned to Matilda and Alice, 'especially any interviews in the company of artists.'

Matilda felt her pulse racing. She couldn't wait to talk with artist Marlon Dominey and she crossed her fingers that Thomas was the detective assigned to the Benjamin Bannon case.

Chapter 4

Later that evening, Matilda left her bedroom and made her way down the stairs for dinner. Cook never minded how many came to dinner at the Hayward household, even on short notice – there was never a shortage of food and leftovers were devoured quickly. But she was a stickler for eating on time when the meal was ready and at its best.

'Ah, I was just about to hurry you along,' Harriet, the Hayward housekeeper, said, standing at the bottom of the stairs, her hand on the banister. She had been with the Haywards from before Matilda was born. On the death of Matilda's mother, Harriet had stepped up, running the household for Mr Hayward with his brood of four boys and Matilda. These days, her hair was greying and worn in her customary neat bun, her grey dress and lace collar a recognised self-imposed uniform.

Voices carried from the dining room.

'Goodness,' Matilda exclaimed on reaching the lowest step, 'don't tell me Elijah and Gideon are gracing us with their company. I'd forgotten they live here, they are so seldom home.'

'They may be three-and-twenty, and spending a lot of time at their club these days, but if I should mention to them that Cook is doing a roast, they somehow find their way here on time,' Harriet said, with a smile. 'Having said that, Daniel's not here.'

As she said the words, the front door swung open, slammed close, and they could hear footsteps hurrying down the hallway. Daniel appeared moments later, pulling off his hat and coat. He smiled at seeing the two ladies.

'Just on time,' he said, looking windblown.

Cook's head appeared around the corner and she gave Daniel a sly smile.

'Lucky, my boy,' she said in her thick Irish accent, 'or I'd be giving your brothers an extra-large serve, I would.'

'Wash your mouth out, Mary,' Daniel said, shocked.

Cook laughed and disappeared back to the kitchen to serve. She had been with the family as long as Harriet. Despite many offers to go to grander homes with bigger salaries, including Aunt Audrey's, the Hayward family suited her lifestyle and now in her mid-fifties, she did not welcome change.

Matilda entered the dining room and greeted her brothers and father. Mr Hayward sat at the head of the table, looking neat and handsome in his ornate waistcoat; as the next eldest present, Daniel took his place at the other head of the table setting.

'Well, isn't it nice to have nearly all of us here,' Mr Hayward said, looking at his brood, 'not that we can expect Amos to dine with us midweek now that he is a married man.'

'I bet he misses it, though,' Elijah said. 'His cook is no match for our Mary.'

Mr Hayward chuckled. 'Best we say grace for fear Audrey hears about it and makes us do extra penance on Sunday. Elijah, why don't you do the honours, I hate to think what Gideon would come up with,' he said with a small sigh and smile at his youngest son.

'Right you are, Pa, but make it quick, Elijah,' Gideon agreed. His twin said a quick blessing and Harriet brought out two large plates of roast vegetables, followed by a gravy boat and a platter of perfectly cooked roast turkey… the roast beef was kept for the Sunday family lunch tradition.

'How was your day, Matilda, dear?' Mr Hayward asked.

'Pa, most exciting. I've been assigned a story, well Alice and I are both to request an interview with Mr Dominey.'

'My artist?' Gideon said, gratefully taking the plate of roast turkey from Harriet's hands and offering it first to his father on his left.

'Your artist,' Matilda confirmed.

'And Alice will be with you if you get the interview?' Daniel asked, his intent obvious.

Matilda smiled at him. 'Do not worry, Daniel, I will ensure that despite how handsome Mr Dominey is, she will not lose her heart to him.'

Daniel looked far from happy.

'Don't worry Dan, Marlon has his hands full with his muse,' Gideon said. 'Miss Sapphire Reubens is quite a beauty. You should have seen her, Pa.'

'Oh, she is so elegant and worldly,' Matilda agreed, and

Daniel looked happier that the artist might not notice his Alice.

'For fear of being indiscrete,' Mr Hayward started, 'did the death of the artist impact your gallery today, Gideon?'

Everyone started talking about it at once now that the head of the family had introduced the topic.

'Surely, Gideon, Mr Dominey, is not under suspicion, he had his own gallery exhibition that night,' Matilda said, serving herself some baked potatoes as Elijah held the platter for her. She served his plate at the same time.

'If he arrived on time, he might be off the hook. But he was late,' Daniel said. 'Depending on what time Mr Bannon died, Marlon could be a suspect.'

'He was late, wasn't he?' Gideon pondered on that. 'We need Thomas here to give us the time of death. I'm surprised you don't know already, Matilda,' he ribbed his sister.

Matilda smiled at her brother; she had not told the family of their courting, although she knew Thomas had asked permission of her father. Then she realised her brother was not referring to her closeness to Thomas but her nose for a story.

She breathed out and tried to save face. 'If I had seen Thomas today or could have got to the scene of the tragedy, I might have more to share,' she said with her chin up, smiling at Gideon. 'It is early days yet.'

'Have you heard anything at the gallery, Gids?' Elijah asked his twin.

'Not about the artist's death, but I must say the bad reviews for Marlon's work did us no damage. I had a steady stream of paying guests today keen to see for themselves just how awful the paintings really were, so I am not complaining,' Gideon said.

'Did you think they were awful when you secured the exhibition or hadn't you seen them yet?' Mr Hayward asked.

Gideon shook his head. 'Marlon showed me several pieces which, while I knew they weren't as good as his past efforts, I thought they had potential. Unfortunately, they didn't reach that potential.' He said and shrugged. 'Marlon is still a big enough name to warrant the exhibition, but next time, we will need to sight his work before agreeing.'

'Do you know if Marlon and the deceased artist knew each other personally?' Matilda asked Gideon.

'Yes, they have met several times. I suspect there's competitiveness between all the artists trying to make their name and living, and maintain patronage,' Gideon said, 'and Marlon Dominey was particularly jealous of his fellow artists.'

Matilda turned to her brother with a raised eyebrow, and he smiled at her.

'Yes, you can tell your detective that, but I'll be sure to share it when he interviews me and no doubt he will, he's thorough,' Gideon said with a smile to Matilda. 'He gets what he wants.'

'He's always been very determined,' Daniel agreed and smiled, 'now more so than ever.'

She looked from one brother to the next. Clearly, word spread fast.

'Really you two,' Elijah stepped in to help his sister.

'Remember what goes around comes around. So, if you persist in teasing Matilda, just remember she is Alice's friend, Daniel, and you might need a good word said on your behalf. And Gideon, you want some stories about your gallery in the *Women's Journal,* don't you?'

'Indeed, thank you, Elijah,' Matilda said smugly, with affection towards her ever sensible, peacemaking brother.

*****

Once dinner was finished and appropriately appreciated, Matilda remained in the company of her father, her brothers having taken themselves to their clubs.

'I wanted the chance to talk with you, dear,' Mr Hayward said, pouring himself an after-dinner glass of port and offering Matilda the same; she declined. They sat fireside, enjoying the quiet of the household. Cook had gone home for the evening and Harriet had retired to her own rooms in a wing of the household where she had resided for many years.

Her father got straight to the point. 'Thomas has spoken to me about courting you. I know you are a progressive young lady and I want you to choose a partner that makes you happy, but it is respectful that he asked. Has he made his intentions clear to you?'

Matilda felt herself blushing. 'He did, Pa, at the art gallery exhibition. When did he speak to you?'

Mr Hayward sipped before answering. 'Last week, but we had spoken about it before.'

'How long before?' Matilda asked, a look of astonishment on her face.

He grinned. 'It's fair to say that young man has held a flame for you for some time. I thought he'd never get to it.'

Matilda's eyes widened with surprise. 'Really? But our affections have only really come to the fore in the last few months, maybe six months.'

'Your affections, maybe,' he said, and smiled at his daughter. 'Thomas on the other hand has looked out for you since you were children. He's a smart enough young man to know not to rush you, and I think it was good for him to live a little in the world before becoming serious as well. He's focused on his career, got his home in order, and enjoyed society a little,' Mr Hayward said with delicacy.

Matilda scoffed. 'I'm sure he has. But you could hardly call us serious at this stage, Pa.'

'No, but you are both of an age to be serious. So, Matilda, if you don't reciprocate his feelings with the depth that he feels, do the honourable thing and release him now,' Mr Hayward said, becoming stern with her. 'He's a fine young man from a good family with a wonderful future. I don't want to ruin his relationship with this family or have his feelings or intentions trivialised.'

Matilda studied her father. 'But what if we begin and the relationship does not survive, will I be shunned from the family? Or would Thomas?'

Mr Hayward chuckled. 'Neither of you.'

Matilda smiled. 'I was just being dramatic. I have genuine feelings for him, Pa, and I don't want to see him with anyone else. My only concern is that he must support what I want to do.'

Mr Hayward nodded. 'It will be challenging, I believe. He won't want you putting yourself in danger when you have a nose for a story. It will be difficult for you, too. With his career, he will be absent often, unreliable with his social commitments, and also often in danger.'

Matilda nodded. 'I understand.'

'But,' Mr Hayward continued, 'you are an independent young lass who will have no problem filling your own time and he may find comfort in having someone to talk with about the trials of his day, and a fresh perspective if he chooses to share his work with you.'

Matilda nodded. 'If he wants a pretty and ornamental lady who will distract him from the ugliness he is often exposed to, then I'm sure he knows better than to court me. I'll be asking him questions about his cases.'

'No doubt. I suspect that won't come as a surprise.' The pair laughed at the scenario. 'But you will still be beautiful while doing so and charm him nonetheless,' Mr Hayward continued. 'Anyway, I am very happy about it, my dear. Your darling mother, if she were here, would have handled this much better than me, asked the right questions, and helped prepare you. I am sorry I can't live up to that.'

Matilda softened. 'Pa, you are my world. I love the opportunities you have created for me, and I am sure Mother is looking down in agreement that you have done a wonderful job. I'm grateful.'

Mr Hayward nodded his thanks, too emotional to speak.

'Having said that,' Matilda lightened the mood, 'I've no doubt Aunt Audrey will have plenty to contribute on Sunday at lunch.'

Mr Hayward gave a resounding laugh as he thought of his sister, who took the role of family matriarch – in the absence of Matilda's mother – very seriously, and had taken it upon herself to try to partner all the children with little success. Except for her favourite Hayward, Amos, the eldest, who married Minnie.

'Yes, there's something to look forward to,' Mr Hayward said and brightened.

Matilda groaned. 'Thank you, Pa.'

He laughed again.

Chapter 5

Thomas stood near the board in his office and stared at his chalk notes concerning the murder of the artist, Benjamin Bannon. He had wanted to call on Matilda last night; she had only just accepted his intentions and now he had spent several nights on this and other minor cases.

'So, that's my thoughts. What do you think?' his partner, Harry asked, pacing nearby.

Thomas looked at him, an expression of panic on his face. He hadn't heard a word.

Harry laughed. 'You've not heard anything I said, have you, son?'

Thomas sighed. 'Sorry Harry, I was thinking.'

Harry narrowed his eyes. 'Not about this case, I imagine.'

Thomas gave him a look of indignation and then gave up. Harry could see right through him.

'You've asked her, haven't you? You've asked to court Miss Hayward?' Harry said, and Thomas nodded and gave a small smile.

'Well, at last. Good on you, Thom. You'll make a grand pair.' Harry looked genuinely thrilled.

'It is early days yet, Harry. But I'm happy,' he said and couldn't help but smile. 'Now, to this case, sorry. We've not got a lot.'

'That's for sure,' Harry said. 'The neighbours heard nothing. The landlady left early that evening to spend the evening with her sister and did not return until after us the next morning, and the housekeeper arrived early only to find Mr Bannon dead.'

Thomas nodded. 'The housekeeper said he had a lady friend, but not a relationship. That's all she'd say, so I don't know if that means a girlfriend, a woman he shouldn't be seeing, or a paid companion – but I doubt she'd refer to her as a lady.'

'She seemed the type who called a spade a spade,' Harry agreed. He pulled a chair out that was tucked under Thomas's desk, swung it around to face the board, and sat down.

Thomas sighed. 'Time of death around 7pm, and we are yet to have it confirmed, but Bannon was most likely injected with a poison. We have a huge clue in the manner in which he was murdered.'

'A work of art,' Harry agreed. 'So, the killer must know Bannon's work.'

'Yes. Suspects for his murder… Did he have a muse or a patron? Was he in a relationship other than the lady friend mentioned by the housekeeper?' Thomas posed questions as they came to him. 'Was he financially stable? Did his last exhibition go well? Who might have been jealous of him? Was he in debt?'

'Woah, woah,' Harry said, 'you're exhausting me. Let's just get back to fundamentals… the basics. We'll eliminate the first round of enquiries and see what turns up, shall we?'

Thomas nodded. This was where he most appreciated Harry's input, when he approached each case with a police officer's perspective. Thomas had been fast-tracked and had not experienced the years on the job walking the beat.

'You're right,' he said to Harry. 'Let's start with the art community and find out where that painting is that he emulates in death.'

'Then we can seek fellow artists who may not have felt warmly towards Mr Bannon,' Harry added.

'Gideon might be able to help us with who the agent is and where Bannon last exhibited. We can get Marlon Dominey's details from him as well.'

'I'm keen to check out just how bad these Marlon Dominey paintings are while we're there,' Harry said, rising.

Thomas grabbed his coat and hat from his desk.

'Trust me, an art connoisseur like you will agree they're awful.'

Harry enjoyed the joke. 'Connoisseur, hey? I won't bring my cheque book then,' he said, and gave Thomas a grin. 'But first—'

'The coroner,' Thomas said finishing his sentence.

They had gone but half way down the hallway when the coroner appeared.

'Ah, I was in the building for other business so brought you your results,' Dr Patrick Nevins said, his limp not as pronounced given he was walking on a level surface. He handed the men a file.

'Thank you, Patrick,' Harry said opening it and showing the results to Thomas.

'Injection, as expected,' Thomas said and looked up at the coroner.

'Yes. Subtle, in the leg. It was a lethal dose and I'd say professionally done. I've kept all the leaves should you wish to study them,' he said with a smile and tipping his hat continued on, their thanks in his ears.

'To the Gallery of Fine Arts then,' Harry said.

'Let's,' Thomas followed him. He was looking forward to seeing Gideon; for that brief time, he'd be in Matilda's world, even if it was her brother he was visiting.

*****

Thomas pushed open the glass door to the *Gallery of Fine Arts*, which looked quite different in the light of day compared to his recent evening visit in black tie with the champagne flowing. Gideon came out of the back room on hearing the chime of the doorbell.

'Ah, I was wondering when I might expect you,' he said, and grinned at Thomas. The men shook hands.

'You remember my partner, Detective Harry Dart,' Thomas said.

'You look a little better than last time I saw you,' Harry said with a grin, and shook Gideon's hand.

Gideon sighed. 'Yes, there's been a few rough nights…

led astray by my twin. He never knows when to stop,' he said and Thomas laughed, thinking of the sober and sensible, Elijah who would never be considered a bad influence.

Gideon continued: 'So, you want to know about Marlon Dominey's movements?' He indicated several couches where they could sit at the front entrance to the gallery.

The gallery was presently empty, but had only just opened. A young woman appeared from the back room; Thomas would describe her as bookish.

'Shall I make tea, Mr Hayward?' she asked.

Gideon looked at his guests. The men all wore dark suits and there was no sign that they were detectives, they may have been art-loving patrons.

Harry spoke up. 'I'd be grateful for a good cup of tea, thank you, love,' he said to her and, without waiting for the consent of the other gentlemen, she headed to the kitchen.

'We want to ask you about Marlon and the deceased Benjamin Bannon, too. But, Marlon first, what can you tell us about his movements that night of the exhibition opening?' Thomas asked.

Gideon sat back. 'He arrived late, as you know. He said he and Sapphire were admiring the light on the river, as you know. You left before he did,' Gideon recalled, 'and he probably stayed about ninety minutes after you. I heard Sapphire was keen to go out and continue enjoying the evening.'

'Any idea where?' Harry asked.

Gideon nodded. 'One guest who is known for having an interest in the arts and deep pockets, suggested they return to his home and enjoy his cellar. He took a small group with him.'

'Marlon would be foolish to say no to a potential patron, I imagine,' Thomas said.

'Indeed. Do you know what time Mr Bannon was murdered?' Gideon asked. He hoped he'd have something to tell Matilda before she knew it.

'Yes,' Thomas said, and gave no detail. 'With your help, we also need to speak with Mr Bannon's agent and to any artists who had an acquaintance with Mr Bannon.'

Gideon nodded and changed to small talk while his assistant appeared with the tea tray.

'I hear you will be courting my sister.'

'A very fortunate man,' Harry answered, before Thomas had a chance to say so. 'A most handsome couple, wouldn't you say?'

'Well one of them,' Gideon teased and laughed at Thomas's expression. 'It's about time.'

Thomas smiled and shuffled uncomfortably 'Yes, I'm delighted that Matilda has agreed to see me. I'll protect her, I assure you.'

'I know you will, but you'll have your work cut out for you,' Gideon joked.

As soon as the assistant left, Thomas returned to the subject at hand – work – which he was more relaxed talking about.

'Can you help us with those contacts – Marlon's details, the patron he left with that night, Bannon's agent and his last showing?' he asked Gideon.

'I'll get my contacts book.' Gideon rose and disappeared into the back office.

Thomas frowned as he thought over Gideon's words. Was his personal life now going to be as challenging as his professional life?

Chapter 6

The canvas mounted on the easel seemed to mock him. He felt nothing. No rush to feel the brush in his hands, the soft sable hairs dipping into his paint, to make his first mark on the canvas or to see the vision once in his mind come to life bigger, better, brighter than he had dreamed. Nothing.

'Damn,' he hissed between clenched teeth. Marlon Dominey wanted a drink but it was only 11am. He ran a hand over his face and threw the brush across the room. There was a reason for his slump and he knew it.

It was her – Sapphire – once his greatest inspiration. But now, anytime, every time he looked at her, he did not feel the same rush of passion and inspiration. Anger rose within him. He was weary of her games, the way she flirted with everyone, and feeling the constant burn of jealousy. He had tolerated Sapphire's behaviour because he needed her and painted better with her in his life. If he was being honest with himself, since the reviews came out for his gallery exhibition, he had felt nothing but pure anger and hatred for Sapphire, for everyone. But especially for her.

He could hear her coming up the narrow stairs to his studio, humming a tune that he had also come to despise. He was the laughingstock of the art world this week and she hums a tune as if nothing has changed in the world.

'Darling,' she said on entering.

Momentarily he was taken by her beauty; any man would be, but it had served its purpose and served him well. She moved closer and wrapped her arms around him, looking up into his eyes. He kissed the top of her head.

She glanced at the canvas and back at him.

'Marlon, my darling, you are an artistic genius. Those critics have never picked up a paint brush in their lives. How dare they presume to judge your work?'

'Thank you,' he said, tired of hearing false statements of inspiration and support. Hollow words of encouragement. Marlon continued to hold her, one hand pressing Sapphire closer, the other hand moving up her back.

He knew she could read him, after all, Sapphire traded in intimacy and knew when she had hooked a man's affection. He had studied her long enough for his canvas to anticipate her beauty. It was only a matter of time until her persuasive ways would bring about the return of inspiration. After all, vanity and pride were foremost in her list of sins.

He allowed her to reach higher to his lips, and just as he was about to touch her lips with his own, he pulled back slightly to watch her. He saw her eyes widen in surprise. She gave him a teasing smile and tried again, but Marlon moved slightly away from her reach again.

He studied her look of confusion, the slow blink of her eyes and the realisation that maybe she hadn't yet got his full attention. And then he ran his hand up her beautiful swan-like neck and touched her face. She relaxed and smiled.

'I love you,' she said, her voice soft and enticing.

Now he leaned down closer, allowing his lips to come within touching distance of hers. His hand travelled back to her throat, and he pressed her tighter against him. Marlon tightened his grip around her throat.

In confusion, she bucked away, and he held her closer.

'Marlon,' she gasped, 'stop, please, you're hurting me.'

He increased his grip, tightening on her throat, watching her fear and confusion unfold. Her beautiful eyes stared at him in shock. She began to fight him, but he was too strong and well-prepared for her reaction.

Sapphire was gasping for air. Marlon watched in awe at the ebb and flow of her life. He studied her struggle, the emotions across her face, and then he released the pressure a little.

'Stop,' she gasped. 'Marlon, why?'

Now he kissed her as she struggled to pull away from him.

'Don't fight me,' he snarled and moved his hand back to her throat. He studied all her reactions as they played across her beautiful features. Then she stopped fighting and her body became limp.

Marlon moved her body to the chaise lounge and laid her across it. He didn't have time to arrange her. It wasn't necessary.

He was full of energy and inspiration. He had to capture it now while she lay still and while her energy filled him.

This would be his finest work. He smiled as he thought about Benjamin Bannon. How envious Bannon would be of him now if he weren't dead.

Chapter 7

As if her ears had been burning from the conversation between the two detectives and her brother, Miss Matilda Hayward entered the Fine Art Gallery accompanied by a rather tall, colt-like woman. The bell above the door announced their arrival.

'Matilda.' Thomas stood on seeing her, and Harry followed.

'Thomas! Detective Dart, how good to see you both,' she said, smiling.

'And you, Miss Hayward. May I say how lovely you look,' Harry said, offering a small bow.

'Thank you, Detective Dart.' Matilda smiled with pleasure. The fitted bright red-coloured dress she wore was a recent gift from Aunt Audrey, who often surprised her niece with dresses she thought might catch the eye of a suitor. Matilda was not complaining.

'May I introduce Miss Georgina Urry, our illustrator at the *Women's Journal*.'

The party exchanged greetings and as Harry spoke with Georgina, Thomas moved to Matilda's side. He took her hand and kissed it. 'This is a pleasant surprise,' he said, his eyes travelling over Matilda's pretty face, her honey-coloured hair tied back neatly and adorned by a stylish, matching red hat with a black ribbon.

Gideon re-entered the room with his contacts book, his assistant trailing behind him.

'Matilda,' he exclaimed, 'back to see the paintings again in the light of day and make up your own mind?'

'Unlikely, Gids,' she said. 'Hello, Miss Warren. We didn't get to talk at the opening, you were so busy.'

'Miss Hayward, it is lovely to see you again. Yes, your brother does overwork me,' she said with a smile and confidence that belied her mousy appearance.

Matilda laughed as Gideon rolled his eyes. When introductions were done, Matilda turned her attention to Thomas and Detective Dart. 'So, what brings you here then?'

'We might ask the same of you,' Thomas said curiously.

'Where is Alice, Miss Doran, today?' Gideon asked.

'She is reporting at a suffragette gathering in the city,' Matilda said and looked at each man in turn challenging them to say something. Not one said a derogatory word. Matilda smiled. 'Well done, all of you!'

Gideon gave her a wry look. 'We wouldn't be game.'

Matilda laughed. 'Poor Miss Urry has had to accompany me as our editor, Mrs Lawson, insists that we travel in pairs.'

'Oh, I am always happy to get out of the office on an excursion,' Georgina assured them. 'An illustrator rarely gets to venture out, and what better place to visit.'

'Ah, our brother Daniel is an illustrator,' Gideon told her. 'He just got a court appointment.'

'Oh, the lucky duck,' she said. 'I would love to talk with him about his experience and find out how he acquired that role.'

Thomas gave Gideon a small shake of his head as a warning; he got his best friend Daniel the job and did not want Miss Georgina Urry pressing him to recommend her.

Matilda continued. 'You are both so talented,' she said diplomatically. 'So, Miss Urry and I are here to seek an introduction to the artist,' she said with a nod to the paintings on the wall. 'Mrs Lawson has commissioned Alice and me to write two articles on Mr Dominey's representation of women in art and on the value of having a muse like Miss Sapphire Reubens.'

'Quite the glamorous lady,' Gideon added.

'You are not intending to meet with Marlon Dominey and interview him, surely?' Thomas asked, his tone abrupt.

The present guests silenced at his tone, and all eyes turned to Matilda.

'Well, that burst of liberalism was short-lived wasn't it, Thomas?' Matilda said.

Harry chuckled and disguised it as a cough.

'I'll write those contacts out for you both then,' Gideon said, addressing the detectives and Matilda. He moved to the counter with his books. His assistant followed.

'Shall we have a quick look at the artwork while we are here, Miss Urry?' Harry asked. 'Let's determine for ourselves if the critics were correct. Being an illustrator, I expect some insights from you.'

'A fine idea, Detective,' Georgina said, taking his arm to tour the paintings.

Thomas moved closer to Matilda. 'He could be our murderer, Matilda. At the very least he is a suspect, so I don't want you and Alice in his company.'

'Do you think he might be capable of that?' Matilda asked.

'Of course. He received bad reviews while I believe Bannon's work is heavily patronised. Mr Dominey was late at his own exhibition opening, which coincidentally was around the same time as Mr Bannon's murder.' Thomas paused, cleared his throat, remembering that she worked for a newspaper of sorts and he did not want to reveal details of the case.

'Is that so?' she asked, wide-eyed.

'I am not giving you any more information, Matilda, and you won't wheedle it out of me with your feminine wiles.'

She smiled. 'Feminine wiles? Well, I guess we all use that which is at our disposal,' she said with a glance to her brother, who was assisting the detectives because of a family friendship. The dig had not gone unnoticed by Thomas.

'That is different. This is a police matter.'

'Of course,' she said. 'Mind you it is all over the newspaper this morning, so I imagine the reporter has a good source, other than yourself. But, rest assured, if Mr Dominey reveals anything to Alice and me about his misadventures, you shall be the first person to know.'

Thomas's lips thinned in a grimace.

'Here you go,' Gideon said, handing both Thomas and Matilda a piece of paper with the details they sought.

'Thank you,' they both said in unison, and looked at each other.

'Good luck then,' Gideon said, intending to move them to the door as more gallery guests arrived.

'I'll see you out,' Thomas said to Matilda.

'No need. Miss Urry and I will take an omnibus back to our office. It's good to see you, Thomas.'

'And you, Matilda.' He took her hand and kissed it, but with a noticeable show of frustration. 'Will you come to dinner with me on Friday evening?' he asked, eager to enjoy an outing away from the brothers now that he and Matilda were officially courting.

'Yes, I would like that, if you can make it,' she added.

He nodded. 'I'll do my best.'

Harry interrupted them. 'Right then, I'll take Thom. Miss Urry, I will hand you back to Miss Hayward and we're best back to our work,' he said. 'To the agent first?' he asked his fellow detective.

Thomas held his hand up to Matilda. 'Don't ask, I'm not telling you.'

'We'll see,' she said and smiled. Kissing her brother on the cheek as she departed.

Thomas felt a flash of jealousy that he got no more than a look and to kiss her hand.

*****

Matilda sat beside Georgina as the omnibus made its way down the street, back to their office. There were plenty of seats now that the morning rush to work had passed. Blessed with beauty, Matilda always attracted attention, and even Miss Urry received the occasional glance from male commuters – she may have been ungainly, like a foal getting used to her long legs, but she was a handsome woman of sorts and confidence had its appeal.

'I am curious to know what you thought of the paintings, as you are an artist,' Matilda said.

'There's talent there, definitely good technique but I concur with the critics. There is nothing to write home about in that lot,' she said, to the point.

'Hmm, I'm struggling to understand how a muse could inspire those works. Not being an artist, I'm not sure I understand the relationship,' Matilda agreed.

Georgina nodded. 'I've seen some of his earlier exhibitions and she appeared in many of the works in some form, but her appearance was graceful. As if he found her beauty in everything, do you know what I mean?'

'I do. Yet these paintings were almost violent, weren't they? The woman in nature – if it was Miss Reubens – was represented with hostility. Do you think that's fair?'

'I think you've nailed it,' Georgina said. 'Angry, violent, even ugly. Maybe it's over with his muse.'

Matilda pondered this for a few moments. 'Thank you, Georgina, you've been most helpful. Your observations will help me with my questions for Mr Dominey.'

'Really? Well, that's good. Anytime I can help, just ask. Here's our stop,' she said, and as the omnibus slowed down on the familiar stretch of road, the two ladies rose and alighted, preparing to walk back to the offices of the *Women's Journal* a short distance away.

Matilda pondered if she had the confidence to ask Marlon Dominey if he really did like his muse, or was their trouble brewing below the surface of his canvas.

Chapter 8

Benjamin Bannon's agent was the type of man that Detective Thomas Ashdown had no time for on any day. Pompous, fussy and arrogant, he also wore a bowtie during the day which Thomas abhorred. Way too flashy. The agent stood in the doorway of his small gallery and allowed them entry once the men had produced their badges.

It was a pristine gallery, all white, glass and mirrors. Even the paintings on the wall appeared to be quite anaemic compared to Gideon's gallery featuring Marlon Dominey's vulgar works.

'We don't open for another hour,' he said.

'We're not here to buy, and we'll be gone before you open,' Thomas informed him. 'A few questions about the artist Benjamin Bannon, if you will? What is your relationship to him?'

The agent sighed and deigned to answer the men's queries. He indicated two couches and the three men took a seat, Thomas and Harry sharing one couch.

The agent began: 'I have represented the work of Mr Bannon for over a decade now and organised the display of his paintings in many fine galleries. He no longer had a dedicated patron – rather several who contributed to his success. His work achieved a most celebrated price. It afforded him the freedom to paint what he wanted when he wanted,' the agent said, pushing his large steel-rimmed glasses further up his nose.

'Wouldn't that be nice, then? Well done to him,' Detective Dart said sincerely. Harry was not one for society, but never felt unwelcome anywhere. He had come from money and had lost money. Now he was a working man and was quite happy with that arrangement.

'Did he have any enemies or rivals?' Thomas asked.

The agent snorted. 'Of course. He's a successful artist, top of his game. Every artist is a rival.'

Thomas sighed. 'Right, so sifting through those rivals, do you know of anyone who might do Mr Bannon harm?'

The agent thought for a moment. 'Benjamin has slighted a few over the years, only because he would not agree to mentor or support them, but the burden on him to do so would inhibit his creativity.'

'Of course, I feel the burden of mentoring myself some days,' Harry said with a glance at Thomas.

Thomas gave his mentor a wry look. Harry smiled and continued with a question to the agent.

'Could you give us the names and contact details of Mr Bannon's patrons and those persons that you believe might have had a grudge with Mr Bannon or sought to harm him?'

'I suppose I could,' the agent said, 'but it might take me a while.'

'You can bring it down to the station later, or we can send a uniformed constable here to collect it tomorrow,' Thomas said, impatient with the agent. 'This is a murder investigation.'

'I'll drop it to the station on my way home this evening,' he said smartly, not wanting the public to see the constabulary at his venue.

Thomas nodded his thanks. 'Where were you last Saturday between 6pm and 10pm?'

'Me! You can't imagine I would want to harm Mr Bannon? If I harmed every artist that I made my living from, where would I be?' he sputtered.

'Where would you be, indeed,' Thomas agreed.

The agent scoffed. 'I was at Marlon Dominey's exhibition.'

'And so was I,' Thomas answered. He did not recall seeing the agent there and by the flush that appeared on the agent's face, they caught him in an untruth.

'I was having dinner with a friend,' he said, clearing his throat. 'A discrete arrangement that I would prefer to stay that way.'

Thomas glanced at the man's hand and saw no wedding ring. 'We will need the name and contact details of your friend to verify your story.' As the agent opened his mouth to protest, Thomas continued shutting him down. 'Did you have a written contract with Mr Bannon to represent him?'

'Yes.'

'Could I see that please?' Harry asked, rising.

The agent hesitated, and then rose and went to a timber cabinet. He pulled open a drawer, rifled through some papers, and produced it. He handed it over with reluctance.

Harry studied the document. 'This contract finished in December last year.'

'Yes, remiss of me,' the agent stumbled. 'I hadn't got it resigned.'

'Did Mr Bannon end your relationship?' Thomas asked.

The agent took the paper back and re-filed it, closing the drawer with more force than necessary.

'He did no such thing. We had not completed the relevant documents, that's all.'

'How many artists do you currently manage?' Thomas asked.

'Several.'

'Mr Bannon being the most renowned?' Thomas continued.

'Yes.'

'So, losing his custom would hurt your business.'

'Of course. Fortunately, that wasn't the case. As you can see, I have several of his works for sale.' The agent pointed to two large etchings hanging on the wall. They appeared to be sketches for paintings, not the paintings themselves. The agent assumed, no doubt, the men would not know the difference.

Thomas studied the tag with the price written on it and the faded one next to it on another artist's work. 'This price is new. Has the value gone up since Mr Bannon's death?'

The agent swallowed. 'Of course, it is now a collector's item. I have a keen buyer coming later today and I expect to sell them.'

'Where are the paintings, though?' Harry asked.

'Pardon?' the agent said most indignantly.

Harry continued. 'If I'm not mistaken, these are sketches for pending work. The number on the bottom of both would indicate that.'

The agent swallowed. 'He did not complete the paintings before his death, which makes the sketches even more valuable.'

'Right,' Harry said.

The death of Mr Bannon might have benefited him, but Thomas could not imagine this small, insipid man murdering anyone even to save his own skin. His alibi, once checked out, would likely reinforce this. Unless he had an accomplice.

'Just a couple more questions, if you will,' Thomas said. 'Mr Bannon's last successful exhibition featured the seasons, I believe?'

'Yes. It was called *Seasons of our Life*.'

'Where is the painting *An Artist Bathing in the Season?*' Harry cut to the chase.

The agent's eyes widened. 'That's the one—'

'Yes,' Harry cut him off. 'Mr Bannon was posed in the fashion of that painting.'

'A lady purchased it, I have her details,' the agent said before being asked, keen to be rid of the two detectives as opening time loomed. He went behind a large timber desk and searched for the name. 'Here is the buyer. Mrs Sophie Cornish, quite an admirer of Mr Bannon's work.' He handed Harry a slip of paper with a name and address.

'Thank you, you have been most helpful,' Harry said, 'but we will need to verify your alibi.'

The agent's lips thinned, but he returned to his desk and wrote a name and address of a male friend on the pad and returned it to the detectives.

Thomas gave a small nod, and the men departed the gallery. When some distance away, Thomas turned back and saw the agent watching them.

'What do you think of all that?' Thomas asked Harry.

'I think he has a motive, but I imagine the thought of murder or mess would make him too squeamish,' Harry said.

Thomas grinned. 'Yes, my thoughts exactly. Unless he has a partner.'

'There's always that,' Harry agreed. He glanced at the agent's list and stopped on recognising a name. 'Ah, I know this fellow – Francis Sparrow – one of Bannon's patrons. Made his fortune on the land boom and got out in time. We have played golf together on the odd occasion when I can get to the club.'

'Would he be working or at the course today, per chance?' Thomas asked.

'He is retired, so let's try our luck,' Harry said, waving down a hansom cab.

The journey of twenty minutes gave them time to review and, stepping out at the course, Thomas stopped to enjoy the vast green view and smell the clean air.

'Yes, breathe that in, good for you,' Harry said with a grin, as they made their way to the clubhouse. Fortunately,

Mr Sparrow had just made his way in from the 9th hole as it was nearing lunchtime.

'Dart, old fellow,' he said, 'not like you to be here at this time of day,' he said, slapping Detective Harry Dart on the back.

'Sadly, it's a duty call, Francis,' Harry told him and introduced Thomas.

'Ah, the young gun,' Mr Sparrow said as they took a seat and the men accepted a glass of water while Mr Sparrow enjoyed a beverage with more bite. 'So what can I do for the city's best detectives, as the press would have us believe.'

Harry chuckled. 'Patronage… you know, of course, about the death of Mr Bannon.'

Mr Sparrow shook his head. 'I was astounded, could not believe it.'

'In confidence, we are considering a number of potential suspects,' Thomas said.

'Of course, not me, I hope,' Mr Sparrow said and laughed.

'No, I think you are in the clear,' Harry assured him. 'But as you move in those circles, did you notice any animosity to Mr Bannon?'

'They are a competitive lot, and that art-world is somewhat incestuous, dare I say,' Mr Sparrow said, sitting back and giving Harry's question some thought. 'I can't say I noticed anything out of the normal.'

Thomas directed the line of questioning. 'Were you approached by the artist Marlon Dominey for patronage?'

'Indeed. I met with him on several occasions and I liked both him and his delightful companion,' Mr Sparrow said.

The detectives exchanged looks, and Mr Sparrow continued: 'But in all honesty, I didn't like his work. I saw his collection when in progress.'

Harry nodded. 'The critics agreed with you.'

'I had to turn him down, and I told Bannon I would support his next collection instead, although Mrs Sparrow wants to support the theatre and not take on any other artists.'

'Did Mr Dominey know you invested what might have been his patronage with Mr Bannon?' Thomas asked.

'I believe I might have said so, or Mrs Sparrow did, but I could not stand up in court and put a hand on heart to it,' he said in jest.

'Francis, you have been most helpful,' Harry said, rising. 'Our apologies for keeping you from your lunch.'

'Not at all. It has allowed me to cool just a little after this morning's round. Plus, I am always at your service, gentlemen,' he said with a small bow.

Thomas thought over his suspect list as the men organised transport. 'Marlon Dominey is definitely of interest,' he said, eyes narrowed.

'Agreed. Let's stay on the patron trail,' Harry suggested. 'Shall we pay a quick visit to Mrs Cornish?'

'It's nearby,' Thomas said, and the two men headed to the next destination.

Chapter 9

The thought of seeing the very handsome Marlon Dominey in his art studio had both ladies most excited. Matilda and Alice stopped out the front of his terrace home in Red Hill.

'Very nice,' Alice said, dropping her eyes from the mansions to the written address in her hand to check. 'This is it.'

'Mr Dominey must be doing rather well then, despite his current showing,' Matilda said in a low voice.

'Indeed, or he has done well in the past. Perhaps a patron allows him to live here,' Alice suggested.

The ladies took the four steps to the imposing front door.

Matilda tapped the lion brass knocker. Within moments, they could hear footfalls approaching. A middle-aged lady opened the door, wearing a worn, printed dress covered by a white apron. She gave them a sour look.

'Good morning, we were hoping for an audience with Mr Dominey, please,' Matilda said.

'I'm his landlady,' she said, casting an eye over both ladies. 'And he's not looking for any visitors or new muses if that's what you are thinking.'

Alice gave a small laugh.

'Madam, I assure you we are not interested in being muses,' she said.

Matilda nodded in confirmation of Alice's fact and continued: 'I am Matilda Hayward and this is Miss Alice Doran. We are writers from the *Women's Journal* and are seeking to interview Mr Dominey about his artwork.'

The landlady opened her mouth to speak when a voice bellowed down the stairs: 'Let them up, Mrs Dempsey.'

'Hmph, you may go up. Two flights and the last room at the end of the hallway.'

'Thank you, Mrs Dempsey.' Matilda smiled, and Alice gave a small nod of appreciation as they passed.

'How exciting,' Matilda whispered to Alice as they lifted their dresses and took the two flights of narrow stairs.

'I know,' Alice said in a low squeal. 'I hope Miss Reubens is posing for him. To think, Matilda, we're going into an artist's studio and watching him work!'

They quietened as they reached the end of the hallway and stopped in the open doorway.

Matilda gave a small gasp, Alice's eyes widened. In front of them, working on a large canvas, was Marlon Dominey, several brushes in hand, spattered in paints of all colours and holding a palette. He was undressed as such, with his white shirt loose over dark pants, and both ladies considered the appropriateness of being in the room with Mr Dominey given his state of undress. They did, however, discount their concern.

The canvas was alive with the passion of the artist – the stream of a river, surrounded by thick, overgrown plants in deep green hues, and in the water lay the image of Sapphire

Reubens. Her body lay in repose, but her face was bright, her eyes captured the viewer.

'Do not talk, do not ask me anything. You may sit or leave, your only options,' he barked, not stopping to look at them.

Alice touched Matilda's hand and indicated the chaise lounge. The ladies moved there. Matilda studied the room but there was no sign of Mr Dominey's muse. He was painting from memory. She returned her gaze to Mr Dominey. He was and remained the most handsome man she had ever seen, not that she intended to tell anyone of that fact – especially her brothers, who would no doubt mention it to Thomas in jest. Mr Dominey was even more dynamic in his own domain, producing work of such beauty and skill.

The ladies watched as he worked feverishly, applying lashes of colour and stopping only to stand back and observe before applying the paint again to canvas, transforming it inch by inch. Time flew but it must have been a good hour before he stopped and placed his brushes and palette down. He turned to the two ladies and bowed.

'Marlon Dominey, at your service. Good morning,' he said and straightened.

Matilda laughed. 'Good morning. Thank you for letting us observe you at work; you are masterful. I am Miss Matilda Hayward and my friend is Miss Alice Doran.'

Alice stared, wide-eyed. 'The painting is truly breathtaking, Mr Dominey.'

'Too kind,' he said, but Matilda could tell from his

confident expression that he knew this was a fact. He stood back to study his work. 'The inspiration quite overtook me.'

'It's stunning,' Matilda agreed.

Mr Dominey reached for a piece of cloth nearby and wiped his hands. 'Forgive me for not offering the usual pleasantries. Were you wishing to purchase a painting? I leave that to the gallery.'

'We were not,' Alice said, rising and moving to the window to see the effect of the light on the artwork. 'We were hoping for an audience with you to conduct an interview. Matilda and I write for the *Women's Journal* and the editor has commissioned us to do two pieces.'

'Two pieces,' he declared, 'my that's generous. Your lady readers must have a fond interest in art then?'

'Amongst other things,' Matilda said, knowing he was slightly mocking them.

'Then you may ask away right now if that suits you. I need to break but only for a small window of time. The canvas is calling me. I shall call for tea for three.' He strode to the door and bellowed, startling both girls. 'Mrs Dempsey, I am breaking briefly. Could we have tea for three please?'

He returned to the room without waiting and pulled up a chair near the chaise, where Matilda remained seated. She had retrieved a notebook and pencil from her small bag and Alice had done the same, re-joining Matilda on the lounge.

'Please, begin,' Mr Dominey said, sitting back and studying the ladies in a manner that rather unsettled them. His intense brown eyes appraising them.

Matilda cleared her throat. 'We like to ask one question

apiece so we can make notes while you are engaged in your next question, if that is suitable?'

'Sounds sensible,' Mr Dominey agreed.

Matilda's eyes narrowed as she sensed he was mocking her again. He gave her the slightest of smiles, which caused her heart to flutter.

Mrs Dempsey arrived with the tea tray and served them, placing their tea on a side table nearby each of them and a plate of fresh biscuits closer to Mr Dominey.

The ladies thanked her and continued.

'I notice Miss Reubens isn't here in person, but clearly she is foremost in your mind,' Matilda said, nodding to the painting. 'Can you tell me about the importance of a muse to your inspiration?'

Mr Dominey appeared to give the question some thought before answering.

'Like all artists, many things have inspired me… nature, light, other artists, music, the feminine form,' he said, running an eye over the ladies. He caused Alice to shift uncomfortably, and Matilda improved her posture. 'But to find a muse, a pure form of beauty and poetry and art, all represented on a face who, when she gazes upon you, halts your thoughts and movements so that all you think of is her… then that inspires this,' he said and looked to the painting.

Matilda thought it must be the most romantic thing she had ever heard, and beside her, Alice looked at the artist in awe. Matilda gave her a light nudge as she hurried to finish writing Mr Dominey's quote.

Alice daintily cleared her throat and spoke in her lovely English lilt: 'Mr Dominey, I have seen two of your exhibitions now and each time your muse is strongly represented in nature. What is the connection for you between woman and nature?'

Mr Dominey leaned forward, entwining his fingers and focusing on Alice, which startled her a little. She sat back and dropped her eyes to her notepad, ready to take notes.

'Miss Doran,' he began, 'I greatly admire the work of a fellow artist that you may have heard of, Mr Cezanne?' he did not wait for an answer. 'Cezanne once said that "there is only nature, and the eye is turned through contact with her." That is how I feel. Nature inspires me with her beauty. She is the creator, and man is the destroyer. To place my muse in nature is to express my admiration for all of life and its beauty.'

Matilda had been studying the painting as Mr Dominey spoke.

'May I ask where is your muse today? We so hoped to meet and speak with her too.'

The artist sat back. 'She is visiting a friend. I can't always ask her to spend every hour in repose waiting for me to release her.'

'Her expression is hard to read,' Matilda said, gazing upon the artist's representation of Miss Reubens.

'Yes,' Mr Dominey agreed. 'It is.' His face softened as he looked at the painting and smiled. 'But it is the most beautiful expression I have ever seen upon her countenance.'

*****

Mrs Sophie Cornish was not what the two detectives expected. She was young, voluptuous, feminine and beautiful, and from the look of the interior of her house, which served as a showroom for many collections of works, very wealthy. She sat after receiving them and offered tea, which they declined. Her dress was of the finest fabrics, a pale lemon that suited her olive skin and tawny eyes.

'My husband passed away last year,' she said in a soft but refined voice.

'We are sorry to hear that, Mrs Cornish,' Harry said, and she nodded her thanks.

'He was quite elderly, so it was not a shock, but I did not expect to find myself alone just yet and having to manage all this,' she said, and coyly looked at Thomas as she spoke.

Thomas cleared his throat. He imagined that indeed Mrs Cornish had fully expected the result from such a union.

'I understand you are quite an admirer of Mr Benjamin Bannon's work and that you have the painting *An Artist Bathing in the Season* in your possession?' Thomas asked.

'Oh yes, I'm an admirer of many of the English artists that have brought their fine art style to Australia. I like traditional paintings, I'm not one for those modern works.'

'Nor am I,' Harry agreed. 'I like to be elevated or taken somewhere when I view a painting.'

'Exactly, Detective,' she said, and looked at the handsome, mature man with more appreciation.

'May we see it?' Thomas asked.

'Of course,' she said, and stood. 'Please come this way.'

She moved in front of them, showing off her figure to

her best advantage. They moved through several large rooms that appeared to feature little but art and occasional furniture. Rounding a corner, Mrs Cornish stopped in front of a wall that featured just two paintings.

'This is it,' Mrs Cornish said, standing back to admire it.

Even Thomas, who held little interest in art, was taken aback. She noted his reaction.

'It's quite dramatic, isn't it?' she smiled.

An Artist Bathing in the Season was a large painting taking up half the wall. The colours were vibrant, the autumn leaves in the bath were very visible and the artist in the painting paled by comparison. Thomas was more struck by the similarity to the death scene than by the quality of the work.

'Without meaning to be indiscrete,' Harry began, 'I imagine the value of this work has risen since the recent death of Mr Bannon?'

'Indeed. I have had several queries from buyers, but I shan't part from it. I love it.'

There was a noise above their heads, and Thomas glanced upward.

'I'm sorry, are we keeping you from guests?' he asked, not at all sorry, but nosy.

'No, that must be the maid, I suspect,' Mrs Cornish answered.

'Did you meet Mr Bannon himself?' Thomas asked.

'Indeed, he was a friend of my husband's and of mine. When my husband was alive, we often entertained and my husband was a great patron of the arts and artists,' she said.

'How did your husband come to be introduced to artists who enjoyed or needed his patronage?' Harry asked.

'He was a supporter of the art gallery and hence we were invited to many events. A dear friend of mine, Dr Robert Humphries, introduced me to Mr Bannon who then requested I pose for one of his paintings,' she said and continued without pausing. 'Robert brought Mr Cornish to see the finished painting and he requested an introduction. That is how I met my husband. We married within three months of our meeting.'

'So, do you continue to attend the gallery events?' Harry asked.

'Yes, of course. Robert often escorts me and I have met many of the artists whose works feature in my home,' she said. 'It's always nice to have company, don't you think, Detective Ashdown?'

'With the hours I keep, Mrs Cornish, I confess to needing little company after hours,' Thomas said.

Harry looked at his younger partner and gave a small sigh of frustration.

Mrs Cornish looked away from them as she spoke. 'I imagine you both think I am a gold-digger.'

'Madam, what I think is of no consequence,' Thomas said.

Mrs Cornish continued. 'Maxwell was a dashing man, handsome, kind, and so interesting. He treated me like I was an angel given to his care.' She turned to look at the detectives. 'I have never experienced that kind of love and devotion. I was swept off my feet. I imagine I will never feel that depth again.' Her voice hitched and Harry reached for his handkerchief and offered it.

'Thank you, Detective,' she said, accepting it and blotting her eyes.

Thomas softened, believing her reaction to be genuine.

'Thank you, Mrs Cornish, for your time and allowing us to see the work,' he said. 'We will trouble you no more, but should you hear anything that you think might be relevant, please don't hesitate to contact the station.'

'I will do that, Detective,' she said. 'Please follow me and I will show you out. It can be a maze otherwise.'

As they caught a ride on an omnibus back to their Roma Street station, Harry sighed.

'Seriously, son, it's no wonder you are single. You all but had an invitation.'

Thomas ran a finger around his necktie, feeling it tighten like a noose. 'Could you imagine?' he said. 'I felt great sympathy for her, but no doubt she is like that with every eligible man she meets and I suspect she would require a great deal of attention.'

'You would be a kept man.'

'The last thing I want,' Thomas said, and then looked at his partner. 'Shame you are married as she clearly likes the older men.'

'Only the rich ones, I suspect,' Harry joked, and the two men chuckled. 'She is not a match for the lovely Miss Hayward though.'

'That we agree on,' Thomas said, the thought of his Friday night date filling him with pleasure and apprehension.

'I can't see Mrs Cornish being a killer,' Harry said, interrupting Thomas's pleasant thoughts.

'She has plenty of artwork to sell if her spending money starts to run out, so I don't think there's a motive there to increase the work's value,' Thomas said with a sigh.

'Unless she was Bannon's lover and was jilted. But you are right… she'd struggle to set up that death scene and get him into his bath, and how would she administer poison to him externally through his skin without him reacting. But the painting was amazing.'

'It was,' Thomas agreed, 'and his murderer has paid a deadly tribute.'

Thomas felt ridiculously nervous. He bathed and dressed in a fresh suit that he had picked up from the cleaners and wore a crisp shirt from his laundry service. He was no stranger to dating and no stranger to the company of ladies, yet he was jittery.

What if the night was a disaster? Should he show his face at the customary Hayward Sunday lunch, of which he was a regular and expected guest? What if he and Matilda kissed and it was terrible? It couldn't be when you shared such an attraction, surely. He took a deep breath. Even worse, what if during his date he got interrupted by a work summons; would she realise this was not the ideal life? It was the only life he knew and the life he wanted, but there was many a detective whose private life had suffered from the job.

He also felt a rush of excitement. The date was just him and Matilda. No best friend, no Hayward brothers, none of Matilda's fellow writers or any family commitments. Just the two of them for the first time. He had thought about this moment many a time in the late hours of the evening when he had returned to his home, and in the early hours of the morning as he lay alone.

Combing his hair once more, he heard voices from the front rooms. He finished up and ventured out to see who his tall, ginger-haired nephew was speaking with. Teddy was not much younger than himself and had come to live with Thomas while seeking employment as a cook. On getting it, he stayed on, which suited them both. In the kitchen, Thomas found his nephew and best friend.

'Ah, here he is,' Daniel said, running an eye up and down Thomas. 'Looking snappy.'

'Dan! What are you doing here?' Thomas asked, at first friendly, and then his eyes narrowed with suspicion.

Teddy chuckled. 'It is better to have Daniel here, Uncle, than lining up with his brothers to interview you at the Hayward household,' he joked, running a hand through his unruly ginger hair that was long overdue to visit the barber's chair. 'Drink, Dan?'

'Ah, no thanks Teddy, I'm meeting Gideon and Elijah at the club, you're welcome to come.'

'Thanks, but I'm off to the pub soon,' Teddy said. 'Just a few boys from the kitchen I work at having a drink,' he said for his uncle's benefit. 'Don't worry, you won't find me in the lock-up later.'

'Make sure of that,' Thomas said, teasing his nephew. 'Can't guarantee you'll make bail.' He turned his attention back to Daniel. 'I thought you were pursuing a date with Miss Doran tonight?'

Daniel waved his hand dismissively. 'She has a commitment with her guardian, who insisted Alice accompany him to some literary event.'

'Right. And you are here because?'

'Ah, yes, that,' Daniel said, running his hands down his coat in a nervous fashion. 'I just wanted to drop in and—' his voice faded off.

'Read me the riot act?' Thomas finished for him, stiffening.

'I'm going to go get changed,' Teddy said, and backed out of the kitchen.

Thomas cleared his throat. 'You know I'll take good care of her, Dan.' His voice was laced with frustration; he of all people did not need to be told to look after Matilda… the girl he'd known since they were children; the girl he had protected many a time from her brothers during pranks – not that he said the latter out loud – and the woman he now loved.

Daniel wandered to the window and glanced out. 'I know you'll look out for her, Thom,' he turned to his best friend. 'But she's the only sister I've got and while she can be sassy, she's not…' he chose his words, 'familiar in the way of men.'

'I hope not,' Thomas said.

'And we are very familiar in the way of women,' Daniel continued.

Thomas understood with crystal clarity what Daniel was saying.

'It's just dinner, Dan.'

Daniel looked a little more relieved and smiled. He moved back to the kitchen table and Thomas stood on the other side of it.

Daniel continued: 'You and I have been socialising together for over six years or more, and we've shown many ladies a good time.'

Thomas held up his hand. 'I won't be taking liberties.'

'We've also spoken about the ladies,' Daniel continued, 'amongst ourselves, but nevertheless, you won't be talking about Matilda at the station or—'

'For the love of God, Dan, do you not know me at all? I have nothing but respect for your sister and will protect Matilda with my life. There will be no liberties,' Thomas said, angered by Daniel's words. He straightened his waistcoat and Daniel lowered himself to the edge of the table, studying his friend.

'Thom, you are my best friend and you're as close to me as my brothers.' He held Thomas's gaze. 'I don't believe there is anyone better for my sister than you, and no one I would want more for a future brother-in-law.' He took a deep breath. 'But I swear if you disrespect her by seeing other women or by loose talk amongst your peers, I don't care if you are an officer of the law or a better fighter than me, I'll have you.'

Thomas's lips narrowed and he took a breath, reining in his anger. Daniel was right, he was a better fighter, stronger and fitter. But it would not go well with the Haywards or Matilda to have warred with Daniel, especially as he was the closest to Matilda.

'Dan, I'll tell you this and you only, so don't repeat it.' Thomas waited until Daniel nodded and then he continued. 'I have dated many women, you know that. But I have always loved your sister, and I have been waiting for her. Consult your father. I spoke with him some years back about my intentions. There is no one else for me and now that she has consented to court me, she will be the only one. I will not speak of our private life again to you or anyone else.'

They glared at each other for a few moments and then Daniel offered his hand to shake and gave Thomas a small smile. Thomas accepted and rolled his eyes.

'Don't tell me I have to go through this with your father now, then Amos, Elijah and Gideon? We'll never get to dinner.'

Daniel grinned and looked a little sheepish. 'No, I told them I would have the talk with you and sort you out,' he said with a wink.

'Hmm,' Thomas said, less than impressed.

'Your hansom is here, Uncle,' Teddy called from the other room.

'Right then, enjoy your evening and don't kiss her yet,' Daniel said.

'Dan, you'll be off then,' Thomas suggested, his voice low, his eyes narrowed. He was rewarded with a laugh from Daniel. The men left the kitchen and headed down the hall. Thomas took one last look at his outward appearance in a well-placed looking glass.

'You look dashing,' Daniel stirred his friend.

'It's the best I can be,' Thomas said, and again felt a flutter of nerves that surprised and annoyed him that after all he had seen and experienced, Matilda rattled him.

Teddy joined them. 'I feel like we're seeing our son off on his first date,' he joked as he looped his arm through Daniel's and they laughed aloud.

'You're both extremely aggravating tonight, which I don't need,' Thomas said in all seriousness.

'It's just what you need, Uncle, now relax. It's a pleasant night out with an old friend. Got your wallet?' Teddy asked, seeing Thomas to the front door and plumping his uncle's hat to look respectable.

'Got it, thanks,' Thomas said, patting his jacket pockets.

'Need any tips?' Teddy asked, then grinned.

Thomas gave him a smirk. 'If I was cooking for her, I'd take you up on that.'

Teddy grinned and slapped his uncle on the back. 'Have a good night and remember I can move out quickly should you wish to get betrothed.'

Thomas gave him a pained look and snatched his hat from Teddy's hands.

'Got a clean handkerchief should Matilda need it?' Daniel called.

Thomas rolled his eyes. 'When did you become the master of etiquette?' he asked Daniel.

'Just one of my many charms,' Daniel said.

Thomas took the few stairs down to the path and to the waiting hansom. He gave the driver the address and settled himself in the cab. When he turned, the two men were still on the veranda and gave him a wave. He shook his head at the pair of them and roused another round of laughs.

The last of the day's light was slipping behind the mountains on the horizon, and he hoped when he arrived at Matilda's home that the entire Hayward household was not waiting to see them off. He dreaded the thought.

Chapter 11

Matilda fussed more than she usually did, which frustrated her given she had known Thomas most of her life and she wasn't the type to fuss. Sitting at her dresser in front of the looking glass, she studied her reflection.

'Does my hair look different?' she asked Harriet, turning to see the sides as best she could. 'I don't want to have the same style I have every day since this is a date after all.'

'Your hair looks wonderful even if I say so myself,' Harriet said.

'You are right, of course, Harriet,' Matilda sighed, watching Harriet studying her handiwork. 'I don't know why I am nervous. It's silly, this is Thomas. I know him as well as I know my brothers.'

Harriet smiled. 'It's Thomas the man, not Thomas the boy you grew up with. A most accomplished, ambitious and handsome man, might I add.'

'Oh, please don't add that.' Matilda frowned at her and Harriet laughed softly. 'I don't know when it all happened. It was only recently that he and Daniel were getting into trouble and annoying me.'

'I have always hoped for it, a union between you and Thomas,' Harriet said, and smiled.

'Have you?' Matilda asked, surprised.

Harriet placed the last pin in Matilda's hair. 'Yes, call me sentimental, but I have a soft spot for Thomas. I was worried one of your brothers' friends might turn your head, but I was never worried about Thomas. He has had his fun, but he's always looked out for you.'

Matilda scoffed. 'That's not how I remember it, he's always competed with me.'

Harriet shook her head. 'Remember when you hurt your ankle jumping the fence while racing Gideon? It was Thomas who helped you back to the house while the other boys continued to race. Remember when your little budgerigar died? It was Thomas who helped you with the burial ceremony while your brothers thought the idea was stupid.'

Matilda studied Harriet. 'I am sure you remember every moment of our lives… you are a walking album, Harriet.'

Matilda heard her father's voice carrying from the bottom of the staircase. 'Five minutes, Matilda,' he called.

'He is a man principled on keeping time,' Harriet said.

'Coming, Pa,' Matilda called and took a deep breath. 'I am ready.'

'You mostly certainly are,' Harriet said. 'You look beautiful.'

Matilda saw the tears in Harriet's eyes.

'Oh Harriet, please don't cry or I will too, and then what a mess I will make of all your good work, and Thomas will regret asking me out,' Matilda said. But she felt the significance of the date and it was not lost on Matilda how much her mother would have loved to have been there with them.

Matilda reached for Harriet's hand. 'What would I have done without you? Thank you.'

Harriet nodded and smiled. 'The pleasure was all mine, it truly was. Now have a lovely night and do your best not to fight too much with Thomas.'

Matilda laughed and enjoyed the break in the tension. 'I can't promise anything.'

'Matilda, Thomas's hansom has arrived,' her father called again.

Matilda rolled her eyes. 'Well, best not to keep the detective waiting.' She gave Harriet a quick kiss on the cheek and departed her room to meet her date.

*****

Thomas waited with Mr Hayward at the bottom of the staircase, feeling like he was a young man attending his first ball. In truth, Matilda's father had known him since he was a boy of seven, and now he was here as a man waiting to take out his most beloved and only daughter.

James Hayward began in a stern voice. 'Now Thomas—'

Thomas turned to look at him, holding back the frustration he felt at getting another lecture. But Mr Hayward just laughed.

'Have a lovely evening,' he said, and Thomas grinned,

exhaling in relief as Mr Hayward gently slapped him on the back. 'I believe Daniel was giving you the lecture on behalf of the family. I did my best to move the other boys out before you arrived.'

Thomas nodded his thanks. 'I appreciate that, Mr Hayward. And yes, I was warned and threatened by Daniel, who decided today was his day to become responsible,' Thomas joked and Mr Hayward laughed again.

'Let's not expect a repeat of that too often,' Mr Hayward sighed.

Thomas looked up as Matilda appeared at the top of the stairs, but unlike the evening of the gallery exhibition opening with Alice where she promenaded down the staircase on display, Matilda came down in her usual hurried style, excited, and greeting the two men. Harriet followed behind.

'Thomas Charles Ashdown, and right on time!' she exclaimed, surprised.

He gave a small bow. 'Of course, Matilda Anne Hayward, you expected anything less?'

He laughed when she made a hmph sound, knowing full well that his work made him completely unreliable.

'You look beautiful, Matilda,' he said, partly because it was expected he would acknowledge the effort of her dressing, and in all honesty, it came off his tongue with sincerity and awe.

'Thank you.'

He enjoyed her look of pleasure as she did a twirl for him in a pale blue dress with embroidered flowers.

'Pa insisted I must have a new dress, but this was my mother's. I had fresh lace applied.'

'It is as beautiful on you as it was on her,' Mr Hayward said. He cleared his throat. 'We might have raised you as a tomboy but I can't see that girl tonight.'

'I'm sure she will come out,' Thomas teased. 'Shall we?' He offered his arm, wanting to have her alone and be done with the awkwardness of the first encounter. He was looking forward to the second date already.

They headed down the path and Thomas offered his hand to assist Matilda into the hansom cab, even though she was capable of getting into it by herself as she reminded him.

He rolled his eyes and joined her after giving the driver the address.

'Let's do our best not to talk about my work tonight,' Thomas said. He reached for her small hand and held it.

Matilda turned slightly to face him. 'But if we don't speak of your work or mine, then we'll be very dull. Once we talk about the décor of the restaurant, the menu and our families, we'll run out of topics.'

'Will we?' Thomas asked, surprised. 'I've never found conversation with you to come to an end. On the contrary.'

She gave him a wry look, and Thomas grinned.

'Would you prefer I talk of things that most ladies talk about? Fashion, gossip… well, not the ladies I know at the *Women's Journal*, but I've heard ladies do talk of those things,' she said.

'Yes, if you like,' Thomas said, knowing full well her unconventional upbringing meant Matilda most likely had no idea what that encompassed.

'Well, Alice tells me the recent suffragette meeting went well and that more men are required to advance our cause.'

'Oh good,' Thomas answered. 'Do ladies speak of that often?'

'I don't know,' she admitted. 'It's important, why wouldn't they?'

'Why, indeed,' he agreed, his experience limited to the ladies from his clubs and the respectable wives he knew. Neither of which had ever spoken of voting and women's rights. This was not how he envisaged the date starting. He tried to steer it on another course. 'Your father was touched by you wearing your mother's dress tonight. I think he was quite emotional.'

Matilda sighed. 'Poor Pa, I worry he is lonely at times. It is a great shame he hasn't found another companion yet.'

'I've no doubt he's had many women try to win his heart and hand,' Thomas said, 'a respectable and accomplished gentleman in possession of a good home and income…'

'Yes, because we are all out there looking to secure a hand in marriage for our betterment,' Matilda said.

He frowned. 'That is not what I meant.'

'Isn't it? You know I don't need to marry, Thomas. I have my own income, so if tonight is about saving me…'

'It is not about saving you,' he assured her. 'But you are welcome to save me. God knows I need it,' he muttered as he turned to look at the street passing by. Thomas steadied himself and gave himself a reminder to curb his responses and not say what he might to Daniel or a younger Matilda. He cleared his throat and tried again.

'I hear Gideon's gallery has not suffered despite the artist's bad reviews.' He knew it was a tenuous link to both of their work but a cultural subject, nevertheless.

'No, thank goodness. I think it has become a curiosity… people are attending to see how bad the artwork is,' Matilda said and smiled.

'People are odd, indeed. It's one safe conclusion I can draw from my work.'

'Which we are not speaking about tonight,' Matilda reminded him.

Thomas gave Matilda a wry look.

'Fine then,' he said, and she laughed and placed her hand on his arm. He looked at her hand and enjoyed the pleasure it gave him.

'This is awkward for both of us,' she said.

He looked up at her, his heart beating a little faster, worried in anticipation of what she might say next. Had she decided accepting his dinner invitation was not a good idea after all?

'But it doesn't have to be,' she added.

'No, of course not,' he said and studied her, still feeling ill at ease and not sure what to do next. 'What are you suggesting?'

She laughed. 'That we be ourselves, of course. It's the only you and me that we know after all.'

He wasn't quite sure what that entailed, and gave Matilda a confused look. She continued. 'This might be a date, but I'm assuming you like me as I am, or you would not have asked me out. I certainly like you… the you that I have known forever. So, let's be ourselves,' she said, and patted his arm.

'Right then, let's do that,' Thomas agreed as the hansom pulled up. 'But Matilda,' he added, 'my feelings are stronger than like.' He held her gaze as her eyes widened slightly. He moved his gaze to her lips. The hansom cab door opened and he straightened up and stepped down, offering his hand to assist Matilda out.

It was going to be a long night, he realised. He just hoped at some point it would become pleasurable.

*****

Matilda thought the evening was beginning to improve – after they got through the awkwardness of ordering and sitting so intimately near each other in the softly lit restaurant, they relaxed.

'It was truly breathtaking and his muse wasn't even there,' Matilda said, telling Thomas about Marlon Dominey's new work.

He frowned. 'Where did he say she was?'

Matilda thought for a moment. 'I think he said she was visiting a friend. I don't know if she posed earlier for him, but he had her in perfect detail in the setting. She was lying as if she was part of the stream. I have never seen anything quite like it.'

She saw the expression on Thomas's face.

'No, it was exceptional,' she tried to convince him. 'I know that might sound impossible given his recent collection, but

84

the colours were so deep and vibrant and Miss Reubens was represented sympathetically in nature… just beautiful,' she sighed.

Thomas cleared his throat. 'Speaking of beautiful, Matilda, I am not one to make idle compliments but please let me say again that you look beautiful this evening.'

She paused and then beamed. 'Harriet paid special attention to my hairstyle.'

'It's your hair, your dress, your bright eyes, and your enthusiasm for life,' Thomas added, 'your inner beauty too.'

She placed her hand on her heart. 'Thank you, Thomas. That's beautiful and almost poetic.'

He looked away, feeling exposed, and then he returned his gaze to her and leant forward. 'I see so many terrible things every day in my work, sights and scenes that I would never want you to come across or bear witness to.'

She reached for his hand and touched it sympathetically. Thomas stiffened.

'So, you must allow me to appreciate beauty when I see it and have the opportunity to fill a void that my work depletes,' he said.

'I understand,' Matilda said. 'I hope I can be that.'

'You are that.'

And then the night came to an abrupt end.

Chapter 12

Thomas held the exit door to the restaurant open for Matilda as she returned from the powder room, the bill paid in her absence. He offered his arm, and she linked hers through his.

'Sir.' He heard a voice and snapped to look to the right, where a constable stood.

Thomas groaned. 'For the love of God, man, not tonight.'

'Ma'am, I'm sorry to interrupt,' the young constable said.

'Then I suggest you don't,' Thomas said. 'Can't you find one of the other teams?'

'Yes. sir, but Detective Dart is on site and it is your case,' the constable said, looking more and more nervous. 'He wanted me to let you know.'

Thomas sighed.

'We must go then,' Matilda said, brightening. 'Where is it you need the Detective?'

'Down at the Botanical Gardens, sir, near the—'

'We are not going, Matilda,' Thomas said before the constable could say another word. 'I am going and you're going home,' he said, stormily. 'I shall take you there first.'

'But it is completely in the opposite direction and Detective Dart is waiting for you. Don't be silly, Thomas,' she said and made the constable smile. It was not often Detective Ashdown was managed.

Thomas caught the smile and the young constable straightened. 'You take this hansom, sir, and I'll get the next,' the young man said.

'That's a good idea, Constable,' Matilda said, smiling at him.

Thomas sighed, not at all happy with the arrangement, nor the satisfied look on Matilda's face. The constable told the driver to return to where they had just come from, then walked behind to the next carriage to tell the waiting driver to follow.

Thomas held her hand as she stepped into the hansom and then followed, sitting next to her.

'You might be waiting a while.' He reconsidered. 'I think it best I take you home.' He moved to tap the roof and inform the driver, but Matilda stopped him.

'I am in no hurry to return home, and I won't be underfoot, I assure you.'

Thomas held her gaze. 'I don't want you seeing anything unpleasant. Trust me, some of the sights I have seen return to visit me regularly,' he said, running a hand over his lightly bearded face.

Matilda looked at him with concern. 'I can only imagine. I will just remain out of the way and not approach.'

Thomas gave her a less than convinced look. 'This might be a good time to establish our work boundaries,' he said.

'I can't have my work or anything I say to you appear on the pages of the *Women's Journal* unless it is an agreed-upon interview, and I assure you, there won't be many, if any, of those.'

Matilda sighed. 'You need not be so high and mighty, Thomas. You are not the source of all news in our town. Other journalists manage to write their pieces through good investigation, and I intend to do just that.'

'That doesn't reassure me,' he said, studying her face and admiring her beauty again for the hundredth time that evening. He desperately wanted to kiss her and he realised, as she delicately cleared her throat, that he had been looking at her lips. Thomas looked away.

'I promise you I will not print anything that you say or reveal to me in our private discussions, not without your consent. However, anything I observe is for me to write as I see fit. Agreed?' she asked, and offered her hand to shake.

Thomas couldn't help but smile. He took her hand in his and, ignoring her shake, turned it over and placed a kiss on her hand.

'Agreed for now, but revisions of our contract may be required.'

'Is that so?' she teased.

He shook his head. 'I am bound to hear from your father and every member of your family that I took you to a crime scene on our first date.'

'So exciting,' she said, and laughed. 'It is the best date ever.'

'Really?' he asked, looking rather pleased. 'The restaurant was excellent, wasn't it?'

'Thank you, Thomas, it really was. I do think my main dish was better than yours though.'

'Perhaps, but my entrée was superior.'

They stopped and smiled at each other. Always competitive, but at least they were back to being themselves. The hansom slowed down and Thomas looked out to see they had arrived. It was not difficult to spot his partner, Detective Dart. A small crowd had gathered and he could see some of the junior constables keeping the crime scene cordoned off. Harry was in the middle of it. The hansom pulled over and Thomas alighted.

'One moment,' he said to Matilda and spoke with the driver. 'If I pay you for the rest of your evening shift, will you remain here for me? I'll include a handsome tip.'

'Right you are, sir,' the driver said, tipping his hat. 'I'd be happy to have an easy night of it plus a good rest for my horses.'

Thomas leaned back into the hansom to speak with Matilda. 'Please remain here. I'll be as quick as I can be.'

'There is no hurry, but I may walk down to where the crowd is, eventually. You go.' She hurried him off without waiting for his reply on her intended movements.

Thomas's lips narrowed as he thought about the wisdom of bringing her here. He stopped, hesitated, and then turning, went to join his partner.

Matilda watched him walk away. She loved to see him in authority. The young officers all stood alert as he approached, and one joined his side to fill him in and take him to the victim. When the crowd swallowed him from sight, she alighted from the hansom cab. The driver jumped down to assist her, and she let him with thanks. Matilda made her way over to join the growing number of people out at this time of the evening, watching a crime unfold.

*****

'You're here. Why are you here?' Detective Harry Dart tipped his hat back off his brow and asked of his partner.

'Did you not send the constable to come and get me?' Thomas asked.

Harry exhaled and looked frustrated. 'Ah, the young one was a bit rattled. I told him where you were and to *inform* you only, so you could meet me later if you chose to do so after your date. I am sorry, Thom.'

'Don't be. Matilda's most excited to be here. The highlight of her evening, I suspect,' he said and rolled his eyes.

Harry laughed. 'Bless her, she's one of a kind that young lady.'

'She'll be snooping for her paper,' he said with a glance around and yes, he found several of the local press had arrived. 'Press is already here. What have we got?' he asked.

'A death in Weeping Fig Avenue,' Harry said, 'and yes, that's what it is called,' he said before Thomas could question him. 'We have found the deceased in a most unusual pose, sitting with his head in his hands, leaning on his knees, as if he is weeping too.'

Harry led him a few feet further towards the start of the avenue, and Thomas stopped.

'He's definitely dead?' Thomas asked, studying the strange scene.

'Most dead indeed. Granted he doesn't look it. We've called for the coroner.'

Thomas walked closer and circled the body and was relieved that there was nothing dramatic about the death should Matilda view it. At least she would not be traumatised on their date, this time at least. At the thought of Matilda, he had a pang of yearning to see her and check on her safety. He looked up, found, as he suspected, the lady herself in her beautiful blue gown amongst the onlookers. He frowned and she gave him a small smile.

'She looks beautiful,' Harry said, with a dip of his hat towards Miss Hayward.

'Hmph,' Thomas grunted, but straightened with pride as he returned his attention to the man before him. 'He is pale. Can you see a puncture wound? Has he too been poisoned?'

'Nothing obvious that I can see from my earlier inspection. Perhaps he has ingested poison and stayed here until it took effect, or he was placed here,' Harry said.

'Ah, here comes the coroner now,' Thomas said as they saw Dr Nevins making his way towards them, the grass slowing him down with his limp and cane.

He arrived at their side. 'Well, clearly you two men have no better way to spend a Friday evening either,' he joked and gave them both a nod.

'On the contrary,' Harry said. 'Thom here was on a date. Impossible to get him married off when he disappears to crime scenes.'

'We are lucky, Detective Dart, that we have found such tolerant wives,' Dr Nevins said. 'Although I sometimes think my wife is so used to my hours that she may not want me at home more should I retire.'

The men chuckled and Thomas glanced towards where Matilda was standing. Now she was talking to a young man, a journalist that Thomas recognised from *The Brisbane Courier*. He didn't like it one bit, and it was not the fact that they might be sharing news that annoyed him. She looked so beautiful tonight, and he was not in her company. As if she read his thoughts, Matilda turned and looked straight at him. Her expression of affection softened him.

'Well, why don't you finish up and see the young lady home, Detective,' Dr Nevins said, noting the look between Thomas and Matilda. 'I'm guessing that is the young lady? Most unconventional to bring her here on your date.'

Thomas sighed. 'Yes.' He didn't elaborate and Harry grinned.

'Long story, Doc,' Harry said. Turning to Thomas he suggested: 'You've seen the victim and site now, Thom, head home and we'll meet in the morning. The good doctor will have some idea of the cause of death and time by then, will you not, Dr Nevins?'

'Indeed,' Dr Nevins agreed and began his work.

Thomas bid the men goodnight and made his way to Matilda. The journalist beside her looked at him keenly.

'Anything you can tell us, Detective?' he asked.

'Yes, we have found a dead body propped against a tree in the Botanic Gardens,' Thomas said. 'Good night.'

Matilda tried not to laugh and wished the journalist good evening. She accepted Thomas's arm as they returned to the carriage.

'That wasn't grisly at all,' she said.

'No, thank goodness. I wish they were all so clean,' he agreed.

'So, no obvious wounds?' she asked.

'Matilda,' he warned.

'I am asking as me, not as a writer.'

'And I'm saying as me, a detective, that I don't want to tell you about murders in our city. It's not for a lady's ears.' He again offered her his hand to enter the hansom cab, and she accepted with a grimace. He gave the driver Matilda's address in Highgate Hill and stepped in beside her.

'Righto, away we are then,' the driver said, with a tap on their roof.

Matilda continued to push Thomas. 'I assure you that this *young lady's ears* are not easily mortified,' she said. 'Thomas, you should know that. If we are not a partnership of equals, as we have been most of our lives, and as father raised me to expect, then there is no point in us pursuing anything more than a friendship, is there?'

She had him there, and he opened his mouth to refute, but he knew to do so might risk losing her before the relationship had barely started.

He nodded. 'Perhaps you are right, Matilda. It's just I have this heightened desire to protect and provide for you.'

She gave him a smile that would melt any icy heart. 'And I am grateful for that,' she said. 'There is no one else I would like to care for me, but I shall care for you, too. And that means sharing our thoughts and feelings at work and at home… whichever home that might be,' she added.

He nodded. 'There are no visible wounds, so we are considering poison,' Thomas told her, reaching for her hand. 'We'll know tomorrow when the coroner finishes his inspection.'

She squeezed his hand. 'It was a good representation, wasn't it?'

Thomas looked at her, puzzled. 'What do you mean?'

'Of the painting,' she said. '*Weeping with the Willows*.'

Thomas hit the top of the cab roof. 'Driver, stop! It's a painting?' he asked Matilda.

'Why yes,' she said, surprised that neither Thomas, Detective Dart nor the coroner had recognised it. The painting had received such positive reviews on its release a few years back.

Thomas leaned out to call to the driver. 'Sorry, can you take us back to the garden, same location?'

'Right you are,' he said, and the hansom turned slowly.

'I didn't know. Who is the artist?' Then he groaned. 'Don't tell me, that is the deceased artist lying against the tree?'

'I am not sure,' Matilda said. 'I can't recall his name.' Her eyes widened. 'Oh my goodness, this could be connected to the death of Benjamin Bannon, your other case. That would be two artists killed in the style of one of their paintings.'

'Yes,' he said through clenched teeth, annoyed that he did not realise the significance of the scene. 'I need to speak to Harry and the coroner before they move the body.' He kissed her hand. 'Thank you, Matilda, you really have helped me,' he said.

She smiled with satisfaction.

The hansom pulled up.

'Please wait for me here.' He rushed out of the hansom as it stopped and raced to catch the two men at the scene.

Chapter 13

Gideon Hayward unlocked the door to the *Gallery of Fine Arts* and entered, locking it behind him. His rostered weekend staff member would arrive before the hour was up and the gallery officially opened at 10am, but Gideon liked to check on things beforehand. Marlon Dominey had not dropped in before the close of business Friday to collect his cheque as planned. The cheque was for sales to date and no artist missed a cheque, ever, even if they weren't significant, as was the case with Marlon's current exhibition. Gideon decided to drop in on Marlon this morning to deliver it personally. He mused that perhaps the artist got distracted in his work or that the thought of returning to the gallery after the bad reviews was not to his creative liking. He could understand that.

Gideon walked around checking the gallery was cleaned to expectations, adjusted a few paintings, lit lamps and was interrupted by the gallery door opening – his weekend manager had arrived early.

'Gideon, good morning,' the bewhiskered young man said with great enthusiasm. 'What a splendid day to be surrounded by fine art.'

Gideon grinned. 'Indeed. it is, Wilkie.'

He had hired Wilkie Watkins to staff the *Fine Art Gallery* on the weekend, in large part due to Wilkie's enthusiasm. He was unconventional, which appealed to Gideon – a snappy but slightly alternative dresser, passionate about art and all things culture, a champion of women's rights, and a poet of sorts. Visitors to the gallery loved Wilkie and he had a way of making them feel like they were the most important person in the room. During the week he worked on translations for his living, but he wanted a role with some human interaction, and both Gideon and Wilkie found the arrangement agreeable.

Mind you, Gideon attracted his own audience to the gallery on weekdays, in particular young ladies with more interest in the manager than in the artwork, which frustrated Gideon no end. This was what he was good at – his eldest brother Amos had a head for law, Daniel was an artist and a court illustrator, his twin brother Elijah had a medical mind and was proving to be a fine young doctor, and his younger sister, Matilda, could write. But Gideon had demonstrated his management skills with the gallery's owner. He had turned the gallery around, brought in a profit, created a profile for it, had secured good stories in the press, and the staff liked him. He was a born manager.

Wilkie looked around. 'Ah, I see the art has not improved overnight,' he quipped and Gideon laughed.

'Sadly no, but it continues to be a curiosity, and that is serving us well. Speaking of the artist, Marlon did not collect his cheque yesterday.'

'Good grief, he's not a starving artist then,' Wilkie exclaimed.

'My thoughts exactly. I'll take it over now and leave you to open.'

As he said the words, a sharp rap on the door startled them both. Gideon's eyes widened at the sight of Detective Thomas Ashdown on the other side of the door. He walked to the door, unlocked it, and let him in.

'Thom, come in, what's going on?' Gideon asked, and then remembering formalities continued. 'Detective Thomas Ashdown, this is my weekend manager, Mr Wilkie Watkins.'

The two men shook hands.

'Gentlemen, I'm sorry to interrupt at this hour. I need your help again, Gids, if you will?' Thomas said.

'Of course. What do you need?'

'Help to find a painting.'

Gideon frowned. 'You're investigating a stolen painting?'

'No, I'm investigating another murder,' Thomas said bluntly, forgetting not everyone worked in finding dead bodies daily.

Wilkie's hand went to his heart. 'Another artist?'

Thomas nodded. 'Sadly, yes.'

'Not Marlon Dominey? He didn't come in yesterday for his cheque!' Gideon said and then quickly calculated the value a deceased artist might add to the less than desirable paintings on the wall.

'No, he's not dead, well not yet to the best of my knowledge,' Thomas said, and resisted a smile at Gideon's look of disappointment. 'But he may be in danger if someone is knocking off the city's artists.'

'Who? Who is the latest victim, Detective?' Gideon pushed.

'Christopher Gill,' Thomas informed him.

'No!' Wilkie's eyes were huge and he leaned back on the arm of the large leather couch near the window. 'Why would anyone do that? His work is beautiful.'

Gideon nodded. 'Maybe that's why. Two artists murdered, both with successful collections.'

'Between us, that's one of our theories,' Thomas agreed. 'I'm trying to find one of Mr Gill's paintings, and whether it is in a private or public collection. Can you help?'

'I'll do my best and if I can't, I'll make some enquiries,' Gideon said and went to his desk, pulling out a large book with the current year on the side and the title *Art Almanac*. 'The annual art bible,' Gideon explained. 'Which painting?'

Thomas looked at his notes: '*Weeping with the Willows*'.

'I love that painting, so beautiful,' Wilkie said. 'I saw it at the State Art Gallery, a wonderful work, such depth.'

Gideon ran his finger down the page, finding the entry and snapping the book closed. 'And that's where it still is, at the State Art Gallery, Thom,' Gideon said. 'My you're getting some culture this month.'

Thomas gave him a smirk, but appreciated that Gideon had not asked about his date with Matilda yet. A young couple appeared at the door and Wilkie glanced at his timepiece.

'Goodness, it's opening time, if that is alright, Detective?' Wilkie asked.

'Of course,' Thomas said. 'Well, thank you.'

'I'm heading over to see Marlon Dominey now. Care to join me? Or is he not a suspect,' Gideon jested.

Thomas smiled and shook his head. 'Everyone's a suspect! But I've got a meeting with Harry and the coroner. Could you warn Mr Dominey to be extra vigilant? Don't mention that I will want to know his alibi for last night just yet. I don't want him planning one if needed.'

'Understood,' Gideon said.

Wilkie opened the door and welcomed the guests.

Farewelling Wilkie, Gideon walked Thomas out. 'So, put me out of my misery, is Matilda still speaking with you?'

Thomas chuckled. 'Of course, it was a lovely evening.'

'No sparring or fighting? Really?' Gideon looked disbelieving.

'Only some, not as much as usual,' Thomas admitted, and Gideon laughed.

'Well, that's good news. See you at lunch tomorrow. I'm looking forward to Aunt Audrey's interrogation. I suspect she'll outdo any techniques you've learnt over the years.'

Thomas groaned. 'No doubt. Hopefully, the first date will suffice and I won't be questioned every Sunday.'

'Don't be ridiculous. When you've got a wedding ring on that finger it might ease up,' Gideon joked as he departed with a wave to see his struggling artist.

Chapter 14

Matilda and Alice were enjoying tea at Bowen's Tea Room. The small venue had become a regular favourite for a Saturday morning chat, a shared pot of tea and a slice of cake or two.

'I confess I missed your brother last night,' Alice said, and looked at her teacup, flushing slightly with being so emotionally open. The English were not prone to be so.

'Which one?' Matilda asked, and then laughed. 'Oh, that one. Yes, Daniel can be endearing.' She reached for Alice's hand. 'He is the brother I am closest to, not in age but we are very similar in nature, I adore him. I am so pleased you like him. I have three remaining sister-in-law positions to be filled and I want you to be one.'

Alice laughed and flushed more. 'Well after one date that might be a bit wishful.'

Matilda became serious. 'Daniel feels the same affection for you as you do for him.'

'Does he?' Alice asked, keen for any news.

'Very much so. I believe he was quite out of sorts that you had a prior engagement last night.'

'Good,' Alice proclaimed and sat up, looking brighter. 'Speaking of which, how was your evening with the handsome detective?' she asked.

'Very exciting. We finished the night at a murder scene.'

'No!'

'Yes.' Matilda leaned closer. 'I believe it is another artist but I haven't heard that officially yet.'

'Oh my. Do you think Mr Dominey and Miss Reubens are in danger?' Alice asked.

'Mr Dominey, possibly so,' Matilda said, topping up both of their teacups. 'I am sure Mrs Lawson will want our articles a little sooner now, just in case – heaven forbid – something happens to him and the articles will be obsolete.'

'Yes, I guess that is how we have to think if we are paid writers,' Alice said and looked a little shocked at the realisation. 'What makes you believe the victim was an artist?'

Matilda lowered her voice and explained the scene she witnessed in which the body was found. 'It's the *Weeping with the Willows* painting, I am sure. Either someone loved the painting enough to emulate it in the victim's death scene, or like last time with the artist Benjamin Bannon, it is the artist himself who is deceased.'

'Terrible,' Alice said. 'I saw that painting in the State Art Gallery, but I couldn't tell you who painted it.'

'Nor I. I think I might go there after our morning tea and see it again for myself. Do you have plans?'

'No, I'd love to come,' Alice said.

'Let us go by home and see if Daniel is there and wishes

to join us,' Matilda suggested. 'I'm sure he would be happy to visit the gallery if you are attending.'

'Indeed, let's do so,' Alice agreed, beaming. 'So, did you kiss?'

Matilda looked confused. 'Oh, Thomas and I, no. But he held my hand and kissed it several times, and we only disagreed a few times. All in all, that was a good effort.'

Alice laughed, and Matilda smiled and gave a small shrug.

'We have a history of being very competitive,' she said sheepishly.

'And some habits are hard to break,' Alice said, eyeing another small cake. 'So, let's not start today by cutting back.' She served them both, and the morning tea continued.

*****

The coroner walked around the prone body of the victim, Christopher Gill, and looked up at the two detectives.

'The small puncture wound is here,' Dr Nevins said, showing a small bruised mark on the victim's back, near his ribs on the right side. 'That is where he was injected with the poison.'

'So, he must have been restrained, asleep or trusted whoever he was with to be lying on his stomach and have received the injection,' Thomas said, thinking aloud.

'Another theory...' Dr Nevins offered.

'Please,' Thomas invited him to continue.

'He has several old injection marks on his body. Perhaps

he was having regular injections of opiates for the relief of pain. I would need to speak with his physician to know more. But perhaps he believed he was receiving pain relief.'

Harry agreed. 'Maybe our killer knew that and thought this injection would go unnoticed.'

Thomas walked to the other side of the victim to study him.

'Possibly. But the dosage was quite large,' Dr Nevins said.

'An amateur poisoner, perhaps,' Thomas said.

'Or someone wanting to finish the job quickly. The dose was much more than was needed to kill the poor fellow. But I'll leave the who and why to you fine detectives. I suspect you need to find the painting as well.'

'It's in the State Art Gallery,' Thomas said. 'I found out this morning.'

'But is it still there?' Harry asked. 'Fancy a trip to see the painting with our own eyes?'

'Perhaps we best, but first a quick stop at the office to see if the constables have completed the statements from last night's witnesses,' Thomas said, and gave his thanks to Dr Nevins.

The detectives departed, making their way back to the station on foot. As they entered the station, Thomas heard his name called.

'Detective Ashdown, a young lady is waiting to speak with you,' the senior desk clerk called. 'I have seated her in your office. Don't worry, I covered your board so your evidence did not offend.'

'Thank you, John, most astute of you,' Thomas said and

felt a rush of pleasure to know Matilda had called on him. He was equally satisfied that she could not get any leads for her story, although he would not put it past her to lift the cover and take a look at his notes on the board. He hastened his step.

'Ah, young love,' his partner said, following him down the hallway to Thomas's office.

Thomas gave Harry a smirk and stopped short in the doorway. It was not Matilda that waited for him but the young, beautiful and wealthy widow, Mrs Sophie Cornish, whom Harry and Thomas had called upon only two days earlier. Thomas grabbed Harry's arm to ensure he followed him into the office and did not leave them alone.

'Mrs Cornish.' The two men gave a small bow, and Mrs Cornish reciprocated. It was impossible not to notice how beautiful she appeared this morning. She had a fine figure accentuated by her wealth and fortune, and many of the police staff took the time to appreciate the fact as they passed the detective's office.

'What do we owe the pleasure of your visit?' Harry asked. 'We could have called on you had it been a police matter to spare you coming here.'

'Too kind, thank you Detective, but I do like to get out into the community where possible.'

Thomas nodded, and maintaining politeness, hurried her to the point.

'What can we do for you, Madam?' He invited her to sit, and made his way behind his desk and lowered himself into the chair, leaning forward slightly to not give the appearance of having all day. Harry stood nearby, not taking the seat nearest Mrs Cornish.

'I have heard of the death of another artist, Mr Christopher Gill,' she said.

Thomas nodded, surprised. 'Yes, I didn't know it was public knowledge yet.'

'You clearly have not seen today's headlines, Detective Ashdown. It is all over the front page of *The Brisbane Courier* and hence my reason for calling.'

Thomas frowned, confused. 'You are acquainted with Mr Gill or are feeling unsafe perhaps?'

'It is fair to say both. Mr Gill called on me only a few days ago. He was a regular guest at my home, a dear friend of my husband and me. In a strange coincidence, I now own both paintings which have featured in the death scenes of the two artists – *An Artist Bathing in the Season* and *Weeping with the Willows.*'

'But we understood that *Weeping with the Willows* was in the State Art Gallery?' Harry said.

'Yes, it is, on loan from my husband and I, well now from me, I guess,' she said with a coy look towards Thomas.

Thomas swallowed. 'I can request that our police force patrols your area more vigilantly and regularly while this investigation is ongoing, if that would give you peace of mind, Mrs Cornish.'

'It would thank you, Detective Ashdown. Should you be in the area, I would feel much safer if you could check in yourself. I know you are busy, of course,' she said, the words soft and whispered with intent.

Thomas ignored the request and continued his

questioning. 'Did you ever entertain where both artists were in attendance at the same time, Mr Bannon and Mr Gill?'

'Yes, there were several times that I held soirees to celebrate the purchase of a work with the artist and the artistic community, and fellow artists attended.'

'Do you have any paintings of Marlon Dominey's?' Thomas asked.

'Two. Why, do you think Mr Dominey will be harmed next?' Mrs Cornish looked alarmed.

'Not at all,' Thomas assured her. 'I recently attended his exhibition opening and was curious.'

'Ah, I didn't know you were an art lover, Detective. I too would have been there but had a prior engagement,' she said.

'Sadly, I'm not an art lover,' Thomas assured her bluntly. 'I was there as a guest.'

Harry spoke up to cover Thomas's lack of charm. 'We were about to visit the State Art Gallery to ensure that *Weeping in the Willows* was still secure there.'

'As was I,' Mrs Cornish said, surprised. 'My carriage is out front, perhaps we can go together now and that will save you time organising your own transport.'

'Excellent,' Harry said, and restrained a laugh at Thomas's expression. 'Shall I see you to the carriage and Detective Ashdown can join us promptly?'

'Yes,' Thomas agreed. 'I just have some paperwork to collect. I'll be there momentarily.'

He watched as Harry escorted Mrs Cornish out, had a quick scurry through the paperwork on his desk, and found the reports he was looking for from the young constables. He glanced through them quickly; there was nothing there that flagged immediate action required. With a sigh, he went to join his partner and Mrs Cornish for a trip to the art gallery.

Chapter 15

Gideon arrived at the residence of Marlon Dominey and noted the curtains were still drawn. He looked at his timepiece; after 10.30am, surely that was not too early for anyone, even an artist. He took the stairs to the front door of the residences and tapped lightly. He could see through the frosted glass panel on the door the shape of a person walking towards him. It swung open and the landlady, Mrs Dempsey, appeared.

'Mr Hayward.' She greeted him with a smile and self-consciously patted down her hair and then apron. 'This is a nice surprise. You're here to see Mr Dominey, then?' she asked, moving aside.

'Indeed, I am, Mrs Dempsey. And how are you on this fine morning?' He greeted her with one of his most charming grins that never failed to win over the ladies of all classes.

'Can't complain, not for a moment. There's worse off, isn't there?' she asked.

'Always. I passed a few on the way here looking a little worse for wear from the evening prior,' he said with a wink that made her chuckle. 'Is our artist up?'

'Not a stirring from him this morning, but high time he was up. I'll bring you both some tea.'

'Too kind, thank you, Mrs Dempsey. That would be lovely.'

Gideon took the stairs two at a time and arriving at Marlon's door, knocked softly and then entered. The room was dark and Gideon could see the shape of Marlon lying full length on the Chesterfield leather lounge.

Marlon's head lifted at the intrusion of light and a visitor into his room.

'Gideon, is that you?' he said, and slowly swung his legs around to sit up. He ran his hands through his hair and then over the stubble on his face.

'It is. I'm sorry to disturb you, but I'm here to announce it is morning,' Gideon joked, and Marlon gave him a small smile and shrug.

'Didn't make it to the bedroom?' Gideon asked. He pictured Marlon and Miss Reubens enjoying a passionate night as one expected lovers, artists and muses might.

'I worked very late. In fact, I worked non-stop. I don't know what day or time it is, but I am glad you woke me,' Marlon said. His European accent was a little thicker when first woken, and when he was not concentrating on his words. Marlon rose, tucking in his loose white shirt.

Gideon made his way to the window. 'Shall I let in the morning?'

'Please, slowly,' Marlon said, and winced as Gideon pulled back the curtains, filling the room with light.

Gideon moved along to each of the four large windows

and pulled back the heavy drapes. It was a beautiful day outside, bright, fresh and smelling of autumn.

He returned to Marlon's side and pulled the cheque from his pocket. 'You forgot to collect this yesterday, and I was worried about you,' Gideon said, and handed it over.

'Ah, yes, my apologies. I was working.' Marlon glanced at the cheque and nodded, surprised. 'A reasonable effort given the reviews were so harsh.'

'Good sales,' Gideon agreed, and turned to see what Marlon had been working on. He gasped.

'What do you think?' Marlon asked.

Gideon never gave an artist his opinion on their work. He was no artist and he did not think it was his business to comment; Marlon knew this.

Gideon stood in awe.

'Tell me. I know you don't like to, but I do value your opinion,' Marlon said.

Gideon turned to look at him. 'Marlon, they are quite exceptional.'

Marlon grinned. 'The inspiration returned.'

'Where is Miss Reubens?' Gideon asked, and looked around as if he expected her to surface from behind a canvas.

Marlon waved his hand dismissively. 'She is off gallivanting and socialising as she does. I am not an artist that requires a model, she is a muse and her inspiration was all that was needed. She knows best not to interrupt me when I am painting with fervour.'

Gideon moved more in line with the first of four large canvases. Two were completed and the third and fourth were underway. He stood staring at the life coming off the canvas.

'I feel like Miss Reubens' life has been suspended in motion and you have captured her spirit,' Gideon said.

'Yes!' Marlon hissed, moving to stand beside Gideon. 'Yes.'

'Dramatic and romantic, but…' Gideon hesitated. He was not a poetic man, but a practical one. 'I feel like I shouldn't be looking, but yet I can't look away from her eyes.'

'Thank you. Do you not feel as though her soul is hanging in the balance of life and the beyond? Is it not?' Marlon asked.

'Yes, exactly, and the way nature has enveloped her in the stream, I am not sure if she is from nature or returning to it.'

Marlon nodded and smiled beside him. He slapped Gideon on the back, delighted with his words.

Gideon moved on to the second painting. Marlon's muse was just below the surface of the water, where her eyes watched the viewer, but they were hazy and out of focus as they were painted immersed. Her sharpest feature that drew the viewer's eye was her small white hand rising above the water as if begging to be pulled from it.

'Amazing,' Gideon said, spellbound. He moved on to the partially finished third and fourth paintings and after some time observing them with great appreciation, he turned to find Mrs Dempsey had served tea and cake and he had not heard her enter the room. 'Marlon, you must have worked non-stop. I am no judge but this is your best work ever, surely. It is truly mesmerising.'

Marlon smiled, excited. 'I feel the same. It flowed from me. I could not get it on the canvas quick enough it has such power over me.' He rubbed his unshaven face, evidence of his inability to do anything but paint for the last few days.

Marlon offered a poured cup of tea, and Gideon accepted it with thanks.

'Will you exhibit it?' Marlon asked.

'Of course, I'd be honoured,' Gideon said. 'But wait, this must be planned carefully.'

'Because of the poor reviews for my current showing,' Marlon said, and sighed.

'No, because you are a genius,' Gideon said, and made Marlon laugh. 'Let me think for a moment…' Gideon said. He walked to the window with his teacup and looked out as he sipped.

The two men stood in the silent room; Marlon finished his dressing while Gideon thought.

'This is what I think we should do.' Gideon turned to elaborate on his thoughts.

Marlon gave him his attention. 'Please, go ahead.'

'I suggest we invite two critics, no more – your two harshest critics from your current exhibition to come for a private preview viewing. Stroke their significant sense of self-importance,' Gideon said with a smile. 'When they arrive, they will find the works as I did… in progress, suspended dramatically as they are now in this morning light. We will tell them they alone may review it in advance and it is an exclusive invitation. The reviews will astound,' Gideon said. He moved to the table and placed his teacup down. 'Then,' he continued, 'the attention that is created from the reviews will heighten the anticipation. My gallery will run several notices in the newspaper promoting the opening of your highly acclaimed exhibition, and we will do opening night differently.'

'How so?' Marlon asked, seating himself on the couch and enjoying the attention promised for his work.

'The opening night exhibition will be a paid ticketed event only. No special guests, no free tickets, paid entry only and the price of entry will be considerable. This opening will be the event every society person will want to attend.' Gideon grinned. 'We will have limited tickets and when we have three-quarters of the tickets sold, we will announce it is sold out. I will have the remainder up my sleeve to offer to the highest and most persuasive bidders.'

Marlon laughed. 'Brilliant.'

Gideon continued. 'We will also ensure the entry price affords only the best champagne and quality canapes are served. I know just the man to organise that for us,' he said, thinking of Thomas' nephew, Teddy. 'The profit from ticket sales will reward us both handsomely before even one painting sells.'

Marlon grinned. 'I am loving this idea of yours, Gideon. You are a born businessman.'

Gideon smiled and nodded his thanks, secretly thrilled, especially with the opportunities it would create to profile the gallery even more.

'There will be no painting sales allowed on the night,' Gideon stated firmly.

'No?' Marlon looked worried. 'But they will be passionate and full of champagne.'

'We will conduct a silent auction and accept bids delivered to us in sealed envelopes. The day following the official launch, we will be open to the public for one month only before the exhibition closes. This will create a sense of desire to get to the exhibition now or be unable to contribute to the talk in society. Then at the end of the month, the winners of the silent auction will be informed of their winning bid, and your paintings delivered,' Gideon said and smiled on finishing his plan.

'That is brilliant,' Marlon said, rising and clapping him on the back again as he passed him to go to his first and favourite painting. 'I am not sure I can part with this one though.'

Gideon nodded. 'See how you feel closer to the end of the month. It will certainly encourage the price to be driven up if we advise you can't part with it. Someone will rise to the challenge of wanting to take it from your hands for their private collection.'

Marlon nodded, but did not take his eyes from his first painting. 'I will finish the other two paintings in the next few days, so invite your critics when you wish,' Marlon said.

'And I shall leave you to it,' Gideon said. He took one last look at the work. 'Please give my regards to Miss Reubens. She has inspired you beyond all measure this time.'

Marlon smiled. 'That she has. She has been the perfect muse and served her purpose well.'

Chapter 16

Matilda looked around in surprise; there were quite a few people at the State Art Gallery this morning. She wondered how many had come to see the 'sacrificial' painting for themselves. The omnibus stopped and Daniel disembarked, offering his hand to Alice to assist her from the ride, and then to his sister, Matilda, who accepted only because they were out in society.

'I haven't been to the art gallery for years,' Daniel proclaimed. Matilda suspected her brother was more thrilled to be in the company of Alice than at the art gallery.

'It is a perfect day to be out and about as well,' Alice said. 'I don't think I shall ever tire of this beautiful weather. At home, it would be wet and cold, but I will say I miss the green countryside.'

'Then we'll have to show you some of ours,' Daniel suggested. 'I have no idea where that might be given I am largely a town dweller, but I shall do my research,' he said, making the ladies laugh.

After the omnibus ride, the ladies brushed down their

patterned skirts and crisp white shirts and straightened their straw sailor hats.

'Right then, shall we?' Matilda asked, walking towards the gallery entrance. 'It is a shame Gideon wasn't home. He might have come with us and given us a professional tour.'

'I suspect because he works in a gallery all week, he is happy to not be in one on a Saturday,' Daniel suggested.

'Look at the newspaper headline, Matilda,' Alice exclaimed, pointing at *The Brisbane Courier* that the young paper seller held. 'Oh my goodness, no wonder there is a crowd here. It must list the location of the painting. Perhaps it includes the artist's name.'

The Brisbane Courier's front page screamed: *Another artist found dead. Posed in the style of his famous painting.*

'Murder in the gardens,' the boy paper seller yelled.

Daniel approached and offered him a coin for the paper and let the lad keep the tip. He returned to the ladies.

'So, the victim is the artist. I did wonder. Who is it, Daniel?' Matilda asked as she and Alice looked over his shoulder.

Daniel scanned the story. 'It says his name is Christopher Gill and his death was designed to look like his famous painting, *Weeping with the Willows*. He was left against the tree – it is unknown yet if he died there, or earlier and was moved to the site.'

'How awful,' Alice said, her hand going to her heart.

Daniel's eyes widened on seeing that he upset Miss Doran. He quickly folded the paper and put it behind his back. 'I'm sorry, that was careless of me.'

Alice shook her head. 'No, Matilda and I were discussing the crime earlier and as we work for a newspaper now, we have to face the fact that violence is around us.'

Matilda agreed.

'No, you don't,' Daniel said, looking at Alice with concern. 'Forgive me. I can only imagine what we have put Matilda through over the years without remembering that she is a lady,' he said, and gave her a wink.

'Yes, fortunately, I am hardy,' she joked with him, and accepted his offered arm as they took to the stairs and entered the cool and spacious surrounds of the gallery.

'What a fortunate man I am,' he said, 'with two beautiful ladies to escort. Look, I am the envy of every man here already.'

Matilda had noted several men had passed and dipped their hats as they entered the art gallery searching for *Weeping with the Willows*.

'I am no detective, but I suspect that is it over there where the crowd has gathered,' Matilda said with a nod toward a large painting where a viewing audience was three rows deep.

'Let's join them and make our way to the front,' Daniel said, escorting the ladies over.

It was not long until they were before the large and dramatic painting, appreciating the artist's skill and subject matter.

Alice whispered to Matilda: 'Was that what it was like, the scene?'

Matilda nodded. 'Exactly so. Quite amazing, really.'

After a few moments, they moved away. 'Let's take tea,' Alice suggested, despite having done so earlier with Matilda.

The British were known for their consumption of tea and Alice was a willing participant.

'Let's have a light lunch instead,' Daniel said. 'I know just the place if time permits?' he asked Alice.

'That would be delightful,' she agreed, and the pair smiled happily at each other.

They walked around the gallery for another twenty minutes and then made their way out for lunch. As they neared the stairs outside the gallery, Matilda stopped.

'There's Thomas and Detective Dart getting out of that carriage… with a woman,' Matilda said, her voice fading as she saw Thomas offer his hand to assist the woman. Daniel and Alice turned to see the three people that Matilda had spotted. 'Who is she, I wonder?'

'She's beautiful,' Alice said. 'I thought at first it was Miss Sapphire Reubens.'

'As did I,' Matilda agreed, 'but it is not.'

'I believe she is the widow, Mrs Sophie Cornish,' Daniel offered.

Matilda had the opportunity to study Thomas without his knowing. She had never experienced jealousy. All her life, as the only daughter, she was cocooned in love. There was no sister to compete with and no suitor whose heart and hand she had lost. Her father and brothers protected her, and Aunt Audrey guided her in the ways of womanhood. But the feeling that engulfed her was surprisingly overwhelming.

'How do you know of her?' Matilda asked Daniel.

'She was in court… a minor matter relating to her husband's will. I did not have to illustrate that session, but

I sat in the gallery for a while until my next work session,' he advised.

'Was she successful in her representation?' Alice asked delicately.

'Very much so,' Daniel answered. 'She is a very wealthy single woman.' He turned to Matilda. 'She is a great art benefactor, I believe. You know her residence, the Georgian mansion on the river at Newstead.'

'Indeed,' Matilda said.

Matilda noted Thomas was being most attentive to the widow, and Matilda bristled. Mrs Cornish had stepped to the ground from the carriage and moved away, but continued to rest her hand on Thomas's arm. Just the evening prior, Matilda had allowed him to hold her hand and profess his feelings. And now, here he was in the company of a beautiful, sophisticated woman but a few years older than herself, his hand assisting her. She was grateful, at least, that Detective Dart was along with them.

The small party was walking towards Matilda, and despite her desire to turn away she could not while accompanied by Alice and Daniel. By now Thomas had excused himself of Mrs Cornish's hold by searching for a notepad in his jacket. But as they arrived at the half a dozen stairs to the gallery entrance, Mrs Cornish took his arm again.

Matilda watched as he led Mrs Cornish up the stairs, looked up, and scanned the small crowd with annoyance. The numbers were increasing, making it harder for him to do his duty if that was the purpose of his visit, Matilda mused. At last, his gaze reached hers and she saw his eyes widened with surprise. She raised a hand and attracted Detective Dart's attention too; the gentlemen with Mrs Cornish in tow, steered towards them.

Each of the group was a study in character: Thomas looked decidedly uncomfortable as he again freed himself from Mrs Cornish's grip. Daniel had a noticeable frown upon his brow, while Alice looked intrigued and Matilda's expression was that of an experienced poker player. Harry looked delighted to see the group and Mrs Cornish sized the ladies up as expected.

'Matilda,' Thomas cleared his throat, 'Miss Hayward, Miss Doran, Dan, what a pleasant surprise.'

'It is, Detective Ashdown. A lovely day for an outing to the gallery with friends,' Matilda said, and raised an eyebrow.

Harry spoke up. 'May I introduce Mrs Sophie Cornish?'

Daniel bowed, and all three of the ladies offered a small curtsey as Harry continued with the introductions.

Thomas explained. 'Mrs Cornish has gifted the painting, *Weeping with the Willows*, to the gallery, and wishes to see it is still in place.'

'Loaned,' Mrs Cornish corrected him.

He nodded, not taking his eyes off Matilda.

'Shall we all go in then together?' Harry suggested, glossing over the tension that existed between Matilda and Thomas. Daniel appeared to have readily accepted his best friend's explanation for being in the company of another woman other than his sister, given Mrs Cornish was tied up in Thomas's investigation.

'We have already seen the painting,' Alice said and addressed Mrs Cornish. 'A truly amazing work by Mr Gill.'

'It is indeed,' Mrs Cornish said.

Alice continued: 'I suspect it will be impossible to get near the painting by this afternoon, the crowds are already gathering.'

Harry nodded. 'I'll just show my badge and we'll work our way to the front of the queue,' he said.

'At least more people can enjoy it now that it is here in the gallery, rather than have it hidden away in a private residence,' Mrs Cornish said, altruistically. 'However, given the circumstances, do you think I should ask to have it removed and brought home for now?'

'No, Mrs Cornish, I don't recommend that. Let it stay here. For your safety we don't want to draw any attention to you or your home,' Thomas informed her, and she nodded her understanding.

'How concerning for you,' Alice said, patting Mrs Cornish's arm.

'Very alarming,' she agreed, and gave Daniel her most vulnerable look. Alice noticed and Daniel cleared his throat and looked away.

Mrs Cornish addressed Alice: 'You are visiting from England, or have you arrived to make this your home?'

'Visiting, but I have fallen in love with Australia so I am not in any hurry to depart,' Alice said without looking at Daniel directly but registering his smile and interest.

'You must come for tea, and you too, Miss Hayward.'

'Thank you,' Matilda said, pleased with the invitation and the chance to see the residence of Mrs Cornish. 'That would be delightful. But for now, we best leave you to your purpose. The crowd is getting larger.'

A glance at the crowds arriving and the jostling on the pavement gave truth to Matilda's comments. They bid the group goodbye, and Thomas tried to catch Matilda's eye. She closely followed Daniel and Alice. He moved to take her arm and nodded to Harry to continue inside. She pulled away from him and he stepped around and in front of her to stop her for a moment.

'A moment, Matilda, please,' he said, and she acquiesced and dropped behind her party.

Matilda looked up at him as Thomas lowered his head to speak in a quiet voice.

'You cannot think for a moment that I am disloyal to you?' he asked, frowning at her.

'Of course not. It is so fortunate that you were on hand to offer Mrs Cornish assistance. She looked most needy,' Matilda said, narrowing her eyes.

'I assure you, I did not seek the company of Mrs Cornish to inspect the painting nor offer myself as her guide.'

'I must go, Thomas. I'm delaying Alice and Daniel, and you are at work after all.' She gave him a brief curtsey and departed before he could say another word.

Chapter 17

Matilda's mind was racing, her heart beating fast, and she had no appetite for lunch.

'Will you think me terribly rude if I excuse myself from lunch?' she asked Daniel and Alice, knowing they would be secretly happy to be in each other's company.

'Are you not well?' Alice asked, concerned. 'I will see you home.'

'No, I am perfectly fine, but thank you, dear Alice. I was planning to go to the *Women's Journal* office this afternoon and finish my piece on Mr Dominey. The timing is perfect now that I am feeling particularly inspired after the visit to the gallery. I am sure you both will find plenty to talk about without me present,' she said with a smile.

'I will do my best to make up for Matilda's absence,' Daniel assured Alice. 'Let me get you a hansom at least, Tillie,' he said, using her nickname.

'No, I think I shall walk. It is not that far, and the day is perfect. Besides, we indulged in sweets this morning so the exercise will do me good,' Matilda said.

'That's true,' Alice agreed, 'so for my part, it will be a light lunch and no supper this evening.'

Alice touched Matilda's arm and turned to Daniel. 'Will you excuse us for just one moment.'

'Of course,' he said and bowed, moving away.

Matilda was always in awe of watching her brothers being so charming in society; it is hardly what she experienced in their rowdy household.

'You're distressed,' Alice whispered.

Matilda gave a barely discernible nod.

Alice continued, 'I can't attest to knowing your Thomas, but I know from observation that he is devoted to you. Wait until you hear what the circumstances are that brought him, Detective Dart, and Mrs Cornish together before you let the situation envelope you.'

Matilda nodded. 'Thank you, Alice. I know that is wise counsel, but I confess I am a novice at romance and I did not expect to be slighted so easily.'

'I am sure you have not been. You have known Thomas for most of your life and you know him to have integrity. Come with us for lunch or let me see you home,' Alice begged.

Matilda took her hand. 'You are a dear and kind friend, but really, I look forward to a brisk walk to clear my head and I do want to finish my story. I had planned to do so this afternoon.'

Alice nodded and accepted Matilda's words.

Matilda departed with a fond farewell to her brother and Alice, and walked away with purpose, a little consoled by Alice's thoughts on the situation. Even as a child, when she needed to be alone after an incident with her brothers or just sought her own company, she would walk or sit in nature. She found it healing. But to be slighted for another woman was something foreign to her, and she walked with purpose while she tried to analyse her emotions.

She thought of the glamourous Mrs Cornish – her youth, beauty, wealth and with all she had to offer, and compared herself. She knew herself to be outspoken… a lady with too many boyish habits. While her father was a man of some wealth – as was Aunt Audrey – should she marry, then her husband would be judged for what he could bring to the marriage, unlike Mrs Cornish who no doubt could keep any husband.

She kept seeing Mrs Cornish's hand upon *her* Thomas's arm.

'I love him,' she said, speaking to herself as she strode along. She had never said those words out loud to anyone, especially not Thomas. Matilda barely noticed the path she walked or those that she greeted as she passed; her mind consumed in thoughts of the incident.

'He loves me. He is respectable and caring and strong. Have I been too flippant with his affections? Does he not know that I too feel committed to him?' After considering this argument for a brief time, Matilda decided surely not. 'We have been friends for so many years that there has only been a recent departure from friendship to love. And yet, was he flirting with the widow?' she asked herself.

She came to the street in which the *Women's Journal*

office was located and walked the remaining length to the building, pushing open the office door and finding several ladies at work. Matilda immediately felt at home and greeted them. A glance at Mrs Lawson's office told her the editor was not in today. Matilda went to her allocated desk to write. She allowed herself to dwell a little longer on her predicament, unsure of how to handle it.

She thought, *what if he realised after our date that he had made a mistake? But no, he said at the gallery that he did not seek to accompany Mrs Cornish there, but yet he did. Maybe I should beg his pardon for how our date ended. Maybe I should not have insisted on accompanying him to the crime scene.*

Matilda sat up straight, removed her straw hat, and took a deep breath.

No, this is me, she thought. *I shall always be like this, so it is for the best that Thomas sees that now and can make the choice his heart desires.*

And with a heavy heart, she opened her notebook to read back over her Marlon Dominey story and edit as needed.

*****

Thomas could not get away from Mrs Cornish soon enough. She enjoyed and indulged in the attention she received, and Harry found the situation amusing. Thomas could not. He had patiently waited and worked at winning Matilda's hand and he had no intention of being derailed by the husband-seeking Mrs Cornish… or at least that was his opinion of her.

On seeing the painting in place and confirming that it was indeed the inspiration for the murder, Detectives Ashdown and Dart bid Mrs Cornish farewell. She intended to seek the curator for a chat and had her carriage and footman nearby to see her home.

'Slow down, Thom,' Harry said, trying to keep up with Thomas, who walked with purpose, his jaw locked in frustration.

He slowed his pace, and Harry arrived at his side.

'Why don't you go visit Miss Hayward and sort this out, son. Your head won't be in your work until you do.'

Thomas exhaled, frustrated, holding the door for Harry as they departed the gallery.

'She has ventured out with Miss Doran and Daniel. I don't know where. I'll visit her residence later this afternoon.'

Harry nodded as they made their way to the street. 'Back to the office, then, and let's go through what we have to date,' he said, knowing how his young protegee worked and how Thomas's mind would need to be methodical in his process.

They hailed a hansom and arrived in time for lunch. Thomas had no appetite but Harry bought them both a sandwich from the dining room on the ground floor of their Roma Street offices and couldn't help but smile as Thomas devoured it despite his earlier protest of not being hungry. Thomas would forget to eat if food was not placed in front of him.

Standing at the board in his office, Harry took the chalk from his hand.

'We need to be able to read this later,' he joked, and took over the writing.

'My writing is not that bad,' Thomas smirked, not caring. He was happy to be hands-free to finish the sandwich. He began, 'So, victims… the first was Benjamin Bannon, 39, who was poisoned and positioned to replicate his painting *An Artist Bathing in the Season*.'

Harry wrote up the victim, the method of death and the name of the painting. Thomas continued: 'The second victim was artist Christopher Gill, 32, poisoned and placed in the Botanical Gardens in the mode of his painting *Weeping with the Willows*.'

Harry scribed this then drew a timeline and several columns labelling them *'People of Interest'*, *'Possible suspects'*, and *'Possible victims.'*

'Right,' Harry continued, 'we know that both of the deceased artists had glowing reviews for their recent exhibitions, unlike Mr Dominey. One of the constables has some information about it in the folder,' he told Thomas, who went to the desk, found the file and opened it.

Thomas drew out several news clippings and glanced over the witness statements.

'There is nothing in the witness statements of much value except how they found the deceased bodies or when they last saw the artist,' he mumbled. Looking at the press clippings, Thomas began to read aloud, 'Hmm, Harry, listen to this. Art critic Lawrence Longman described Benjamin Bannon's exhibition, *Seasons of our Life,* as "breathtaking and original. Mr Bannon's artistic strengths are best realised when depicting nature". Longman's review of the other artist, Christopher Gill's exhibition is generous as well. He describes the work as "displaying Gill's fine luminism and evoking emotions and reactions as only an artist of this calibre can achieve." High praise,' Thomas said.

'Longman was the critic that suggested Marlon Dominey wash out his paintbrush, was he not?' Harry asked.

'Yes. Add the critic Longman to our potential victims' list, and Marlon Dominey to the suspects' list – jealousy and anger are powerful motives for murder and two of his fellow artists enjoyed exemplary exhibitions and reviews while Dominey was lashed.'

'Done,' Harry said. 'We'd best drop in on the critics, especially Longman, and warn them to watch their backs. I suspect they are no stranger to receiving a few threats.'

'Their job is like ours… thankless unless you are delivering good news,' Thomas said, his heart still heavy, his head distracted. He took a deep breath and fired several more names at Harry. 'Miss Sapphire Reubens is a possible suspect. Does she love her artist, Mr Dominey, enough to orchestrate the death of his competitors?'

'She may be a potential victim too if someone is bumping off artists. The muse may well be in their sight,' Harry suggested, and put her in both columns. 'Mrs Sophie Cornish could go in both columns, too. She owns the paintings so are the attacks somehow a veiled threat to her, or did she organise killing the artists to increase the value of her paintings?' Harry wrote her name in both columns.

'Good thought. We should check out exactly how much her husband left her and if she really is the rich widow that she makes out to be,' Thomas said. 'There's another name we need to add to the list… Gideon Hayward.'

Harry snapped to look at him. 'I wondered if you would get to Mr Hayward. If you are out of favour now with Miss Hayward, you can be sure that won't put you in good stead.'

'I know, but she need not know. Besides, I don't believe it, but if I didn't know him, he would be on the list,' Thomas said. 'The other artists exhibited with different galleries and the one artist that went with Gideon's relatively new gallery – Mr Dominey – had a disastrous showing.'

'Except we know that the bad reviews have brought in a crowd and if Mr Hayward was our killer and trying to improve the value of the artwork of his artist, he would have considered taking Marlon Dominey's life,' Harry said.

'That's all true,' Thomas said, 'even so, he is worth considering and I didn't want you to think I was biased,' he said and gave his partner a grin.

'You? Never.' Harry chuckled. 'Anyone we've missed?'

'Most likely. On Monday I'll chase up the coroner and see if we have any clarification on the type of poison used and we can start narrowing down suppliers. The next thing is probably to visit Marlon Dominey and the critic, Lawrence Longman,' Thomas said, feeling weighted down with little evidence to go on, two dead artists, and a slight from Matilda.

Harry read him as he always did. 'Why don't we call it a day, Thom? This case will not get solved overnight and we both might benefit with an afternoon's separation from it.'

'You are probably right.'

Harry covered their board with a large black sheet. 'You need to visit Miss Hayward and clear the air.'

Thomas sighed. 'Yes. I can't believe she would think I was distracted by Mrs Cornish and welcomed her attention.'

Harry walked to the hat rack and grabbed both of their coats and hats. 'If you look at it from her perspective, you have arrived at the art gallery with an attractive woman of her own age on your arm, and Mrs Cornish was holding onto you as though you were the catch of the day. You didn't call in and invite Miss Hayward to attend the gallery with you even though she did tip you off about the painting, did she not?'

'Yes,' Thomas grimaced. 'I think Mrs Cornish is fishing for her next husband.'

'She is that,' Harry said, and put his coat on. 'Let me know if you need a kind word spoken on your behalf to Miss Hayward. Otherwise, I'll think about the case and let's confer on Monday morning. If we have no other artists dying in the interim.'

'God forbid,' Thomas muttered. 'Thank you, Harry.'

'Good luck mending bridges with your lady, Thom,' he said, departing with a wave and walking off down the hallway to head home to his loving and patient wife, Therese.

Thomas knew Harry was right, he had to call in at the Hayward household. He just hoped Matilda was home by now.

Women's Journal
Tuesday, 29 May 1888
Fortnightly edition Vol.1, No.14.
Price, 3d.

The Artist's Muse
by Matilda Hayward

Special feature: An interview with the artist Mr Marlon Dominey.

Imagine possessing the capability to inspire an artist to create works in literature, on canvas, or on stage. Is this the exclusive domain of the beautiful or is there an undefinable quality that enthrals an artist to capture a subject forever in their creation? Does that quality rest solely in the eyes of the creator?

Artist, Mr Marlon Dominey, has enjoyed success throughout his career. While his recent collection may have disappointed his loyal following, and received the ire of the critics, Mr Dominey has gone to pains to ensure the responsibility for his artwork rests with him.

'Like many artists, many things have inspired me - nature, light, other artists, music, the feminine form,' Mr Dominey said. 'But sometimes the inspiration does not get reflected in the artwork. The fault lies with me. But an artist does not create just to please. We create to agitate, motivate and sometimes to cast out our own demons.'

Mr Dominey would not expand on the latter other than to say that being far from home, it gratified him to be received so warmly into the breast of the community, and he was settling into his newly adopted city.

'My next collection will not only reflect the importance of nature to my soul, but the influence of my current homeland, and the impact my beautiful muse, Miss Sapphire Reubens, has upon me.'

I have had the privilege to preview the works in progress and can concur that they will satisfy the harshest critic.

When asked how Mr Dominey was introduced to his inspiration, Miss Reubens, he said: 'The moment I laid eyes upon her at a gallery, many years past, now, I was mesmerised. I could not continue to paint until I had met her, and from that day on, she became part of my life,' he said.

Miss Sapphire Reubens of European descent is a classic beauty of olive skin, amber eyes and long dark tresses.

Mr Dominey explained: 'To find a muse – a pure form of beauty and poetry and art all represented in a face – that when she gazes upon you, halts your thoughts and movements so that all you think of is her – is a blessing that inspires your best creativity,' he said.

But it would take a woman of some character and fortitude to be a muse. Was there always a person waiting to take her role? Did she worry she may fail to inspire, thus threaten her own security? Or does she worry she may age and her beauty decline in the artist's eyes? What then becomes of her? Of this Mr Dominey had no answer as it seemed an impossible fate.

The recently deceased artist, Dante Gabriel Rossetti, married his muse, Elizabeth Siddal. She departed this earth before him, but Mr Rosetti continued to paint her after her death, their love having no bounds. The artist we know as Rembrandt married his muse, Saskia van Uylenburgh, drawing her with tender accuracy and care. She too departed this life before him.

The celebrated French artist, Claude Monet, painted his muse and wife, Camille Doncieux in the beautiful painting, Femme Cueillant des Fleurs. But Camille died young, after the birth of their second child. While Mr Monet has remarried, Miss Doncieux or rather, Mrs Monet, will live on forever as he captured her.

Let us hope this is not the fate of the artist's muse, as the beautiful Miss Sapphire Reubens may well have inspired Mr Dominey's best work yet. The separation of hearts in love is too painful to consider, as poet Mr Shelley said, "What is all this sweet work worth, If thou kiss not me?"

Chapter 18

Matilda arrived home mid-afternoon, relieved to be back in the comfort and security of her home, especially while feeling so shaken by Thomas's duplicity.

'Ah good,' Harriet said on seeing Matilda come through the front door. 'I like you home before the dusk falls, and these autumn afternoons can turn chilly quickly.'

Matilda smiled gratefully at Harriet. 'I was just finishing my article at the *Women's Journal*, but I confess I am feeling weary. I might lie down for a while.'

Harriet helped Matilda remove her hat and gloves.

'Perhaps you are taking on too much. Are you unwell?' Harriet touched Matilda's forehead as she did when Matilda was a child.

'No.' Matilda smiled at her action. 'But I have been out most of the day and did a long walk from the gallery to the office. I'm feeling quite spent,' she said, heading towards the stairs. 'Should anyone call, please say I am unavailable.'

'Including Thomas?'

'Especially Thomas,' Matilda said.

Harriet narrowed her eyes, understanding the source of Matilda's state of distress. 'Have you had a falling out?'

'Nothing more than our usual bantering, but I don't feel up to company.' Matilda embellished the truth a little.

Harriet nodded. 'I'll be leaving shortly. I am off to a birthday party tonight. Cook has cold meat and salads for tea as requested by Mr Hayward, so rest until then.'

'I will. Thank you, Harriet, have an enjoyable evening.'

Matilda took the remaining stairs to her room, entered, and closed the door. She made her way to sit at the dressing table. She removed the pins from her hair, letting her blonde waves loose and feeling the relief from freeing the tight hairdo. She removed her garments, not needing Harriet's assistance as every clip was within reach, and put on a lighter dress suitable for home and dinner. She still felt restless, but lay on her bed.

Just for a little while, she told herself and closed her eyes. Her thoughts wandered. *Did Miss Reubens or Mrs Cornish ever suffer from fears of their chosen finding someone else?* Matilda wondered. *If they were married and he ceased to be inspired by her, she may stay on as a wife while he takes a mistress, but if they were not married, was she discarded? She only had her beauty to trade on.*

Her thoughts drifted to the rich widow. *Poor Mrs Cornish, to be widowed so young. That must have been terribly sad, but at least she has been looked after.* She couldn't imagine losing Thomas just when they were beginning.

Speaking of which, she heard the knock on the door downstairs and sat upright. Matilda wasn't sure if she had drifted off, but the light was softer outsider, perhaps she had slept for an hour or more. Straining to hear the conversation, Matilda could only make out the timbre of Thomas's voice and Harriet's soothing tone. The door opened and closed again five minutes later, and she breathed a sigh of relief.

I need to lick my wounds and think of my position before I face Thomas again too soon. Perhaps we are best to remain friends and as close as siblings, then he will always be welcome in my home. Except when he marries, I don't want Thomas and his wife here!

Matilda realised the situation was perilous. She rose, went to her dressing table and straightened her dress and brushed her hair. Matilda was not one for lying around and thus decided to see who else was home and maybe have a cup of tea if Cook didn't chase her out of the kitchen so close to the evening meal time. She opened her bedroom door and wandered down the hallway to the staircase, holding her dress as she took the descent. She gasped as a man rose from the seat near the entrance hallway. He held his hat in his hands, his jacket still on.

'Thomas!' her eyes widened. She dropped the skirt of her dress and gingerly touched her free hair.

'Matilda,' he gave a small bow, but not taking his eyes from her. She looked feminine and beautiful, and he wanted to embrace her.

'I thought you had departed,' she said, shocked, with a glance to the door and back.

'That was Harriet departing. I sought permission to wait for you.'

Matilda scoffed. 'You hardly need it. You have spent so many years in this house, it is surprising you don't have a bedroom of your own.' She coloured slightly on saying the words.

'Please, let me speak with you,' Thomas said. Seeing her reluctance, he added. 'I must insist upon it.'

'Must you?' she asked, surprised, stopping on the bottom step and nearly at eye level with him.

Thomas held firm, not removing his gaze from Matilda.

'I am not departing until we have spoken and while I know how long you can play this game for,' he said with the hint of a smile, 'I suggest you let me win on this occasion.'

Matilda sighed. 'Very well then, let's go to the drawing-room, no one is there I believe.' She led the way and Thomas followed, closing the door behind him. He reached for Matilda but she pulled away, maintaining a distance between them.

Thomas's jaw locked and then, taking a deep breath, he said, 'It is not how you perceived the situation to be, I assure you. Mrs Cornish is a widow who owns both of the paintings related to the last two victims.'

'Oh.'

'Yes, exactly. Her husband was a rich and senior man…'

'I understand, Thomas,' Matilda cut him off, her voice wavering. She did not wish to hear any more. 'She is attractive and wealthy—'

Thomas snapped. 'I don't desire her, Matilda, for goodness' sake! Far from it. We called on Mrs Cornish prior when we discovered she owned *An Artist Bathing in the Season*, and then she arrived at the station to tell us of her ownership of *Weeping with the Willows* once the news had broken of the murder. As Harry and I were departing for the gallery to see the painting for ourselves, Mrs Cornish offered a ride in her carriage as we were all heading in the same direction. It was fortuitous.'

Matilda nodded and walked to the window. Thomas studied her, but what he wanted to do was wrap her in his arms and kiss her, run his hand through her long blonde tresses and feel her softness against him.

'I understand you must make the best connection for yourself, and Mrs Cornish would be an advantageous match.'

Thomas threw his hands up in despair.

Matilda continued: 'I was thinking this afternoon, that perhaps you just decided on me because I have always been here. It is an easy and convenient relationship now at an age when you wish to settle.'

Thomas moved to Matilda in two quick strides and pulled her against him. She gasped in surprise.

'I don't know where these thoughts have originated from but hear me, Matilda, and understand this – I am not interested in bettering myself through marriage except with you. I am not in the least bit interested in Mrs Cornish or any other lady for that matter, my heart is in your hands,' he said, gazing upon her face framed by her loose hair. 'You are not an easy or convenient choice, trust me,' he said with a small smile, and Matilda accepted his tease with a smile of her own. 'I would walk from one end of the earth to the other for you, and I am not losing your hand in mine for anything.'

Matilda was a little overcome by emotion. Such beautiful words had never been spoken to her and she would not have expected such intensity from Thomas. She blinked away tears as Thomas touched her face.

'I am sorry, Thomas,' she said. 'I don't want to be that person who is suspicious and claims her man as if he were her property. I was jealous for the first time – it's a terrible feeling.'

'You have no grounds to be jealous of my affections ever,' he assured her. 'Nor do I want to feel that from you.'

Matilda nodded. The intimacy of their discussion was new to them both, and she continued: 'You are the first man to court me, to kiss my hand and tell me of his feelings,' she said in a quiet voice.

Thomas swallowed. 'And those feelings have increased tenfold if that is at all possible.'

They looked at each other for what felt like a long spell, and Thomas lowered his head to kiss her lips for the first time. The touch almost there when the door banged open and they both looked up, alarmed, Thomas stepped back.

'Ah, here you both are!' Daniel exclaimed. He looked from one to the other and back to Thomas. 'Oh, sorry, did I interrupt something?'

Matilda cleared her throat and looked away.

Thomas gave his best friend a frustrated look as he reined in his desire for Matilda. 'I was just telling Matilda, confidentially, and that applies to you, Dan, that Mrs

Cornish owns both paintings belonging to the victims and is thus to be treated with caution.'

'Is she a suspect in the murder? Really?' Daniel laughed.

'Women do murder, and do it very well,' Thomas said with a look to Matilda, who smiled smugly. 'But no, at this stage she is not a suspect, but she is involved whether or not she wants to be. Of course, I wouldn't have made the connection between the second murder and the painting until the victim was identified, if Matilda had not recognised the painting at the scene of the crime.'

She smiled up at him. 'See, I am useful.'

'I know that,' he assured her, 'in so many ways.' They held each other's gaze.

'Right then,' Daniel said, interrupting them again. 'Cook wants to know if you are staying for tea, Thom.'

Thomas turned to Daniel. 'No, but please thank her. I have some work to do on this case.'

'But you will be here for lunch tomorrow?' Matilda asked.

'I will be, indeed,' Thomas said to Matilda. He then turned to Daniel, who continued to stand there as if he were a chaperone.

Thomas rolled his eyes, and Matilda stifled a laugh.

'Best back to it, then.' He reached for Matilda's hand and kissed it. 'Matilda.'

He walked past Daniel. 'Dan,' he said.

'I might drop by your place later this evening,' Daniel called after him and Thomas called back that he was welcome. Matilda watched him depart and turned to find her brother looking at her.

'What?' she asked, frowning.

'Lucky I came in when I did, especially with you dressed so informally.'

Matilda scoffed. 'I assure you, brother, you should know both of us better than that.'

'Exactly,' he said.

Matilda smiled thinking how her world was now so much better again.

She passed him with a teasing glance, but not before mentioning, 'There may be a favour you want regarding Miss Doran. Just remember that before you decide to play the big brother with me.'

With that, she went to see what her father was up to and exchange stories of their day. She smiled as she heard Daniel call her name in pursuit.

Chapter 19

Lunch on Sunday after church was a tradition at the Hayward household that went back to when the boys were little and Mrs Hayward was still alive. Since her death many, many years ago, Mr Hayward's sister, Audrey, stepped in to act as the family matriarch. They were close as siblings go, and while Mr Hayward might not tell her often, the female influence – even if it was just once a week and on special occasions – was appreciated amongst his largely male brood.

Of course, that was changing now, evident with a glance around the table. Amos's wife Minnie was a gentle and compliant soul, but ambitious for Amos. Daniel had invited Miss Alice Doran again, given she was in the country with very few living relatives and was happy to attend church – a fact which won her Audrey's approval. And while Thomas had not yet begun to attend church regularly – that might have to change should he marry Matilda – he rarely missed lunch. With the four ladies around the table, the numbers were beginning to even out. The only Hayward missing at today's lunch was Elijah, who was on duty at the Brisbane hospital, a position he had secured since completing his studies at the Melbourne University and returning home.

Before sitting in his position as the other head of the table, Mr Hayward briefly appeared in the kitchen door to thank Cook. 'You are most tolerant, Mary,' Mr Hayward said. 'Thank you for accommodating our extra guests and growing family.'

'I like a large brood, Mr Hayward, you know that. And I appreciate when a meal is enjoyed. You need not be thanking me,' she said, but her embarrassed smile said she was pleased he thought to compliment her.

'You know Audrey will try to poach you again, and maybe Minne will try as well. I won't be offended if you choose to go to a household with more prestige and opportunities for your skills and fewer Sunday interlopers,' he said and sighed. 'But it will devastate me.'

Cook laughed. 'Yer need not worry about that, Mr Hayward. I have more than enough challenges keeping up the family's favourites and soon, who knows, we might have a youngster or two to feed as well.'

Mr Hayward smiled and nodded. 'I'm sure Audrey will remind Amos and Minnie that it is their duty to do so.'

He rolled his eyes, got another hearty laugh from Mary, and disappeared with a wave as he heard the laughs rising from the dining room.

'Lunch will be served now, Mr Hayward, if that suits you?' Harriet asked.

'When you are good and ready, thank you, Harriet. Do let us know if you need a hand and I'll put some of those children of mine to work.'

She smiled. 'I have it under control. You go and enjoy seeing their faces around the table again.' It was true that as the family was all now young adults, it was only once a week that the faces around the table numbered more than a few.

Mr Hayward joined the table and took his seat at the top, opposite his sister. He noticed that Thomas now sat next to Matilda, and smiled at the handsome pair they made.

'It is lovely to welcome you again, Miss Doran,' Mr Hayward said. 'Please don't stand on formality and wait for an invitation but join us every Sunday after mass.'

'Thank you, Mr Hayward, you are too kind,' Alice said in her crisp English accent. 'It is lovely to be in the breast of a family again.'

As expected, Aunt Audrey began her interrogation, starting with Thomas.

'I understand, young man, that you took my niece on a date Friday evening,' she said, turning to him.

'I had the pleasure of doing so, Aunt Audrey,' Thomas said, addressing the formidable grey-haired woman by the name he had called her since he was a boy.

'And?' she insisted.

'I am not engaged yet, Aunt Audrey, but being irresistible, it is only a matter of time,' Matilda cut in and the family laughed.

Aunt Audrey gave Matilda a small smile. 'Yes, well, let's hope your beau finds you irresistible. I imagine giving your unconventional upbringing not everyone will be so brave as to take you on.'

'Indeed not,' Thomas said and laughed as Matilda elbowed him in the ribs.

'Where did you go?' Aunt Audrey persisted.

Thomas mentioned the restaurant and Audrey raised her eyebrows, suitably impressed.

'And then the date took a turn for the interesting,' Daniel teased his best friend, 'and they went to a crime scene instead!'

Thomas frowned at Daniel, and Matilda kicked him under the table.

'Ouch,' he exclaimed and frowned at her, not at all hurt but adding to the drama.

'No!' Aunt Audrey exclaimed.

'Well, that was an unconventional date,' Amos said with a glance to his wife. 'I just took Minnie for tea.'

'Rightly so,' Aunt Audrey said, patting Amos's hand.

'So romantic,' Gideon said, and enjoyed the grimace Thomas gave him.

Thomas took a deep breath. 'I assure you, Aunt Audrey, I did my best to ensure Matilda stayed in the hansom, while I just quickly checked on my officers. I attempted to drop her home first.'

'Well, that would be no fun, would it?' Matilda said and saw Minnie's shocked expression. 'Thomas insisted I stay in the hansom, Aunt Audrey, but of course I could not. There might have been a story to write.'

'It wasn't a brutal crime at least,' Alice contributed, trying to help.

'Not in the least, it was a work of art, Aunt Audrey,' Matilda continued.

'Hardly conversation for the lunch table, I am sure,' Aunt Audrey said, feigning shock.

'Audrey is right,' Mr Hayward said with paternal solemnity as he gazed fondly at Matilda and then his daughter-in-law, Minnie and guest Miss Doran. 'It was remiss of me with young ladies present to allow it to go on for so long. So, Thomas, we are delighted that you have escorted our Matilda on a date, and let's hope they don't all end up that way,' he said, and Thomas smiled and gave him a nod of agreement.

Gideon spoke up. 'Dan, stop staring at Miss Doran and pass me the bread, please.'

Alice flushed, embarrassed, but Daniel just laughed.

'It is hard not to be drawn to beauty when Miss Doran is in my line of vision,' he said, and passed the bread to his younger brother.

'Do you want to swap places with me then so you can eat without distraction?' Gideon asked.

Daniel looked shocked. 'And look at Thomas all through lunch? Let's not go to extremes.'

Thomas grimaced and Matilda touched his arm. 'I think you are a very handsome man and I would happily gaze upon you, Thomas. Ignore Daniel, who can't even control that unruly hair, should we be discussing handsome.'

'It is rather unruly today, isn't it?' Minnie agreed, teasing her brother-in-law, who looked nothing like his fair-headed brother and her husband, Amos.

Mr Hayward cleared his throat for attention. 'As Audrey suggested, perhaps a more gentile topic. Would one of the ladies like to suggest one?'

Aunt Audrey sat back, satisfied with the suggestion, and

gave her brother a nod of approval, while Minnie looked terrified at the prospect of being put on the spot.

'I shall then,' Alice said, speaking up and winning another look of admiration from Daniel. 'The suffragette meeting went very well last week. You know there is talk of forming the Queensland Women's Suffrage League. It is so exciting.'

There was silence around the table as the men thought about what they should say.

'That is excellent news,' Matilda agreed. 'Will you join, Aunt Audrey?'

All eyes turned to the end of the table for Aunt Audrey's reaction; she was often unpredictable, but always proper.

'I will do so, Matilda,' she said, and gave a firm nod. Minnie gasped beside her, and Alice and Matilda beamed. 'We could achieve so much more with access to the right circles.'

'Hear, hear,' Mr Hayward agreed and raised his glass. 'To the ladies.'

'To the ladies,' the group echoed, and Matilda and Alice exchanged smiles. The times were a-changing.

But despite all good intentions, the subject of murder raised its head again.

'I hear that the artist's exhibition is progressing well at your gallery, Gideon, despite the critics' reviews,' Amos said.

'It is, brother, I am most relieved. So is the owner, I assure you,' Gideon said. 'People are funny, are they not? They have come out in droves to see just how bad the paintings are for themselves, thank goodness.'

'His new collection is breathtaking, is it not, Gids, Alice?' Matilda asked them both.

'It truly is amazing. I was mesmerised,' Alice said. 'Will you represent it, Gideon?'

'Yes, we've already discussed that I shall.' Gideon beamed. 'We'll be launching it in a week.'

'That soon!' Matilda exclaimed.

'I have a strategy,' he said with confidence, and all eyes turned to him. He told of using the critics to create anticipation, and his plan for a private opening launch.

'You are confident they will review it positively?' Thomas asked.

'Without a doubt. I've seen enough to know what appeals to their standards,' Gideon said, and shook his head at the thought of dealing with them.

Matilda added: 'I was hoping to meet Miss Sapphire Reubens when we visited, but she wasn't there. She clearly inspired his collection.'

'She wasn't there when I called either,' Gideon said, 'although Marlon said that once he felt inspired, he does not need his muse to pose.'

Thomas's eyes narrowed. 'What is the subject of the new collection, Gids?' he asked.

'It is varying versions of Miss Reubens lying in the water, amongst the reeds as if she is part of the riverbed, but her features are sharp while the landscape is soft making it even more dramatic,' Gideon responded. 'Wouldn't you say so, ladies?'

'Definitely,' Alice answered. 'She looks so full of life, and for fear of being poetic—'

'Goodness, let's not be that,' Daniel said, and she laughed and continued.

'It is as if her soul is on display, and she has returned to nature.'

'Yes, exactly, Alice, so well said,' Matilda agreed. 'He illuminated her eyes as if in the throes of life, death, or passion,' she said, flushed at the thought of the latter.

'I can't wait to see the paintings again when they are finished and properly displayed,' Alice said.

Matilda turned to the other ladies at the table. 'You will love them, Aunt Audrey and Minnie. I am sure and they are very modest,' Matilda assured them.

Thomas's brow furrowed.

'What is it, Thomas?' Mr Hayward asked him.

Thomas leaned in closer to include Mr Hayward, Matilda, Alice, and Gideon in the discussion. 'So, it has been well over a week and no one has seen Miss Reubens, and yet the subject of the painting is her body floating lifeless, the soul on display?'

There was silence while the group thought about the seriousness of Thomas's question.

He continued, 'Before that, Marlon Dominey was uninspired and now, he has his talent restored?'

'Yes, I see where your thoughts are going, Thomas,' Matilda said. 'You think it might be a death portrait.'

Alice gasped.

'I shall go over straight after lunch,' Thomas said, knowing he could not leave in the middle unless it was a dire emergency. 'Gideon, will you come with me to assist with entry? I don't want to look too official yet. Perhaps I can do so on the ruse of warning Mr Dominey to take care while I see the paintings for myself.'

'Of course, I am happy to accompany you,' Gideon said. 'But if you think Miss Reubens has been murdered, could you come to that conclusion after my showing and once the paintings are sold?'

'Gideon!' Matilda exclaimed, and he chuckled. 'I am coming along too.' She stopped Thomas as he was just about to speak. 'I insist, this time.'

His lips thinned, and Mr Hayward, Alice and Gideon hid a smile.

'I think she's coming with us, Thom,' Gideon said.

'Hmph,' Thomas said with a frown.

'You'll be there to protect me,' she said, smiling at him. 'What could possibly go wrong?'

'What are you talking about in your little group, down there, brother?' Aunt Audrey invaded their discussion.

He saw Thomas's satisfied look. If he revealed the young people's plan, Audrey would forbid Matilda from attending. He knew his daughter, Matilda, had no intention of doing that.

'We are discussing art muses, Audrey,' he said, which was true. 'But of course, muses are not just for the artist. I am sure the ladies around this table inspire us all to be better men.'

Naturally, his comment won him the affection and grateful look of every lady at the table. But Mr Hayward had primarily said it for Minnie's benefit. He often thought Minnie, with her traditional upbringing and conventional ways, felt slightly out of sorts with the more progressive ladies around the table. He nodded to his son, Amos, knowing he would understand and take the opportunity to compliment his wife.

Amos smiled. 'So true, Pa. I don't know where I'd be without Minnie's support and encouragement.' He looked at his wife's small face upturned to him. 'Ensuring I provide for her security and comfort is my greatest pleasure and inspires me to work harder.'

Minnie swooned and Gideon groaned.

'I hope to one day provide for a lady's comfort too,' Daniel said, 'even if that lady is like Matilda and independent.'

Mr Hayward noted Alice blushed at Daniel's words meant for her and that Thomas continued to look distracted as he thought over the artist's muse. He imagined lunch could not finish soon enough for the young detective.

Chapter 20

Gideon led the small party to the residence of Marlon Dominey and, with a glance to the top floor, noted that this time the curtains were wide open. He knocked on the lower-level door, not expecting the landlady to answer on a holy day. The entry serviced three townhouses, and Gideon tried the door and let himself in. Thomas and Matilda followed to the top floor rooms of the artist. Gideon rapped lightly on the door and waited.

The door opened moments later and Marlon Dominey stood in the doorway. He was slightly dishevelled, dressed but unshaven, his hands covered in swatches of paint colour.

'Gideon! Great to see you, I have just finished and needed someone to celebrate with.' He saw Matilda and gave an exaggerated bow. 'The beautiful writer, welcome back, Miss Hayward.'

Matilda blushed. 'Mr Dominey,' she said and smiled.

'Sorry for the intrusion,' Gideon said. 'Might I introduce a family friend and member of our fine constabulary, Detective Thomas Ashdown.'

'Ah, I know my last collection was an offence but not a crime surely?' he said, being his most charming self.

Thomas smiled despite himself, and the men shook hands. 'I assure you, I am just here to check on your safety.'

'Too kind. Please come in.'

'Is Miss Reubens here?' Matilda asked with a glance around Marlon's studio. 'I am so longing to meet her.'

'No, Lord knows where Sapphire is,' Marlon said. 'She gets petulant when I'm painting because I can't take her out and show her off. She'll arrive once she gets word that I have finished, no doubt, keen as ever to enjoy the nightlife of the city.'

He grabbed a rag and wiped his hands.

'I should have come bearing champagne,' Gideon said. 'You are finished, magnificent!'

'Take me out for a celebratory drink instead. I have not seen the outside world for close to a week,' Marlon said. He stood back and smiled at his collection of paintings. 'I am doing my best not to keep touching them – they are wet and I have retouched them too many times. But yes, I am pleased.'

'May I?' Thomas asked before presuming to see the works.

'Be my guest,' Marlon invited him.

The afternoon light was soft in the studio and showed the paintings to their full advantage. Thomas moved from one painting to the next, his focus remaining on how Miss Reubens was represented. He had to agree, they were stunning.

'I am neither a judge nor a critic of art, Mr Dominey, but truly they are wonderful,' Thomas offered as he felt some comment was expected.

Marlon nodded. 'Thank you. I was caught up in a moment, a look from Sapphire and the inspiration came to me. Sometimes that is all it takes.'

'That sounds simple,' Gideon said, standing in front of the first painting, 'but that spark of inspiration is not easily come by.'

'You are correct, my friend,' Marlon said, slapping him on the back and full of good humour from their compliments. 'Gideon has arranged for two critics to come tomorrow for an advance and private viewing. That will be telling.'

'What if they weren't finished?' Matilda asked.

Gideon gave a small shrug. 'That would not matter a great deal when the promise is all there to be seen. It was a risk worth taking,' Gideon said, noting their expressions. 'Then we shall do a private and exclusive opening, display the works for one month only and sell them to the highest bidder.'

'Oh my,' Matilda said, 'how exciting.'

'Indeed,' Gideon agreed. 'We will feature them with the same energy with which you created them.'

Marlon smiled and gave a satisfied nod to Gideon.

Thomas worked his way around the artworks and stood again in front of the first painting. Gideon joined him.

'What were Alice's words?' Gideon asked, trying to recall them. 'Ah yes, "*It is as if her soul is on display and she has returned to nature*" – very apt.'

Thomas nodded and lowered his voice to speak to Gideon only. 'I have seen people struggling in the last throes of life with their eyes illuminated, gasping for life, as Mr Dominey had captured Miss Sapphire Reubens. It could very well be a portrait of the last moments of her life.'

Gideon looked around for Marlon and seeing he was talking with Matilda asked Thomas: 'You think that he has murdered his muse because his inspiration dried up and in doing so, been empowered by the life seeping from her?'

Thomas raised an eyebrow and said nothing.

'Mr Dominey, you have heard of the death of two artists?' Thomas began.

'I have, Detective, a terrible thing. Do you know why?' Marlon asked.

'No, do you?' Thomas asked.

Marlon laughed and then realised that the Detective was being serious.

'No. I have no idea. I barely knew the men.'

'But you knew them?' Thomas asked.

'The art community is a small and, some might say, a somewhat incestuous one,' he said with a nod of apology to Matilda.

'I ask you then to please be careful and take extra precautions with your safety,' Thomas said. 'I'd like to speak with Miss Reubens and ensure she understands the situation as well.'

'When I see her, I shall warn her. Do you really think we are in danger?' Marlon asked, surprised.

Thomas nodded. 'We don't have a motive for the two

murders yet and without a motive, then everyone in the art world is in danger, including you, Gideon.'

'No!' Matilda said, looking at her brother.

Thomas recanted slightly. 'There's no need to be alarmed, just wary,' he said.

'Thank you, Detective, I will heed your words,' Marlon said with sincerity. Then he turned to Gideon. 'Now take me out for a celebratory drink. Will you join us, Detective, Miss Hayward?' he moved closer to Matilda.

Before they could answer, he said, 'You have a most delicate face, Miss Hayward.' Marlon studied her, and when his hand reached out to touch her face and Thomas stepped forward.

Gideon cut the detective off, blocking his way, and hurriedly interrupted. 'Come then, Marlon, clean up and we shall go. Matilda and Thomas have other plans.'

'We do, but so lovely to see you and your works again, Mr Dominey. My article is running this week. I hope you will be happy with it.'

Marlon stepped back. 'I look forward to reading it, and thank you for presenting me to the ladies of this city through your newspaper.'

He gave a brief bow, and Thomas harnessed his anger as Matilda looped her arm through his. Gideon saw them out, sensing his potential income running through his fingers unless Miss Reubens showed herself. Tonight, he would be on the lookout.

Chapter 21

'It is not at all amusing, Matilda,' Thomas said, his jaw locked, his lips thinned as he looked out of the hansom delivering Matilda back to her home.

She smiled and reached for his arm. He turned, feeling her hand on his.

'You need not worry; he is not seeking a new muse nor am I likely to fit that mould.'

'It is not just his gaze upon you that maddens me. For all we know, he might be the killer. I don't want him near you, seeing you, touching you or being inspired by you,' Thomas snapped, breathed out and looked away again. Then he turned back. 'Can you imagine the devastation that would descend on your family if harm were to come to you, and the responsibility I would carry for that? It would be unbearable.'

She narrowed her eyes, studying him. 'And would that devastation extend to outside the family?'

He sighed. 'I swear Matilda, your teasing is not always welcomed.' He wanted to kiss her speechless, with no permission or apology offered.

Then he acted upon those feelings with no warning. Thomas reached over and pulled Matilda to him. She yelped in surprise. He wished her hair was down so he could thread his fingers through it, but instead he touched the back of her neck, feeling her warm skin on his, as his other hand cupped her face. He lowered his face to touch her lips, waiting for her remonstration, but none came. Matilda pressed back, reciprocating the kiss.

A city could have come to its knees, a murderer confessed, Thomas didn't care. Right here, right now, he was aching for her. He would have sold his soul at that moment to make time stop. All the years he had been beside Matilda, her friend, her brothers' playmate, and now that he had tasted her, she was his.

Matilda drew away and he reluctantly let her. Her breathing was quickened, as was his, her lips moist and her expression incredulous. She studied him, surprised by his spontaneity, their faces but inches from each other. Thomas moved to kiss her again, this time slower, gentler, not taking her gaze from him.

The hansom pulled over.

The driver tapped on the roof abruptly, interrupting their moment with his call: 'Your destination, sir.'

They broke apart but continued to stare at each other, not moving. Thomas did not want to leave her, nor for the kiss to end so quickly, to feel the pull of separation. He straightened and swallowed, taking Matilda's hand. He kissed it, then alighted from the hansom and assisted her down. Not that she needed it.

'Can you take me on to Roma Street?' he asked the driver.

'Right you are, sir,' the driver responded.

Thomas lowered his head and spoke in a quiet voice. 'I believe I have kissed you speechless. That might work to my advantage in the future.'

Matilda pulled back from him to give him a well-deserved admonishing look.

Not wanting to ruin the moment, Thomas whispered in her ear, 'I will ache until I can next kiss you, Matilda.'

Her breath hitched, and she felt herself flush.

'I best be getting inside,' Matilda said on seeing her father appear on the veranda.

'Yes, of course,' Thomas said, but he needed more, a security of sorts that said she felt the same, that the kiss meant something to her.

But as Mr Hayward walked down the path to enjoy the afternoon and accompany Matilda inside, she moved away from Thomas towards the company of her father.

He waited until she had secured her arm in her father's and raised a hand in a reciprocal wave to Mr Hayward. Now matters of the heart felt as frustrating to him as the matters of the head with a case going nowhere.

Chapter 22

Matilda arrived at work early on Monday, ready for the editorial meeting with the writers and illustrators of the *Women's Journal*. The office was alive with energy; at every desk sat a lady with a particular skill for the task, and Mrs Lawson had assembled a talented group. Matilda had only been in the position for four months and was in awe of the experienced writers, but mostly in awe of Mrs Lawson, the editor. She was a formidable presence, kind and passionate, with so much knowledge to share and it thrilled Matilda to benefit from her tutelage.

'Matilda,' a mature voice called her name.

She glanced up to see Mrs Lawson in the doorway of her editor's office. She beckoned for Matilda to join her. Adrenaline pumped through Matilda as she grabbed her notebook and pencil and headed over to speak with the editor. Perhaps she did not like the *muse* piece and was going to ask for it to be rewritten.

'Come in, Matilda. How are you this fine morning?' Mrs Lawson asked and indicated that they should sit at the meeting table.

'Very well, thank you, Mrs Lawson, and you?' Matilda asked nervously, taking a seat.

'The same, I am pleased to say. I just wanted to speak with you quickly before the meeting begins in five minutes to congratulate you on your muse piece,' Mrs Lawson said, and smiled at Matilda's obvious relief.

'Thank you.' Matilda tried not to look too excited by the praise which Mrs Lawson gave when due.

'I very much liked that you did your research and found artists and their muses from history, and the piece will compliment Alice's story on the influence of nature nicely.'

'My brother has a fine collection of art and history books. They were a great source of reference,' Matilda said. 'I would have liked to have included quotes from Miss Reubens herself but, despite several attempts, I could not reach her.'

'I understand,' Mrs Lawson said, as she studied Matilda. 'I felt your article had a little more emotional depth than your past work. I wondered if perhaps you experienced some private distress, which of course you need not reveal. But there was an emotional balance to the piece particularly from the perspective of the vulnerable muse.' She stopped, allowing Matilda to discuss her state of heart and mind, should she wish to reveal that.

Matilda nodded. 'Yes, there was an incident, but I did not realise it might be reflected in my writing.' Matilda cleared her throat. 'You know of Detective Ashdown from previous visits?'

Mrs Lawson nodded.

'He has asked to court me and we are…' Matilda hesitated.

'I guess we are transitioning from childhood friends to a relationship, and I have much to learn. It wasn't the easy road I thought it might be.'

Mrs Lawson smiled and nodded. 'It is a vulnerable time when you are first in love and your heart is in the hands of another.'

'I wish I had said that,' Matilda said, and made Mrs Lawson laugh.

'If I may offer a small piece of advice?'

'Please.' Matilda invited her mentor to continue.

'I found that a close friend or two in which you can share your fears and excitement will ensure that you never feel truly alone. Also, I think this is a good learning exercise for you, Matilda.' Mrs Lawson held up her hand. 'Don't be concerned, I will not start assigning stories to you that require you to tap into the heartbeat of the ladies of the nation. However, I'd like to suggest as you continue to grow in this role, you seek more opportunities to witness human joy and suffering.'

Matilda nodded, her brow furrowed with concentration and confusion. 'Do you mean I should interview people who have loved and lost?'

'No, not necessarily anything that dictated. Just take the time to study life and people. Artists and poets do so, and as writers, we should as well,' Mrs Lawson said. 'For example, I am sure your beau, Detective Ashdown, is witness to all life's best and worst moments – coming across tragedy, witnessing how the family reacts, delivering the good news of rescue and other stories and being exposed to the emotions of loss and anguish. That makes us more empathetic, rounds out our character and adds depth to our work, but there is nothing like having personal life experience. Often that comes with age.'

'I understand, I think,' Matilda said. 'My brother, Elijah, is a doctor having recently completed his degree. He has shared the occasional encounter when he has had a troubling case or when he has celebrated a patient's recovery. I imagine it is raw and new for him.'

'Exactly!' Mrs Lawson said, pleased that Matilda had grasped her meaning. 'Perhaps in due course, you might understudy both Detective Ashdown and Elijah. But don't rush in to bury yourself in drama. Remember, there is an emotional reward in victory and beauty as well,' Mrs Lawson warned. 'As mentioned, our best work comes from empathy, and that is gained with experience. You, Alice, and some of the other young ladies are just starting. When you get as senior as our deputy editor, Betty, for example, your work will have a different quality. Don't be disheartened, your youth also brings a freshness and different perspective to our writing, and that is appreciated as well.'

Matilda and Mrs Lawson saw the staff members making their way towards her office for the 9.30am meeting.

'Thank you, Mrs Lawson. That feedback has been invaluable,' Matilda said.

'You are welcome, your work is coming along nicely.'

Georgina, the illustrator, stuck her head in the office door. 'Ready for us, Mrs Lawson?' she asked in her usual blunt manner.

'I am, come in please,' Mrs Lawson said, and Matilda thanked her again and rose to sit further down the table and think about all that Mrs Lawson had said to her. She smiled at Alice, who dropped in the chair beside her.

If Thomas hoped Matilda would steer clear of his work before, he was now going to be most frustrated as she intended to study him and integrate herself much more to view the lives and actions of those around her.

*****

Detectives Thomas Ashdown and Harry Dart had only just walked into the Roma Street offices after returning from giving the two art critics a warning about their safety when the desk sergeant came running down the hallway after them.

'Detectives, there's a man at the front desk. He thinks he has stumbled across a murder scene,' the desk sergeant said.

Thomas groaned, and the men turned to return to the front desk, coats still on, hats in hand.

'Not another,' Harry muttered behind him.

The desk sergeant introduced the man who nervously fumbled with a beret as Mr Alfred Poyser. He was a short, stout man, with a weathered face that said he had worked hard; he had hands to match.

He started speaking as he saw the two detectives approaching: 'It might be nothing. I just didn't want to trample in and find something I didn't want to find,' he said, talking quickly.

'Then you did the best thing coming here, Mr Poyser,' Harry assured him. 'Shall we follow you and you can tell us all about it on the way?'

'It's not far, down by the river, in the mangroves,' he said and led the way.

Thomas's thoughts immediately went to Marlon Dominey and his water paintings. As he followed Harry and the stout man, he mentally prepared himself to find Miss Sapphire Reubens in a state of decline, having been immersed in water for some days. He cringed, the smell in his nostrils already drawn from past experiences.

Fortunately, there were few people around except for a ferryman in the distance.

'I was walking along here, I often do in my lunch break,' the man said. 'I work in the city saddlery. Then I came upon this,' he pointed.

From where they stood, the men could see a shoe and what looked like a lady's scarf.

'Thank you, please remain here, My Poyser,' Thomas said.

'Happily,' Alfred Poyser agreed, standing back further on the path and watching their progress.

Harry led the way into the mangroves, hesitating as the ground softened, and the mangroves became thicker.

'Should have brought our rubber boots,' he said and stopped on seeing the other red shoe. Thomas pulled up beside him and breathed out as he examined the scene.

'Thank Christ,' Thomas said.

'Weird though,' Harry frowned.

In front of them, laid out in the river, floating, was a

gold shawl, pinned between several mangrove branches and opposite, two red shoes between the mangrove vines. If there was once a body in between, it was no longer there.

'Couldn't have sunk,' Thomas said. 'The reeds would have held it in place and there's not enough depth there.'

'I agree,' Harry said. 'These items could have floated here, the body dumped in the river, but it doesn't seem right.'

'No,' Thomas said and stepped back again. 'This has been set up. Harry, I've seen this.'

'What do you mean?'

'Come back over here and get this scene in your mind,' he told his partner. Then, on seeing Mr Poyser was still there, Thomas returned to the nervous man.

'My Poyser, I'm happy to report it is women's clothing only, no body.'

Alfred Poyser's hand went to his heart, and he breathed out with relief. 'I'm sorry to have wasted your time then,' he said.

'Not at all. I wish all citizens would do as you did,' Harry said, joining them.

'Thank you,' Mr Poyser said with a brisk nod. 'Will you leave the items there?'

'No, we'll retrieve them,' Thomas assured him. 'They still might be part of a crime that may surface in time, so to speak, so we appreciate you showing us. It is irregular.'

'That's what I thought. Well, I'll be heading off then, back to work,' he said, hesitant whether to shake hands with the men or keep going.

Harry offered his hand for a quick shake, but Thomas had already turned to study the scene.

After Mr Poyser had departed, Harry studied his partner. 'What is it, Thom?'

Thomas narrowed his eyes at the scene. 'The artist, Marlon Dominey, has just created some of his best work – Gideon's words, but I've seen the paintings, they are impressive.'

'And?' Harry prompted him.

'This is the painting,' Thomas said and stood back. He indicated with his hands. 'This scene, the shallow water, the vines and mangroves around the muse, Miss Reubens.'

'Don't tell me she was wearing a gold shawl and red shoes?' Harry asked.

'The first painting is upper body only, the others are full body but I believe her feet were bare. I can't speak for the shawl, but the colour is the same as in the painting… the red and golds.'

'What are the chances these clothes are labelled and belong to Miss Sapphire Reubens?' Harry asked.

'If they've been to a cleaner regularly they might be, or a seamstress might recognise the shawl or the distinct red shoes.'

'So, you're saying this scene didn't just wash up?' Harry said.

'No, it's a display, I'm sure of it. The artist has either done it for attention, or it is a warning from the murderer or…' Thomas glanced around again, looking for something more. Harry finished his sentence.

'Or the body is out there somewhere.'

'Yes. The artist has not seen Miss Reubens for close to a week,' Thomas said. 'Burn this scene to your memory,

Harry, I need you to see the painting next.' He found a large dead mangrove stem and snapped it off. With that, Thomas unsnagged the shawl and pulled it towards him. He lifted the dripping gold wrap from the water and Harry took it from the stick while Thomas repeated the same for each shoe.

'I think a visit to the artist is in order,' Harry said, turning over the label on the shawl where the initials S.R. were stitched in an elaborate style. 'S.R. – Sapphire Reubens? Odd coincidence if these are not her items.'

'I agree. We are nearby the coroner's office and I want to know more about the cause of death of both of our artists. Shall we?'

'Lead on,' Harry said.

Chapter 23

Marlon Dominey paid a visit to his exhibition manager, Gideon Hayward, at the *Fine Art Gallery* at the civilised hour of 11am that fine Tuesday morning. He had beamed with confidence and happiness all the way in, and laughed with pleasure as he paused at the entrance to read the sign on the front door:

Mr Marlon Dominey's exclusive exhibition launch this Wednesday is now SOLD OUT. Management apologises for any inconvenience. The exhibition will open to the general public from Thursday 9am for one month only.
Mr Gideon Hayward, Manager.

Marlon pushed open the door of the gallery to enter. Gideon looked up from the desk in the corner at which he worked.

'It worked, you are a genius,' Marlon grinned as Gideon rose to greet him, offering his hand to shake. Marlon enveloped him in a hug and, grinning, pushed him back away, holding him by the shoulders. 'The reviews from the harshest two critics… they are glowing.'

Gideon laughed, and pulling away, turned to grab his newspaper from his small desk in the corner.

'Don't I know it. You have them eating out of your hand,' Gideon agreed. 'Congratulations, Marlon, you deserve this.'

'It was as if inspiration came from nowhere and poured from me. It has been many years since I have felt that rush, that passion to put the paint on the canvas.'

'That is evident in the work,' Gideon agreed.

Marlon continued: 'But your plan to get the two top critics in for a special preview was brilliant. They are full of their own importance most days and stroking their egos pandered to them perfectly, especially Lawrence Longman.' Marlon said his name with distaste.

'And he has written the most glowing review we could hope for and mentioned the exhibition opening dates,' Gideon agreed. 'I have also booked some advertising in *The Brisbane Courier* which will feature from tomorrow.'

Marlon sighed, as if the world had fallen off his shoulders. He moved to the couch area near the window, and Gideon followed. The men sat and accepted the offer of tea from Gideon's assistant.

'I feel reborn, invigorated,' Marlon said. 'It's all happening so quickly, I love the energy surrounding the collection.'

'I feel relieved, not that I doubted your success with this showing for a moment, mind you,' Gideon assured Marlon. 'But I had pre-sold forty tickets to the launch on Wednesday evening promising that once the early reviews came out, there would be no tickets available, and warned buy early or be disappointed.'

Marlon laughed. 'Well from the sign on the door, that is true?'

'With the critics' reviews in the paper today, I sold the remaining forty tickets by 10am, and all for the price we agreed upon,' Gideon said. 'Prepare to make your grand entrance on Wednesday night.'

'I best find Sapphire and buy her a new dress, I supposed,' Marlon said still smiling.

'She is the major feature,' Gideon agreed.

*****

Dr Nevins was studying the dead body in front of him and looked up at the sound of the door opening.

'Ah, good, you were on my list of people to follow up with today. You have saved me a trip, Detectives,' he said, acknowledging Thomas and Harry.

'We're always thoughtful,' Harry joked.

'Don't tell me that's a fresh one?' Thomas asked, studying the body on the table. It was another middle-aged man, hopefully not an artist.

'Don't concern yourself,' Dr Nevins assured him. 'This poor fellow died of a long-borne illness.' He pulled up the covering to hide the corpse's face and allow some dignity to the dead. 'Now gentlemen, I have the official cause of death for your two artists and I can't say I am surprised.' Moving to a small table in the corner of the room, he invited the men to take a chair. The small hardwood table seated four but had seen better days and looked far from sturdy.

'Poisoning?' Harry asked, taking a seat. Thomas sat on the edge of a seat opposite.

'Yes, everyone's favourite these days,' Dr Nevins said with an attempt at humour. 'But we are seeing less and less of it.'

'Since the tighter restrictions have come in on its sale?' Thomas asked.

'Indeed, and with its enforced indigo colouring, it makes it easier to identify in the body,' Dr Nevins said. 'So, both of your victims were poisoned, injected with arsenic through one spot on the skin. But don't rush off just yet… it is not that clear cut.' He saw Thomas's face and smiled. 'Sorry, Detective.'

'And I was counting on you to keep it simple.' Thomas smiled.

'You'll have to blame the art community, not me. There are traces of arsenic in both bodies, enough to kill, but how it got there may be a little harder to prove,' Dr Nevins said. 'The quantities were enough to kill reasonably quickly, so my first prediction still stands – that the poison was injected, which is a little different as most amateur killers try to disguise it in food and drink.'

'So, this person might know what they are doing and have access to some medical equipment or at least a syringe?' Harry asked.

'Yes, it is likely, but proving your case might be hampered because both of your victims are artists,' Dr Nevins said.

'How so?' Thomas asked, tapping his knee with impatience. He liked to cut to the chase.

'There is most likely arsenic in their studios, in their paints and materials. I had an artist die many years ago when I worked in another city, and he died a long slow death. It turned out he used to lick his brushes occasionally to achieve a finer point, digesting a bit of arsenic each time. Some paints are full of poison too,' Dr Nevins said.

'Do the artists not realise this?' Harry asked.

'Yes, these days there is quite a bit of information around about paints and their toxicity. But I have met artists who were prepared to risk it because the colour from these paints is so much more intense.'

'Delivering their work at all costs,' Harry said, shaking his head.

'Some might say the risks you men take for your job to get results are not dissimilar,' Dr Nevins said with a raised eyebrow.

'Like Scheele's Green,' Thomas said, thinking about arsenic in the paint colours.

'Yes!' Dr Nevins said, surprised. 'The intense green paint that is rife with arsenic. How did you know of it?'

'I read it somewhere, I am sure,' Thomas said. 'It was used in paintings, wallpaper and even in jewellery.'

'Indeed, it was. What is a little arsenic when you have such a beautiful colour, hey?' Dr Nevins chuckled. 'Well, that is all I have for you.'

'That is all we need. Thank you, Doctor,' Thomas said rising. The men shook his hand.

'Always a pleasure to have a break from the corpses and talk to the living,' the doctor said with a smile.

Chapter 24

Mrs Dempsey, the landlady at Marlon Dominey's residence was not quite so charming to the two detectives as she was to Gideon and Marlon's occasional other visitors. She wasn't a fan of his muse, but on most occasions kept that to herself.

'He's not here,' she said. 'I can take a message.'

'I'm sure you have enough on your plate, Mrs—' Harry hesitated. He had the gift of charming the ladies when necessary.

'Dempsey,' she answered, and gave a nod of thanks.

'Mrs Dempsey,' Harry repeated. 'We just wanted to see Mr Dominey or Miss Reubens or even the paintings – a bit of safety check-up.'

'Ah,' she nodded and smiled at him. Thomas stood by patiently, lips thinned, trying not to ruin Harry's efforts.

'The paintings have gone,' she said. 'They were all taken out of here over the weekend to get them framed for the launch, according to Mr Hayward.'

'Of course,' Harry said, as if he were an art connoisseur.

'As for that Miss Reubens, the last time I saw her here was several weeks back now.'

'Is that normal, Mrs Dempsey, that she comes and goes like that? From your experience, of course.' Thomas prodded her with an attempt to make her information seem that much more important.

'Well,' she said, standing a little taller and crossing her arms over her chest, 'if you ask me, she's a little too loose with her time. She'll be away for days at a time and then come back and stay for a week or more, then she's off again. She likes to socialise and if Mr Dominey is working, she'll go out without him.'

'So, it is about two weeks since she was here, would you say?' Harry confirmed.

'About that. She's like an alley cat,' Mrs Dempsey said nastily.

Thomas cut the interview short. 'Thank you for your time, Mrs Dempsey. No need to alert Mr Dominey of our visit unless you feel inclined. I'll seek Mr Hayward instead and check up on all three.'

'Now he's a lovely young man,' she said. 'Well, best back to it.'

The gentlemen tipped their hats and stepped away as Mrs Dempsey went back inside and closed the door.

'Two weeks,' Harry said. 'But she could be staying with a friend.'

'True,' Thomas agreed, 'but it's time we find that friend and confirm her whereabouts. You need to see the paintings,

Harry, and tell me if I'm imagining it. Let's swing by Gideon's gallery and see if they are back from the framer.'

The men saw the omnibus coming from a little further down the street and hurried to get on board.

*****

Miss Warren, Gideon's assistant, met the two detectives at the reception desk of the gallery. She looked bland and officious in a long grey skirt and crisp white shirt, a small black ribbon tied around her neck.

'I am afraid that Mr Hayward is not here,' she said. 'Can I take a message?'

'For the love of God,' Thomas muttered. Where was everyone when he was trying to get some work done? 'Do you know where he is or when he might be back, please?'

'I don't think he will be back today, Detective. He had some appointments including calling on the caterer to check on the launch details, and then I believe he was heading home after that,' Miss Warren said.

'And Mr Dominey? Was he with Mr Hayward?' Harry asked.

'They left together, but I believe Mr Dominey had some of his own errands to run, including picking up his suit from the tailor. If it is an emergency—'

'No, that's fine. I'll catch Mr Hayward at home, thank you,' Thomas said and sighed. 'By chance, are Mr Dominey's painting here yet? I understand they were getting framed.'

'Yes, they arrived a few hours ago.'

Thomas brightened. 'Excellent, are we able to see them, please?'

Miss Warren hesitated and glanced around as if she needed to seek permission first, and the decision was above her status at the gallery.

Thomas continued. 'I assure you it is a police matter and I have seen them several times at Mr Dominey's studio while discussing his safety during this period. There is a detail I want to check.'

'For the case, the murder case?' Miss Warren's eyes widened.

'No, regarding his inspiration, the subject of his painting,' Harry interrupted, not wanting to give anything away. 'We want to talk with Miss Sapphire Reubens and there was something in the painting that we wanted to cross-check.'

Miss Warren wrung her hands and looked confused. 'Oh, well I guess that will be alright, then. I'll just lock the door while we are in the back room.' She moved to close the front door and then indicated for the gentlemen to follow her.

'Have you seen Miss Reubens of late?' Thomas asked.

'No Detective, but I normally don't move in their circle,' Miss Warren said. 'The last time I saw her was at Mr Dominey's previous launch, here.'

She stood aside at the entrance to the backroom, and the men entered. The four artworks took up the entire back room and Harry gasped at seeing them.

Miss Warren smiled at his reaction. 'They are superb, are they not?' she said with pride that the *Fine Art Gallery* had scored the exhibition.

'Absolutely stunning,' Harry said. Then he stepped right in front of the first painting in the collection and saw the scene for himself – the scene they had just left by the mangroves. Miss Reubens floated in the water, immersed in nature, and drawing the viewer's eye with her piercing gaze. Around her shoulders was a gold shawl floating gently in the river and snagged on a vine.

Harry turned. 'Right, we've seen what we need. Thank you very much, Miss Warren, you have been most helpful.'

'Oh,' she said, surprised. She had expected them to stay and look at each piece with equal duration and with as much admiration. 'Well, that's my pleasure. I'll let you both out.'

Thomas and Harry thanked Miss Warren again on departure and waited until they were further away before speaking.

'Two artists dead, and a muse possibly missing,' Thomas said.

'I am thinking we need to get the river searched around the mangroves,' Harry said.

'I am thinking the same thing,' Thomas agreed. 'Let's do that and then I'll drop in on Gideon at the end of the day.'

'I'll come with you if you make it on my way home,' Harry said. 'If the launch is tomorrow evening, one would expect Miss Reubens to be there. If she is not…'

'Then,' Thomas continued Harry's train of thought, 'Miss Reubens may well be missing, or dead, and that might be her death, her last moments captured for everyone to admire on canvas.'

Chapter 25

Lamps were being lit at the Hayward house as Thomas and Harry arrived. It was just after 4.30pm but the autumn late afternoons cast shadows in the house and added to the chill in the air.

Given Harry accompanied Thomas on this visit, Thomas did not presume to enter without announcement and knocked for admission. Harriet opened the door and looked surprised.

'Thomas, family don't knock!'

'Harriet,' he said with a smile and a small bow. 'As I'm here on official business, I thought I'd best not barge in. You remember, Harry,' he said.

'Of course, Mr Dart,' Harriet said. 'Oh, Detective Dart I should say.'

'Harry, please,' he said with a grin and removed his hat.

'Come in, come in,' Harriet ushered the gentleman in. 'So, who is under arrest this time?' she said with a smile.

Thomas laughed, pleased that she didn't assume their visit was to deliver bad news. 'There are a few likely suspects to choose from, granted,' he bantered back. 'But we just need to talk to Gideon if he is in, please?'

'You are in luck. Mr Hayward is out having his evening walk. Daniel and Elijah are not in but, I can round up Gideon,' she said, indicating the window bay seat if they wanted to be seated.

Just as she headed up the stairs to fetch Gideon, Matilda came out of her room on hearing the voices and proceeded downstairs.

'Thomas, Detective Dart, is everything okay?' she asked, worried.

Thomas came to the end of the staircase. 'Fine, nothing to worry about at all,' he said and, taking her hand as she came into reach, applied a kiss to it.

'It's a query about Mr Dominey and his muse, Miss Reubens,' Harry assured her.

'Ah, the exhibition launch is on tomorrow night, and she is expected I am sure,' Matilda said. 'Mind you, Gids has not come up with any free tickets for us this time, sadly. I'm glad we've seen the paintings. That is some consolation.'

'That's because the paying guests are more important than you lot,' Gideon said, running down the stairs behind her. 'Thom, Harry, can I offer you a drink?'

'No, best we don't since we're on business, but thanks Gids,' Thomas said.

Gideon looked serious. 'No, don't tell me… Marlon has been murdered,' Gideon said, and stepped back.

'No, no, I assure you that everyone is alive and well,' Thomas said, holding up his hands in a calming manner.

'Well, to the best of our knowledge,' Harry agreed.

Gideon's hand went to his heart. 'Thank God.'

'We won't keep you long,' Thomas continued. 'I just wanted to ask if you have seen Miss Reubens recently?'

Gideon came down the final few stairs and stood beside Matilda, opposite the men.

'No, not since the last exhibition opening, actually. But Marlon said earlier today that he was going out to spend money on a new dress for her for the opening. Why?' He frowned.

'It's just that no one has seen her for some time,' Harry said, 'and with—'

'With a murderer at large, you think she may have been harmed?' Matilda asked.

'No. Yes.' Thomas shook his head. 'We don't know. That's why we are looking for her.'

Gideon pulled up straighter and looked from Thomas to Harry and back. 'You think she might be a victim of this murderer?'

'We honestly don't know,' Thomas said again. 'All we know is that no one has set eyes on her for close to two weeks and this morning we found in the mangroves by the river, a gold shawl bearing the initials S.R., and a pair of red shoes.'

'No!' Matilda said. 'But you didn't find Miss Reubens herself?'

'No,' Harry assured her.

'Christ,' Gideon said, the word hissing between his teeth as he thought of all the implications.

Thomas watched Gideon, knowing that the youngest Hayward male was prone to being reckless – he was the least checked and the one with the shortest temper. He read his reaction to be genuine and that he honestly did not know of Miss Reubens' whereabouts.

'Are you expecting her to be… washed ashore?' Matilda asked, trying to be as diplomatic as possible.

'We hope it has not come to that, but there is a small team combing the waterways now,' Harry told her.

Thomas warned her. 'None of this is for your newspaper.'

'Absolutely not!' Gideon said, turning on Matilda. He ran a hand through his short dark hair, his deep brown eyes squinted as he thought. 'If this gets out—'

Matilda frowned and assured him: 'I am asking out of concern for Miss Reubens, not as a writer, Gids, stay calm.'

She was asking all the right questions though, Thomas noted.

'Calm,' Gideon muttered. He stepped down in front of the men into the open area of the room and paced. 'Christ almighty,' he swore, 'I've sold out the exhibition for tomorrow night, and if word gets out that you think Sapphire has been murdered or even worse…' he realised, and turned to face Thomas. 'No, no way. Marlon has been painting non-stop for those two weeks, he adores her.'

'But he got his inspiration from somewhere when it was dried up,' Thomas said, his voice low and calm. 'Everyone so far that has seen his paintings comments on the soul and life depicted in Miss Reubens' eyes.'

Gideon's jaw locked in anger. 'You think that's a death

portrait? That Marlon drowned Sapphire? No, no way. I don't believe it.'

'Gids, there is no evidence yet,' Matilda said, attempting to calm him down and frowning in Thomas' direction. 'Miss Reubens might be staying with friends,' she suggested.

'Exactly,' Gideon agreed, and turned to Thomas, his voice raised. 'Have you asked around?'

Thomas gave him an exasperated look. 'No Gideon, we jumped straight to conclusions like we do every case,' he said wryly. 'Just hold up, we're not rushing in to arrest your artist, we are asking you about Miss Reubens' whereabouts.'

'If word gets out that she is missing and then the water-themed paintings of Marlon's are displayed, it won't take a minute for the newspaper and public to put two and two together,' he snapped. 'If you've got nothing, Thom, you can't do this to Marlon, to me!'

The raised voices brought Harriet back to the room. The front door opened and everyone turned, expecting to see Mr Hayward back from his walk, but Daniel came in.

'Hello, what's going on? Thom, Harry,' he said acknowledging the visitors.

No one spoke as Thomas and Gideon resumed their act of glaring at each other. The tension in the room was palpable. Neither of the men, both tall, dark, similarly matched in height, was intimidated or intended to stand down.

'Let's just think this through,' Matilda said, trying to be the peacemaker. Gideon cut her off.

'Tell me you are not going to arrest Marlon before his opening night, are you? You've got nothing.'

'No, if we find a body we'll store it until after your opening and you sell the paintings, shall we?' Thomas shot back.

'Right then,' Daniel said, looking from Matilda to Harriet and back to Gideon. 'Should we take this outside, away from the ladies?'

Gideon ignored his brother and challenged Thomas. 'There are two other artists murdered, is there not? Why would Marlon kill them?' Gideon asked, clawing at possibilities.

'We're done here,' Thomas said.

'I need to know what you are going to do now,' Gideon demanded.

'At this stage, we are not going to do anything that will affect your showing unless we find a body or evidence of Miss Reubens' death, Mr Hayward,' Harry assured Gideon, trying to water the situation down. 'I assure you, all we want to do is find Miss Reubens and we're here asking for your help. Talk to Mr Dominey, subtly ask around, and if she does appear safe and sound let us know immediately.'

Thomas and Gideon glared at each other.

'Did you know that Mr Dominey was slighted by a patron who instead invested in the deceased artist, Mr Bannon?' Thomas asked. He could tell from Gideon's expression that he had not heard this. 'On the strength of this, the subject of the paintings, and the items we have just found, we are treating Mr Dominey as a suspect and we will be searching his premise,' Thomas warned Gideon.

'I'm running a business and if you start casting aspersions on a man who has so far done nothing, then soon that beautiful artwork will be tagged a death portrait and trust me, it will ruin the gallery and Marlon's future earnings,' Gideon said almost in a hiss.

Matilda stepped closer to her brother. 'That's not going to happen, is it, Thomas?' she turned to her beau. 'You are only here asking if we know where Miss Reubens is and why some items of clothing, that are possibly hers, are in the river, correct?'

'At this stage, yes,' Thomas said.

Gideon shook his head. 'I swear Thom if you ruin this with speculation, I will—' He stepped forward and Harry stepped forward at the same time – pure instinct.

'Just let us know if you see her as soon as possible, Mr Hayward, if you will,' Harry said, grabbing Thomas's arm.

Thomas did not move. 'Would you prefer I don't do my job and let a woman be missing or murdered, Gideon, so your artist can make a living? If it was Matilda missing, would you feel the same?' Thomas asked.

Gideon snapped, charging at Thomas. Harriet yelped in surprise – she was used to the boys fighting but not grown men.

Thomas stumbled backward, taken unaware at Gideon's charge. He felt Gideon's hard shove in his chest.

'Gideon!' Daniel roared and barged in along with Harry, pulling the men apart.

Daniel held his brother back, while Thomas righted himself, and Harry apologised to the ladies as he pushed Thomas towards the door.

Gideon shouted after Thomas. 'Sapphire is not missing.

All you have are a few items of clothing, they could have been stolen! Marlon was talking about attending the opening with her tomorrow evening.'

Thomas turned. 'Good, we look forward to laying eyes on her and ending that line of query.' He acknowledged Matilda and Harriet.

'Thank you, Harriet, Miss Hayward,' Harry said, keeping his grip on Thomas's arm and steering him to the entrance.

'I'll see you out,' Daniel said with a glance to Gideon. Matilda followed, and they walked with the two detectives out of the house and down the path.

'I am so sorry about Gideon's behaviour, Detective Dart, he's under a lot of pressure,' Matilda said.

'No apology necessary at all, Miss Hayward, I assure you,' Harry said in his usual charming manner. 'I suspect we could have been a little more patient and diplomatic.' He glanced toward Thomas.

'Might be a good time to go let off some steam. Fancy a box?' Daniel asked his best friend. 'We haven't done that for a while. Harry, come and show us how it's done,' he said, acknowledging that, despite the years that Harry had on the men, he was a better boxer and had once been quite a successful local champion.

'That's not a bad idea, Dan,' Harry said. 'The missus has her church committee tonight and Lord knows you could do with some tension relief, Thom.'

Thomas nodded. 'I'm in.'

Daniel talked with Harry, and Thomas turned to speak quietly to Matilda.

'Do you think I am in the wrong?' Thomas asked with raised eyebrows.

'I think you could have handled Gideon better,' Matilda said in her brother's defence.

'Of course, you do,' Thomas said, acknowledging that blood is thicker than water.

'What does that mean?' Matilda asked at the gate as she held it ajar for them.

'Miss Hayward,' Harry said with a small bow, and Matilda reciprocated.

'Tillie, can you tell Harriet I'm not in for dinner,' Daniel said and continued to walk on with Harry.

Thomas reached for Matilda's hand, which she withdrew. He studied her for a moment, gave a brief bow, and following his partner, he departed. Leaving both parties hot, bothered and feeling self-righteous.

*****

Harry sighed. 'Thom, you can't blame Gideon for wanting to succeed, and you can't blame Matilda for defending him. She might have known you for many years and be your girl, but they are blood.'

Thomas shook his head as they walked towards the omnibus that would take the men to the boxing ring and bar that they frequented a lot more in their younger years.

'Are you alright, Thom?' Daniel asked after conversing with Harry and noticing Thomas was barely saying a word.

'I don't know if it is going to work, Dan, Harry,' Thomas said in a low voice. He glanced away as he said the words, uncomfortable with revealing too much about himself. He'd grown up in the breast of the Hayward household, his own parents not interested in having him underfoot and his only brother much older. He had learnt to deal with things on his own.

'Thom.' Harry looked at his partner. 'It's early days and you and Matilda have always been competitive, it's what makes you well-matched. Keeps the spark alive,' Harry said with a wink.

'Absolutely. Alice and I are always teasing each other,' Daniel said with a grin.

'This is not teasing. She took Gideon's side straight away,' Thomas said.

'Of course, she would,' Daniel said. 'He was around five or six years before you appeared on the doorstep looking for friends. Or perhaps she just thought Gids had more to lose.'

Thomas raised an eyebrow and considered Daniel's words.

'That's a fair call,' Harry said.

Thomas nodded. 'Maybe.'

'Everything will look much different in the morning light or after we do a few rounds in the ring,' Harry said, now looking forward to it. 'If we send you back bruised, Matilda is bound to want to care for you.'

Thomas scoffed. He exhaled, moving the conversation to safer ground. 'Later or in the morning, let's go see the artist, Mr Dominey. I want to search his rooms. I want to see if arsenic is present in any form besides the paints, and I want to know where Miss Reubens is now.'

Harry agreed. 'We'll see what the night turns up. Hopefully, we won't get a call out but we'll leave work now for the day,' he said with a glance to Daniel.

Thomas nodded, getting his meaning. He'd forgotten the company he was in. He turned to Daniel. 'I won't do anything unnecessary that will adversely affect Gideon, you can tell him that when you get home.'

'I will,' Daniel said.

As they took seats in the omnibus, Thomas said privately: 'Thanks, Harry.'

'Anytime, son.'

Chapter 26

Mr Hayward had returned from his walk to find his two youngest, Gideon and Matilda, distressed.

'I go out for a thirty-minute walk and something has happened?' he asked, concerned to sense their frustration. 'Come in, let's talk about this.' He moved into the drawing room and offered them both a brandy. Gideon accepted, Matilda did not. 'Tell me what has happened,' he said, pouring the glass of amber fluid and handing it to Gideon. 'Matilda, darling, take a seat.'

She did so, and Gideon took a seat opposite. Mr Hayward sat next to Matilda and sipped his drink. He told his father all that had transpired. Then he turned to Matilda. 'What do you think, Tillie?' he asked.

Matilda sighed and began, 'It's hard for me to be impartial. I think Thomas is putting Gideon's client and business at significant risk with little in the way of evidence, but I understand he has a job to do.'

'Does Thomas think you may have a part to play in this, Gids?' Mr Hayward asked.

'Me? No. I don't know. Surely not,' he said, and turned to Matilda.

'He didn't say that,' Matilda said.

'What would you do in his shoes, Gideon?' he asked of his youngest son. 'Think before you answer and tell me what you would do.'

Gideon's jaw locked with frustration.

'I would be out looking for her,' Gideon said.

'Where?' Mr Hayward pushed him.

Gideon sighed. 'Where she was last seen, at her lover's place. I need this collection, Marlon needs it.'

'But the bad publicity for Mr Dominey's last collection has worked in your favour, hasn't it?' Matilda asked.

'Yes, but only in attracting an audience to the gallery and increasing the gallery's profile. It has not resulted in many sales for Marlon. This new collection is bound to do so.'

Mr Hayward nodded his understanding.

'What would you do now, Pa, given what's happened and might aspire?' Gideon asked, finishing his brandy in a gulp and rising to top up his glass. Mr Hayward declined.

'If it were me, the first thing I would do is go to your client – Mr Dominey's residence – right now and advise him if he has any knowledge of where Miss Reubens is, this is the time to reveal it or ensure she is there tomorrow. Then, if Miss Reubens does not appear tomorrow evening, I would run the silent auction as planned but I would start it at the beginning of your exhibition and I would end it after a few hours. Advise your buyers that the works must remain on show for the month to the public but they are on sale tonight exclusively to them, and it is their chance to get in before everyone else. What follows should not matter when it comes to the quality of the work and the purchase of a painting.'

Gideon leaned forward. 'Yes Pa, that's brilliant. Then, no matter what happens, if Sapphire doesn't come or heaven forbid, Marlon is arrested, he has sold the paintings and both the gallery and Marlon have the money in the bank.'

'Very clever, Pa.' Matilda smiled at him.

'I have a few tricks up my sleeve,' he said with a wink.

She laughed. 'I am sure during your legal career you saved many a skin and not just from the gaol cells.'

'One must think outside the box,' he agreed. 'But son, you need to put yourself in Thomas's shoes. He has all the same pressures bearing down on him. The police hierarchy, the press, community expectations… don't think on him too harshly.'

Gideon finished his drink and rose. 'Thank you, Pa, I'm going to Marlon's now, and I'll persuade him to come out. We need to find Miss Reubens.' He turned to Matilda and said, 'No.'

'No what?' she asked, confused.

'You are not coming just in case Thom is right and Marlon is dangerous.'

She rolled her eyes. 'Then you best be careful too, Gids. Anyway, I prefer to stay here. Thomas might come back with Daniel and I feel terrible for sending him off so abruptly.'

'You will have to get used to that, my dear,' Mr Hayward said. 'If you are a detective's wife, you would always be sending him off or waiting for him. Best not to part on an angry word or you may never forgive yourself.'

*****

Gideon knocked on the downstairs entry door to Marlon Dominey's terrace block, but did not expect the landlady to answer at dinner time. He waited a few moments, entered, and took the stairs to Marlon's private rooms. Marlon opened the door promptly.

'Gideon, what a pleasure. Come in,' he said and on seeing Gideon's face, he frowned. 'This is not a social call… is everything alright?'

'Yes and no,' Gideon said, entering.

'I am having a lovely red wine. Will you join me?' Marlon asked, picking up a glass and swirling the wine in it.

'Thank you,' Gideon said, and did not speak until Marlon poured the wine and presented him with the glass. He followed Marlon to the small couch area in the apartment and took the invited seat opposite. 'Have you seen Miss Reubens yet?'

'No, and it is the longest she has stayed away. I hope she doesn't miss my opening tomorrow night. She would have heard about it in our circles, I am sure,' he said, sipping his wine. 'I am ready for some company, especially female company.'

Gideon nodded. 'I want you to stay calm but I need to let you know what is going on.'

Marlon leaned forward, frowning.

'Has a reviewer turned on my work?' he asked, his voice wary.

Gideon shook his head. 'Nothing like that. In the river, near the mangroves, the police found a few items of clothing belonging to Miss Reubens this morning.' Gideon studied Marlon's reaction.

'I don't understand,' he said.

'No one has seen Miss Reubens for some time. You were, I believe, the last person to see her when she inspired you and then you began painting again.'

Marlon scoffed. 'But that is not unusual. Sapphire has friends in the art and theatre circles, and we are not exclusive.'

Gideon continued. 'Two artists have been murdered and now your muse is missing, or the police believe her to be.'

Marlon stood quickly. 'They think I have killed her! They think I would kill Sapphire?' he asked, his voice raised.

Gideon placed his wine down. 'They think she might be missing and with a shawl found in the river bearing her initials, and your painting depicting her floating in water…'

'Her shawl was in the river? My God,' Marlon said and turned, running his hand over his face. 'No. This can't be happening. So, if they do not find her, I am ruined?'

Gideon raised his hands to placate him. 'I have a plan.' He waited to speak, but Marlon moved away, pacing and not inviting him to share the plan.

'I don't know where she is. Why would her shawl be by the river? It must be some sort of prank.' He exhaled heavily and then looked at Gideon. 'I don't know where to start looking… the jazz clubs, I suppose. She loves to sing there, or maybe…'

'Hear me out,' Gideon said, cutting him off. 'Let's assume Miss Reubens is perfectly safe—'

Marlon went to speak and Gideon stopped him again.

'And we know you didn't harm her, so this is the plan.' He told Marlon his suggestion for bringing the auction to a close that evening and selling the paintings by offering guests at the VIP event the first bite of the cherry.

'Brilliant, yes, let's do it. But what if Sapphire does show up? Do we delay the sales then?'

Gideon shrugged. 'What do you think? I'm inclined to go with it anyway unless you hope that waiting might draw out a large price in the silent auction as the paintings garner more exposure.'

'There is that,' Marlon agreed.

A knock on the door interrupted them. Gideon rose and answered it to find Thomas, Detective Dart, and Daniel present.

'I thought you were going to do some boxing,' Gideon addressed his brother.

'We were, but we decided to come here first, or rather Thom wanted to come here first,' Daniel said.

Marlon recognised the detectives and before they had even entered his rooms, he was saying: 'You think Sapphire is missing or dead and that I did it?'

Detective Dart closed the door behind them.

Thomas, on making eye contact with Gideon, held up his hands. 'Let's just sit and slowly work through this,' he suggested. 'No one is accusing you of anything Mr Dominey. We just want to set eyes on Miss Reubens and we want to ensure your safety and catch a murderer.'

Gideon nodded at Thomas, remembering what his father had said. He was keen to still persuade Thomas to at least wait until the day after the gallery event and auction before casting aspersions on Marlon's character, so he endeavoured to remain calm.

He turned to his client. 'Marlon, take a seat, let's hear what the detectives need from us,' he said, calming his client. He took up the introductions. 'This is my brother, Daniel.'

'Another sibling?' Marlon asked. 'Welcome, Mr Hayward,' he said, his manners still intact. 'Are there more of you?'

Gideon nodded. 'You have met Daniel and Matilda. There is also my twin brother, Elijah, a doctor, and our eldest brother, Amos, is a lawyer.'

'That could come in handy,' Marlon said. He welcomed the men to sit, but Thomas and Harry remained standing.

'Have you seen Miss Reubens yet?' Thomas asked.

'No, not for days. What if something has become of her? Why would she be murdered along with those artists? What is to be gained from Sapphire's death?' Marlon asked.

'We don't know and we are not sure she is missing, but given the murderer is still at large and several items of clothing were found in the river, one piece bearing the initials S.R, we need to set eyes on Miss Reubens,' Harry said.

'Can you give us a list of her friends, people she might call on?' Thomas asked.

Marlon shook his head. 'She has a cousin and some family friends locally. I have called on her cousin but she has not set eyes on her.' He wrung his hands, leaning forward in his seat as he thought. 'Sapphire has several jazz and theatre acquaintances in Brisbane but I have not met them. Or if I have, I don't know how to contact them. We only arrived here five months ago, and I have been working on two collections during that time. When we went out, we went to clubs and we met many people. When I was working, she went without me. I don't know where to start.'

Gideon saw Thomas and Harry exchange looks; the story seemed implausible.

Daniel came over and sat beside Gideon. 'We could go out to some clubs tonight and look out for her or ask around,' Daniel offered.

'No! Thanks, Dan, but no,' Gideon said. 'We have the launch and auction tomorrow night. I don't want anyone wondering why we are looking for Miss Reubens, let alone if the press heard of our search,' he said with a look at Thomas.

'I need to investigate this and I can't be seen to favour this situation because of friendships,' Thomas said.

'There is no situation yet and I need to deliver for my client and the business owner,' Gideon said, and rose. 'So, one more day will not make a great deal of difference. Can't you focus on the murdered artists instead of Miss Reubens?'

'She often does her own thing,' Marlon mumbled, interrupting the brewing argument between Gideon and Thomas. 'Once in Barcelona, we did not see each other for a month while I was working. That is why we suit each other.'

Harry, always the peacemaker, spoke up. 'Can I offer an outsider's perspective?'

'Of course,' Thomas said, inviting him to speak.

'It seems to me, Thom, Mr Hayward,' he addressed Gideon, 'that you are both being loyal to the same thing and it isn't family. Thomas is seeking to do the right thing for the community and his job; Mr Hayward, Gideon, you are seeking to do the right thing by the artist you represent and your job. May I suggest that neither of you loses your focus on responsibility, but consider that you are family of sorts, maybe soon to be brothers-in-law? How can *both* of you protect each other's jobs and responsibilities?'

The two men studied each other warily and Daniel added, 'Couldn't have said it better, Detective Dart. So, what do you propose?'

Harry nodded and continued. 'Thomas and I need to search your rooms, Mr Dominey. I'm sorry but we at least need to do that much. We can go get a few constables to assist us, but they will be seen arriving. Or we can do it now, while we are here if you remain seated with the Messrs Hayward. Then, Daniel and Thomas will go visit a couple of the clubs you have frequented in the past, if you could write us a list now. They will not ask around after Miss Reubens and will look like two friends out for some entertainment. They will see if they can find Miss Reubens or hear of her. Please write down any other leads you can think of at this stage.'

'What are you looking for in my studio?' he asked.

Thomas glanced at Harry and then decided to tell him since Marlon Dominey was now not free to rise and clean up.

'Evidence of a struggle or fight, blood and arsenic,' Thomas said.

'Arsenic!' Gideon said, surprised. 'Doesn't every artist have that in their rooms?'

'We know that is a consideration and will take it on board,' Harry said.

Marlon Dominey shook his head. 'I have no arsenic on the premises unless it is in the paint itself.'

'Are you consenting, so we may proceed?' Thomas asked.

'And if he doesn't?' Gideon asked.

'Then one of us shall remain here while the other fetches the appropriate paperwork and manpower,' Thomas answered.

Marlon Dominey sat back and sighed. He waved his hand around. 'Please search as you must. I will make you a list of venues.'

'Stay there, I'll get a notepad and pencil for you,' Gideon said. 'We don't want the detectives thinking you hid something while fetching writing material.' He gave Thomas a wry look.

Forty minutes later, the men concluded their search, finding nothing suspicious on the premises. Gideon watched as the two detectives conferred in the corner. He felt Daniel's eyes upon him and turned to his brother.

'You think I am over-reacting?' he asked.

Daniel leaned forward, resting his elbows on his knees and speaking to Gideon and Marlon.

'I think the detectives are genuinely worried that something has happened to Miss Reubens, especially finding that clothing this morning. Thom said there were a few days between the two murders. Now a few days after, they have made this discovery. I don't want to alarm you, but if someone is out there playing games, your event tomorrow night could be targeted,' Daniel said.

Gideon groaned and rested his head on the back of the couch. He closed his eyes, only opening them when he heard Marlon speak.

'Am I under arrest?' Mr Dominey asked.

'No, but we have all we need for now,' Thomas said.

'What do you have?' Gideon asked.

The detectives ignored him, and Thomas accepted the list from Marlon. He asked of him, 'Is there anyone you can think of who might want to harm Miss Reubens or yourself?'

Marlon thought for a moment. 'To be honest detective, we don't know that many people here.'

'Then, is there anyone that might want to frame you for a crime, someone you have slighted?' Harry asked.

Marlon and Gideon exchanged looks of surprise. Gideon explained. 'We were only just talking about this the other day. Marlon was to show at another gallery space but I persuaded him to come to the *Fine Art Gallery*.'

'The other gallery owner was angry,' Marlon explained, 'but nothing was in writing, and I don't imagine he would be angry enough to retaliate by killing two artists and harming Sapphire or me.'

Gideon rose. 'So, until the opening and auction can we keep this contained?' he asked.

Thomas nodded. 'Unless we find Miss Reubens has come to harm.'

Harry turned to Marlon. 'Mr Dominey, I would do your best to find your muse and have her walk in on your arm tomorrow night.'

Marlon nodded. 'That would solve everything.'

'No, we'd still have a murderer at large, but you would not be the first in the spotlight,' Thomas said, and added 'At this stage.'

Chapter 27

Matilda slept fitfully. She had waited, hoping Thomas would return and they could re-establish good terms. Had she been a man she would have gone to his home to speak with him, but that was impossible at the late hour of the night. She could not ask her father to accompany her and might have asked Daniel, had he returned home.

Why did she speak so thoughtlessly? She scolded herself. It was her role now, her duty, to support Thomas or at least, should she not agree, not take a side against him so blatantly.

Matilda saw every hour of the evening and early dawn, distressed and resolving to never let this happen again, if Thomas would forgive her when the morning broke.

*****

It was a bright, crisp and sunny Wednesday morning, and Matilda and Alice were excited as they rode the omnibus across town. Mrs Lawson had given them the morning off work to accept the promised morning tea invitation which arrived from Mrs Sophie Cornish.

'I cannot wait to see her home. How kind of her to remember,' Alice said, dressed in a pale lime gown that complimented her dark hair and bright blue eyes. She juggled a large bouquet of gaily coloured flowers.

Matilda wore a sky-blue gown – her best colour – and both ladies wore their straw hats with matching ribbons. On Matilda's lap sat a small tin with some shortbread delicacies within baked by Cook.

'I so very much need this distraction today,' Matilda said. 'Thomas and I had a less than pleasant encounter last night and I did not sleep a wink for worrying about him and going over it in my head a thousand times.'

'Oh no,' Alice said, giving her a sympathetic look. 'Is everything alright now?'

'I haven't seen him to make amends,' Matilda said, and lowered her voice. 'It's all because of this dreadful artist situation and with Miss Reubens missing—'

'Sapphire Reubens is missing!' Alice exclaimed in a hushed gasp.

'Oh, do keep that to yourself or Thomas will never trust me again,' Matilda said, eyes wide with alarm.

'Cross my heart,' Alice promised. 'She is not a victim, is she? I couldn't bear it.'

'I can't say because I don't know,' Matilda assured her. 'All I know is that no one has seen her for a couple of weeks. While Mr Dominey is not concerned and told Gideon that her disappearance was quite normal when he was working, the detectives are worried given they already have two dead artists!'

'Rightly so,' Alice said, and they stepped from the omnibus as it stopped at their destination in Newstead. It was a brief walk up the road to the home of Mrs Sophie Cornish, and the day was pleasant for a stroll.

'Don't mention it today, please,' Matilda said.

'Of course not. But isn't Miss Reubens expected to attend the opening tonight for Mr Dominey's showing?'

'Well, that is what everyone, especially Mr Dominey, is expecting,' Matilda agreed. 'Gideon is sick with worry that his artist will be arrested and his gallery's reputation ruined.'

Alice stopped in her tracks. 'They think Mr Dominey might have harmed her? But he adores Miss Reubens, or so it seemed when we saw them together last.'

Matilda nodded. 'If she is missing, he has to be suspect, but there surely would be others.'

Alice looped her arm through Matilda's and began walking again. 'It is positively awful. So, what were you and Thomas fighting about?'

'It wasn't a fight as such, but I thought Thomas should have been more considerate of Gideon's situation, and all he could think about was the job at hand, naturally. But if he was discrete, they could both get through this until more evidence appeared.'

Alice grimaced. 'Dear me, that is difficult. Is there any evidence? Oh, I'm guessing you probably can't tell me that.'

Matilda bit her lip and said softly, 'A shawl was found in the river with the initials S.R. on it, and last night Daniel and

Thomas were intending to visit some of the venues that Miss Reubens liked to frequent. I believe there was no sign of her.'

They arrived at the grand entranceway to Mrs Cornish's Georgian mansion. As if by magic, a young groundsman appeared and opened the large iron gates to allow them entry.

'Hello ladies,' he said with a confident bow for such a young lad, 'Mrs Cornish asked me to look out for you. Just make your way up to the veranda and she will be sure to meet you.'

'Thank you kindly,' Alice said and gave him a smile that ensured he stared at her for several moments after she passed.

'Beautiful day for gardening,' Matilda added.

'It is Miss, and just beautiful in the garden too, now,' he said, looking from one young lady to the other.

They smiled at his attempt at flattery, bid him good-day, and continued up the path.

Matilda studied the upstairs windows and saw movement. She noticed the same at one window downstairs. Mrs Cornish must have quite a few staff on hand, probably necessary for a house of such proportions.

'How imposing,' Alice said, as they continued their walk to the front entrance. 'It's a large place for one young and newly-single woman.'

'I imagine she won't be single for long,' Matilda said.

'Maybe we won't be either,' Alice said with the hint of a smile.

Matilda turned in surprise. 'Really?'

Alice laughed. 'I'm teasing you. Your brother and I have

only been on a few outings. We barely know each other. Not like you and Thomas.'

Matilda groaned at the reminder of her heart pain. She looked up at a flash of colour to find Mrs Cornish herself greeting them from the doorway.

'Miss Hayward, Miss Doran, welcome, you are here, at last. I should have invited you much sooner,' she said, giving the ladies a warm smile.

'The pleasure is all ours,' Alice said, passing over the flowers to her hostess.

'Thank you for the kind invitation, Mrs Cornish, a lovely surprise,' Matilda agreed.

Like Alice, Mrs Cornish wore a fitted gown of pale green but with a delicate red rose embroidered throughout the fabric. It spoke of wealth and good taste. She inhaled the bouquet and sighed.

'Beautiful, thank you. You need not have come bearing gifts. But fresh flowers make a home, don't they?' she said.

Matilda presented the tin of biscuits. 'A small gift from our cook, Mary. She's Irish and makes the best shortbread.'

Mrs Cornish's eyes widened. 'Ooh, lovely. Did she include the recipe?'

'No,' Matilda laughed, 'I think there might only be three ingredients, but the trick, according to Mary, is to get your hands on Irish butter.'

Mrs Cornish nodded and smiled. 'I will remember that. Would you like a tour of the house? And please, call me Sophie.'

Matilda and Alice insisted on the same informality. They followed Sophie through the mansion, admiring the workmanship, the marble, timber and plaster features, and crystal shades. Each room was like a gallery with at least three or four large framed paintings adorning the walls.

A noise above them made both ladies look up, and Sophie laughed.

'Not ghosts, I assure you, although this home has some history. That is just some of my staff.' She stopped outside a room with a closed door and with her hand on the doorknob asked, 'The gallery returned the late Mr Bannon's work to me as they felt the crowd coming to see it after his murder was somewhat macabre. I have both paintings here now by the two deceased artists. Would you like to see them, or would that be too distressing?'

'I would love to see them, please,' Matilda said.

'Indeed, as I would I,' Alice said. 'How sad to think of the artists no longer with us. But clearly someone else felt equally as passionate about their works, enough to copy them as a death statement.'

Sophie nodded. 'That is exactly what I thought too, Alice.' She opened the door and led them into a room that featured a majestic grand piano, and a deep brown chesterfield lounge perfectly placed to sit and view the first of the paintings, Christopher Gill's *Weeping with the Willows*.

Matilda gasped. 'It has so much more impact when isolated and presented as such.'

Sophie smiled her thanks. 'Yes, it is quite something indeed. Christopher was only thirty-two, a great loss.'

'Did you know him well?' Alice asked.

'I met him through my husband and we had met on

several occasions. He was prone to melancholy, hence *Weeping with the Willows.'*

'It is just how I remember the scene that evening,' Matilda said.

Sophie turned to her. 'Oh, you saw it? You saw him in the park?'

Matilda nodded. 'I wasn't meant to, but I was present at the time and I immediately recognised the way he was positioned. It was oddly quite beautiful.'

Sophie nodded and the three ladies turned again to admire the white figure in the painting leaning back against the weeping willow in a laneway of willows.

'If you come this way, I can show you Benjamin Bannon's work, *An Artist Bathing in the Season.'*

'This is so exciting,' Matilda said, 'to see them privately and be able to get so close to them.'

'This one is my favourite,' Sophie admitted. She opened the door to another large room which featured a wall of books and again a lone chesterfield lounge, and on the wall in front of them was the painting in question, full of all the autumnal tones with the artist sitting larger than life in his bathtub filled with coloured leaves.

Alice laughed in surprise. 'It is amazing.'

Matilda inhaled a scent she recognised – floral, but with a hint of herbal. She could not place where she had last enjoyed the scent but saw Sophie studying her.

'It is as if I can smell autumn,' Matilda explained.

Sophie smiled and admitted, 'I have a secret... but I might have to tell you both since you are such admirers of these works,' she teased.

'Please do, we are intrigued now,' Matilda begged.

Sophie looked at the painting. 'Benjamin, that is Mr Bannon's painting *An Artist Bathing in the Season* was part of an exhibition called *Seasons of our Life*. I met Mr Bannon through some friends, a doctor actually, and Mr Bannon insisted I model for him.'

'Of course,' Alice said, 'I can imagine you have been asked many a time.'

Sophie smiled, flattered. 'Thank you, but not that often. Nevertheless, I did model for this very collection, and that is how I met my husband. He came to see the collection, immediately bought this one of the artist in his bath, and on seeing my portrait bought it too and insisted on meeting me.'

'That is very romantic,' Alice said, and sighed.

Matilda narrowed her eyes at Sophie and with a teasing smile said, 'So, your portrait adorns the walls of your home, somewhere in here,' she said, looking around. 'Are you in a bath as well, dare I ask?'

Sophie laughed. 'It does indeed have a place on one of the bedroom walls and rest assured, I am not in the bath. However, my husband thought it somewhat risqué and hence kept it in our bedroom. Shall I show you?'

'Absolutely,' Alice insisted. 'We would love to see it.'

'This way then,' Sophie said, closing the door behind them. She walked down a hallway to a large bedroom with a full bay window overlooking the river. 'I warn you, it is called *The Lady Sleeps in Season*.'

She stood aside and watched as Matilda and Alice both

gasped in amazement. A framed painting of Sophie laying on a white bed, covered in a blanket of leaves of autumn colours, filled the entire wall adjacent to the large bed. Parts of her olive skin revealed to the viewer.

'Oh my, it is truly stunning,' Matilda said, and walked from one end to the other, studying the painting.

'Breathtaking,' Alice agreed. 'I can see why your husband had to possess it.'

Sophie smiled, pleased with their reaction.

'The canvas has captured you for all time,' Matilda said.

'It is gratifying,' Sophie agreed. 'My beautiful cousin and I are both represented in art.'

'Are you? What a wonderful thing. Is she here? Do you have that work?' Alice asked.

Sophie shook her head, 'Sadly no. It belongs to the artist, but maybe in time I shall own it and I will hang them together.'

Matilda sensed melancholy when Sophie spoke of her cousin, so she did not ask her any further questions.

'How I'd love to have a female cousin or my sisters living here with me,' Alice sighed.

'As would I,' Matilda said. 'I have four brothers.'

'Oh, you poor thing,' Sophie teased. 'Come, we best get you a cup of tea then.'

The ladies laughed and followed Sophie back to the sitting room for morning tea. Matilda glanced back once more, but there was no scent in this room or by the painting.

Most odd, she mused.

Chapter 28

It was early when Gideon descended from the hansom cab at his gallery, but Detectives Thomas Ashdown and Harry Dart watched from afar. They were comfortably seated, waiting at what was an omnibus stop, but with no intention of catching a ride. Their position offered a discreet but full view of the gallery. It was too early for the guests to arrive but night had fallen and now it was a waiting game – waiting for the man of the evening, Marlon Dominey, to arrive with his muse, Miss Sapphire Reubens, on his arm.

'If the artist has harmed her, he's done a fine job of hiding any evidence,' Harry said as they sat waiting and watching.

'Indeed. Not even any arsenic to be found amongst his studio material. He seemed relaxed about her disappearance. I'm not sure what to make of that,' Thomas said.

'Yes, as if we were making a mountain out of a molehill.'

Thomas suddenly stood up from his seat and peered at a woman alighting from a hansom. 'For the love of God, what is Matilda doing at the exhibition? And that is Miss Doran and a man I do not recognise with her. I wonder if Daniel knows him.'

'Perhaps he is Miss Doran's guardian,' Harry suggested.

'I suspect you are right,' Thomas agreed.

'The ladies might be covering the story for the *Women's Journal*,' Harry reminded him. 'Do you mean what is Miss Hayward doing there without you?'

Thomas turned to his partner, gave him a wry look and sat again, returning his attention to the two ladies ascending the stairs of the gallery. Even from afar, he could see how beautiful Matilda looked – her small face, attractive figure, and wearing a dress he had not seen before. He wondered if Daniel would arrive next and he had simply not told Thomas that he wasn't invited to spare his feelings.

'She told me Gideon couldn't get them in this time because it was only potential buyers,' Thomas muttered.

'Perhaps Miss Hayward is her brother's guest for the night in the number count. Has he got a lady?' Harry asked.

'Depends which week you ask,' Thomas said. 'Nothing serious, I believe.' He watched as Gideon came down the few stairs at the front of the gallery and greeted the ladies. For a moment before entry, they stopped and Gideon pointed toward Thomas and Harry. Matilda looked, raised her hand in a small wave, knowing she wasn't blowing their cover as they were there for anyone to see. She then turned and entered the gallery with Gideon.

'Well, they know we are here,' Thomas said drily. 'I won't be winning any favour with Gideon for my surveillance.'

'That's okay,' Harry assured him. 'Gideon also knows you are not interfering.'

Thomas exhaled with the drama and emotions swerving

around inside him, and Harry clasped his shoulder for a moment in solidarity.

'Let it unfold as it should,' Harry said. 'You go back a long way with the Haywards and surely an incident like this will not break those foundations. Besides, Daniel is not here with Miss Doran, so it appears Gideon invited neither of you and it is not a slight.'

Thomas nodded, wishing he felt as confident of that, especially now with Matilda's heart in his hands. They sat for some time in silence before Harry said, 'The artist will be the last to arrive, I imagine.'

'He was last time, making a grand entrance with his muse. They were more impressive than the artwork on that occasion,' Thomas said, and both men chuckled.

For the next thirty minutes, they waited patiently before the guests began to arrive. Carriages and hansom cabs pulled up out the front and the guests alighted, dressed in their finery. Through the glass windows of the gallery, the gaiety could be witnessed. Potential buyers and their guests toured the gallery with champagne glasses in hand, laughing, talking, and admiring the work. The detectives were not close enough to see if any cheque books were pulled from the gentlemen's jackets or bids written for the silent auction.

'I believe it is going to be a great success,' Harry said.

Thomas nodded, leaning his elbows on his knees and watching the activity. 'Let's just hope that Gideon sells all the paintings tonight, just in case.'

As the last of the guests arrived and it was fifteen minutes past the hour, a hansom cab pulled up near the front stairs. Thomas rose and Harry stood beside him.

'This has got to be the artist, surely,' Thomas said.

He was right. Marlon Dominey, looking resplendent in black tie, stepped out. He extended his hand.

Thomas's breath hitched as they saw a small gloved hand appear through the hansom entry way. The lady eased her way from the hansom in a gold gown, her brunette hair pinned beautifully with small glittering diamonds that caught the light even from where the detectives stood.

'It's her, Miss Reubens,' Harry said, amazed. 'I must say, I wasn't expecting that.'

Thomas stared and then squinted.

'No. I don't believe it,' he said, the words hissed through clenched teeth.

'What? What is it?' Harry snapped to look at him and then looked back to watch Mr Dominey lead the lady up the stairs.

The art gallery door opened and Gideon welcomed them both. They could hear the applause as it broke out on seeing Mr Dominey. Gideon glanced up the hill to the detectives and looked away just as quickly.

Thomas turned to Harry. 'That's not Miss Reubens.'

'Are you sure?' Harry asked, trying to see her again but she had moved too far away to see any redeemable features. 'Then who is it?'

'It's the widow, Mrs Sophie Cornish. She is Marlon Dominey's muse tonight.'

Matilda's eyes widened on seeing Mrs Sophie Cornish enter on the arm of the artist. Where was Miss Reubens? How odd that Sophie had not mentioned she was attending the gallery exhibition tonight when they were at morning tea.

She watched her brother as he welcomed them. A look passed between himself and Mr Dominey that spoke of despair for those who might recognise why.

After the applause died down, Gideon welcomed the artist and his guest and invited Mr Dominey to speak. The speech was similar to before and within minutes Mr Dominey and Mrs Cornish began to circulate. Matilda caught Sophie's eye and Sophie looked pleased to see her, giving her a little wave and blowing a kiss.

Gideon returned to his sister's side.

'What am I going to do?' he whispered.

'Nothing,' she assured him and smiled as if they were having a normal conversation about art. 'You are going to mingle, take bids, remind everyone that they have a window of opportunity to buy and advise the lucky bidders who they are as soon as possible.'

Gideon nodded, taking in her words. He was breathing too fast, his eyes scanning the room as if he expected Miss Sapphire Reubens to step down from her painting.

Matilda continued. 'Gids, you need to stay calm. I am going to go and speak with the Detectives and persuade them to wait until tomorrow or after tonight's party has finished to speak with Mr Dominey.'

'I don't doubt you have some influence with Thomas, but I'm not sure you have enough on this occasion,' Gideon said.

'Gids, please, look at me,' Matilda said. 'I have some information that I gleaned today which might make him agreeable to that arrangement. Trust me, steady yourself, and we will talk later. Yes?'

He breathed out, kissed her on the cheek, and stepped back. 'Yes, thank you.'

Alice appeared at her side. 'Are you feeling alright, Gideon?' she asked.

'A little tense,' he admitted.

Matilda turned to Alice and said in a low voice: 'I am going to speak to the detectives. Do you wish to accompany me? There is no need if you prefer to stay here.'

'I am coming with you,' she said and turning to Gideon advised him, 'I have put in my guardian's silent bid for the painting he desires. He had to leave on business not long after arriving. I hope I secure it.'

Gideon allowed himself to smile. 'Thank you, at least I know of one bid,' he said, relieved.

Matilda nodded and, touching Gideon's arm, said, 'Go

and get your silent auction moving along. Leave the rest with us.'

The two ladies made their way to the door, intent on persuading the two detectives not to interrupt the social gathering, which was proving to be a great success.

✶✶✶✶✶

Harry looked alarmed. 'Are you sure that is Mrs Cornish, Thom? Your younger eyes are better than mine but they look mightily similar, those two ladies.'

Thomas nodded, pacing as he thought: 'They do, I agree, but I am sure it is Mrs Sophie Cornish.' He stopped dead and stared towards the gallery. 'What are they doing? It's Matilda and Miss Doran, they're leaving the gallery.'

They watched as Matilda and Alice walked down the stairs and onto the street.

'I need to go escort them,' Thomas said. 'It's late and they shouldn't be walking out at night.'

'Bring the ladies here if you like and we can see them home,' Harry called after him, but the ladies were already walking towards the two men.

Thomas rushed down the rise towards the gallery and met Matilda and Alice on the way.

'You look beautiful,' he said, arriving in front of her and forgetting all that was going on at that moment. He took her hand and kissed it. 'Miss Doran,' he said with a small bow.

'Thank you, Thomas,' Matilda said and smiled. 'I thought you might still be angry at me.' She looked up at him.

'I have spent several nights awake, worrying about you,

but that's quite normal,' he said, with affection. He was not the emotive or expressive type and least of all in front of another lady.

'As have I. Worried about you, that is, especially when you didn't return after our words. I wanted to come to you but...'

'I'm sorry,' he said, knowing her limitations, 'I too—'

'I understand, you have a lot happening.' Matilda smiled, feeling relieved and more settled having cleared the air a little with Thomas. 'Alice and I need to talk with you and Detective Dart.' She saw Thomas's expression. 'I promise I am not here to beg my brother's case, but we have some interesting and odd information to share.'

Alice agreed. 'We want to tell you first,' she said, 'but the *Women's Journal* will pursue the story if you are not interested.'

Thomas nodded and offered his arms to both ladies. Matilda looped her arm through his.

Alice did not. 'Thank you, Detective, but I should be able to walk unaided,' she said with a teasing smile to Matilda.

'I thought you could not secure tickets for tonight,' Thomas said as they walked up the rise. He felt slighted and only somewhat mollified by Daniel not being in attendance.

'Gideon relented when he found out Alice was attending as a guest of her guardian,' Matilda explained. 'I am his partner for the night, as such.'

Thomas nodded, pleased with the explanation. Alice walked slightly ahead to greet Detective Dart, and Thomas took the opportunity to speak with Matilda.

'It pains me when we are at odds,' he said, slowing his walk.

'I barely slept for the turmoil I felt,' Matilda said gazing up at him. 'I have never felt anything like this before, the feelings I feel for you.'

'I should hope not,' he said and smiled delighted. 'It is the same for me, I assure you.'

'Except for...' she started saying and Thomas frowned, not knowing what to expect.

Matilda continued: 'Do you remember Bertie?'

'Who the hell is Bertie?' Thomas asked, his thoughts immediately going to his work colleague, Burton.

'My pet frog when I was twelve. I loved him dearly.'

Thomas put his head back and laughed. An unusual sound that delighted Matilda. They arrived, and Detective Dart rose from the bench.

'How good it is to see you smile, Thom,' Harry said and to the ladies: 'I'm afraid we are under-dressed Miss Hayward and Miss Doran,' he joked.

Matilda laughed. 'Well, you are both not the company we expected to keep, so the fault is with us.'

Harry brushed down the seat for the ladies and, thanking him, they accepted and sat. They were alone, the omnibus having stopped its service for the day.

Thomas indicated the seat beside Matilda to Harry.

Preferring to stand, he started: 'Tell me was that Mrs Cornish on the arm of Mr Dominey tonight?'

Matilda nodded. 'It was indeed.'

Thomas shook his head and looked away. 'Miss Reubens

has met with foul play, I am sure of it, and we are probably already too late.'

Matilda started to speak and Thomas cut her off. 'I know you want Gideon to have a successful night and secure the sale of Mr Dominey's works. I want that for him too but—'

It was Harry who cut him off. 'Thom, we do not have enough to raid the gallery or haul Mr Dominey out for questioning. We can do that tomorrow morning or later tonight after the exhibition. All off the record, of course,' he said with a glance to Alice.

Matilda gave Detective Dart a grateful smile.

'Yes, we agree this discussion is off the record,' Alice said. 'If we may, we did come up here for a reason. Scarlett…'

'Yes, some insights that might help,' Scarlett said.

'Ah yes, your information, please…' Thomas invited her to speak.

'Today Alice and I had morning tea with Sophie… Mrs Cornish. She extended the invitation when she met us at the gallery that day.' Matilda reminded the gentlemen. 'But several curious things happened while we were at her residence.'

'Go ahead,' Thomas indulged her. Matilda noted this and turned her attention to Detective Dart.

'When we arrived today at Sophie's Newstead home, I saw the shadow of a figure upstairs and another downstairs. Sophie said it was staff, but we never saw them, which was a little odd because we toured the house and usually you see staff at work.'

She looked at both men, and Thomas nodded, unconvinced.

'Please continue,' Harry said, encouraging her.

'Sophie said she met her husband after posing for your first deceased artist, Benjamin Bannon.'

Thomas looked to Harry. 'She did mention that to us when we first spoke with her. A doctor friend introduced her to the artist, and she met her potential husband when he came to view Mr Bannon's paintings, if my memory serves me correctly?'

Harry nodded. 'Yes, that's my recollection.'

Matilda continued. 'Did she mention that she features in one of the paintings in his *Seasons of our Life* collection – the very collection featuring the painting which depicts Mr Bannon's murder?' Matilda said.

Harry clicked his finger. 'She did. Well, no, she said he asked her to pose.'

Thomas concurred and turned to look at Matilda. 'Did she pose? Did you see her painting?'

'We did. It is beautiful. She is lying in repose on a bed covered in a blanket of autumn leaves,' Alice informed them.

'No wonder the husband bought it once they were betrothed,' Thomas said.

'How did Mrs Cornish come to know the doctor?' Harry asked.

The ladies looked at each other.

'We don't know,' Matilda said. 'But *The Brisbane Courier* reported the victims died from an injection, if memory serves me. That is an interesting connection is it not – the artists and the doctor in their circle.'

Thomas raised an eyebrow, impressed, but not wanting to

encourage Matilda or Alice to play detective – or journalist for that matter – he tempered his response.

'Well, that's interesting. She has a friend who is a doctor who knows how to administer an injection and has access to drugs. And Mrs Cornish knew both victims. I wonder if she knows Miss Reubens?'

'As she is escorting Mr Dominey tonight, there is every chance she has met the artist and his muse on previous occasions,' Harry said. 'Also, just as importantly, how did Mrs Cornish come to befriend this doctor, I wonder?'

'I wonder if her husband did die of an age-related complaint,' Thomas said under his breath.

'There's more,' Matilda said. 'Sophie said that both she and her cousin now featured in paintings but did not say which ones, or who her cousin was. I was not in a position to ask, but I wondered… given the similarity—'

'Good Lord,' Thomas said, 'could Mrs Cornish be Miss Reubens' cousin?'

'Do you know Mrs Cornish's maiden name?' Harry asked, and Matilda and Alice shook their head in the negative.

'Ladies, this is very helpful,' Thomas said, forgetting his reticence.

'One last thing,' Matilda said, looking pleased with herself. 'It is an odd observation.'

'Go ahead,' Thomas encouraged her now, impressed with all her observations.

'While I didn't see any staff, I smelled perfume, a fragrance both sweet and woody in the room featuring the painting of the artist in the bath. I remembered where I had smelt it before.'

Alice gasped. 'Me too! At Mr Dominey's first exhibition.'

'Yes, exactly,' Matilda said with excitement. 'Tonight, when I saw Mr Dominey walking in the door with Mrs Cornish on his arm, it was as if he was wandering in that first showing with Miss Reubens on his arm. That's what triggered my memory – it was her scent. That was where I first inhaled it and again today at Mrs Cornish's place. I think Miss Reubens could be Sophie's cousin or at least acquainted with her, and I believe for some reason, she is hiding at Sophie's home.'

Chapter 30

Thomas was alive with energy, his thoughts running in a hundred directions. Until now, he had felt like he and his colleague, Harry, were treading water. There had been no strong leads and it was as if the killer was taunting them with clues.

'Matilda, I could kiss you,' he said.

'Really?' she laughed.

'Well don't let me stop you,' Harry said, smiling, and Alice laughed.

'I suggest we head straight to Mrs Cornish's home now,' Thomas said, refocusing.

'I agree,' Matilda said.

Thomas shook his head. 'No, it could be dangerous. You two should return to the party or else Mrs Cornish or Mr Dominey might notice you have slipped out and be suspicious.'

'I don't see why they would be,' Matilda said, giving Thomas a wry look.

'No,' Alice agreed. 'We are two friends who came and left together after seeing the art and sharing a champagne.'

Thomas stood straighter, searching for a new argument and knowing he was going to be outdone.

'Besides, you might need us,' Matilda said. 'We could knock on the door and ask to see Miss Sapphire Reubens and see if the staff fetch her or deny she is there. You could stay out of sight. She may appear to two ladies.'

Matilda saw the men exchange looks.

Harry nodded. 'I think that is a valid idea and we can be close by so that Miss Hayward and Miss Doran are not in any danger.'

Thomas frowned. 'Only if you ask for Miss Reubens but do not enter. I cannot risk the servants closing the door and having you inside with Miss Reubens, who may be a murderer, or maybe desperate enough to keep her secret that she will harm either or both of you.'

'We can do that, but I have my own condition too,' Matilda said.

Thomas rolled his eyes and Harry suppressed a smile.

'We get to report this as it unfolds and we get to include a comment from both of you in our story.'

Thomas groaned and Harry spoke up. 'Deal. Negotiated like a professional, Miss Hayward. Let's depart.' He hailed two hansom cabs before Thomas had the chance to reopen negotiations.

*****

The house was lit, the glow from lamps slipping through cracks behind closed curtains.

228

'Thank goodness, the gates are open,' Alice said as they arrived at the entrance to Mrs Cornish's mansion.

'It truly is impressive,' Harry said, peering out of the hansom cab he shared with Miss Doran.

'Wait until you see inside, Detective Dart,' she said. 'Without meaning to be indelicate, Mrs Cornish must have inherited a significant amount to manage its upkeep.'

It was the first time Harry had the chance to speak with the young lady.

'Are you enjoying your time here?' he asked.

'Oh, I love it, and I am so grateful to have made Matilda's acquaintance and to have work at the *Women's Journal*. This is so exciting tonight.'

Harry grinned. 'Yes, I suppose we forget that after becoming jaded old detectives. But you never tire of closing the case and bringing someone to justice who deserves it. I hear you have made the acquaintance and won the heart of another Hayward.'

Alice blushed. 'Yes, he is rather lovely.'

'I've known Daniel for as long as I've known Thomas, they are good young men. I was worried you were arriving with Daniel tonight; Thomas would have been most slighted – it is a difficult situation he is in.'

Alice bit her lower lip for a moment as she thought and then said: 'Matilda might have been upset with him, but I doubt she would lie to Thomas, especially given he would be likely to find out in conversation that they both attended.'

'True,' Harry agreed. 'I suspect she would say upfront that he was not invited.'

Alice laughed. 'Indeed.'

The two hansom cabs came to a stop as directed just past the entrance stairs and close to the side of the house, out of view from the windows upstairs. Harry alighted and assisted Miss Doran down the step. The two men turned and faded into the shadows. The ladies then took the first small steps to the imposing front door.

Matilda knocked and they stood back.

'Did he deliver on that kiss?' Alice whispered for Matilda's ears only and Matilda laughed.

'He might have done so,' she said and blushed.

Within minutes the door open and a young maid appeared. She gave a small curtsey. In her peripheral vision, Alice saw Harry and Thomas move closer. They remained screened, courtesy of greenery around the entrance doorway.

'Good evening,' Alice said in her crisp British accent. 'We are here to visit Miss Reubens please.'

'I'm afraid she is out. Oh, sorry, did you mean Mrs Cornish?' the maid corrected herself.

'No, her guest, Miss Reubens,' Matilda added.

'Do come in,' the maid stood aside and within seconds a middle-aged house steward appeared by her side and took over, correcting the maid.

'I'm sorry, there is no one here by that name. Perhaps you have the wrong house,' he said, standing straight. The maid fled from their sight.

'I believe she is expecting us,' Matilda said, pushing the truth. 'We've just been at the exhibition in which she featured and had the pleasure of talking with Mrs Cornish.'

For a moment, a look of doubt crossed the steward's face and he directed them: 'Please, wait here.'

He turned, leaving them standing in the doorway. Harry and Thomas moved closer to view what might proceed, and in a matter of minutes, Miss Sapphire Reubens appeared at the top of the stairs. Matilda gasped at seeing her. She was as beautiful as the ladies remembered, wrapped in a dark blue gown with small gold slip-on shoes. As she approached, yellow bruising was visible around her neck.

'You are alive and well,' Matilda said.

Miss Reubens turned to steward. 'Thank you. I will talk with the ladies,' she said, dismissing him. She turned her attention back to the ladies. 'Was there a fear I was dead?' she asked, surprised.

Thomas and Harry stepped into the light and Miss Reubens gave a cry of surprise. Her hand went to her heart.

'Fear not, Miss Reubens, Detectives Ashdown and Dart at your service,' Harry said, indicating himself and Thomas.

'Detectives, you frightened me,' she said.

'We are pleased to set eyes on you, Miss Reubens,' Thomas said. 'Can you explain why clothing items belonging to you may have ended up in the mangroves of the Brisbane River?'

Miss Reubens' eyes widened with great theatrics.

'I have no idea, Detective. I cannot say I noticed any items in my possession were missing. Which items?'

'A shawl with the initials S.R. and a pair of red shoes,' Harry said.

'Well, I possess both of those items. How peculiar,' she said, giving nothing away.

'Do you think we might move into your sitting room while we discuss this?' Alice asked.

Miss Reubens looked less than pleased with the suggestion. 'I was just about to retire and I'm afraid the hostess of the house is not home,' she said.

'Your cousin?' Matilda asked.

Miss Reubens did not answer and Matilda continued, 'Were you here when we visited the other day?'

'I don't recall your visit. I might have been resting.'

'I think it best we take a seat inside, Miss Reubens,' Thomas said.

The small party followed as she turned sharply and led them into a large sitting room. The lamps were lit and the room was imposing and silent.

'Can you tell us how you received that bruising around your throat, Madam?' Harry asked.

Miss Reubens' hand automatically went there. Before she could respond, a carriage could be heard coming up the path at a fast rate. Thomas rose and went to the door, leaving Harry to keep an eye on Miss Reubens and ensure the safety of the ladies.

Chapter 31

Matilda momentarily excused herself and found the steward.

'I need to get an urgent message to my brother. Would you have a boy who could take it?'

'Of course, miss,' he said and indicated a small table near the entranceway, where she could find paper and pencil. Matilda thanked him as he departed to fetch the boy.

She scribbled Gideon's name and the gallery's address on the front and wrote: *'We have found Miss Reubens safe and sound at Mrs Cornish's residence.'* and signed her name. Folding the note, Matilda retrieved a coin from her purse. The steward and boy returned, and she pressed both the note and coin into the boy's hands.

'The payment is unnecessary, miss,' the steward said haughtily, with a glance to the boy.

Matilda nodded her understanding and said to the boy, who was the cheeky young teenage gardener they had previously met, 'I am grateful for you taking it so quickly at this hour.'

'Of course, miss, I am on my way.' He smiled appreciatively and departed before the steward could change Matilda's mind on the handsome sum received.

Matilda thanked the older man again and returned to the sitting room.

Sapphire Reubens was explaining that she was simply having some respite.

Alice asked in a low voice: 'Are you alright, Miss Reubens? Were you in fear for your life?'

Miss Reubens' face softened. 'Thank you. I confess I am not used to the tenderness of women. They often find me to be a threat. But there was an incident,' she said hesitantly.

'Mr Dominey did this to you?' Matilda asked, touching her own throat.

'He gets passionate about his work sometimes and—'

Mrs Sophie Cornish rushed into the room, Thomas in her wake.

'What has happened? Are you okay?' She dropped on her knees in front of her cousin, touching Sapphire's face.

Miss Reubens took her hand. 'I am fine, Sophie, do not distress yourself. The ladies and the detectives thought I was dead.'

'Why would you think that?' Sophie asked, turning around to address them. She rose and lowered herself on the seat next to Miss Reubens, continuing to hold her hand.

'Why indeed?' Thomas asked. 'Perhaps you can explain.'

'I have no idea what you mean,' Sophia said. She looked from Alice to Matilda and then back to the detectives.

'Can you confirm that you are cousins?' Harry asked.

The two ladies looked at each other and Sophie gave a brief nod.

'Sophie Reubens? Was that your maiden name, Mrs Cornish?' Thomas asked.

'Yes.'

'Why did you attend tonight as Mr Dominey's guest?' Thomas continued.

'Sapphire was not feeling up to it and I am a patron of the arts. I contacted him to ask would he care to escort me. Is that a crime that I should be aware of?' she asked curtly.

Thomas grimaced in annoyance. 'I suspect you are well aware of what I am asking, Mrs Cornish. Mr Dominey did not know that you were harbouring your cousin. In fact, he told us he had contacted Miss Reubens' cousin and was told she had not been sighted.'

'Then I mustn't have sighted Sapphire when he asked,' she said, defiantly. 'May I ask why you are all here?' Sophie addressed Matilda and Alice.

Alice nodded to Matilda to explain.

'We were frightened for Miss Reubens,' Matilda said, looking from Mrs Cornish to Miss Reubens. 'We saw the beautiful paintings featuring you lying in water as if in death, and then the clothing was found in the river, laid out almost as you appeared in the painting. For over a week Mr Dominey could not attest to your whereabouts, we feared you might be the next victim, especially with a murderer on the loose.'

Miss Reubens smiled at Matilda, and Sophie softened.

'It was kind of you to worry, especially as we had not

been formally introduced and I am a stranger in your city,' Miss Reubens said.

'But of course, you intended for that to happen, for suspicion to be raised around your whereabouts, didn't you?' Thomas asked the two ladies. 'The question is, why? Are you both, along with Mr Dominey, involved in something underhanded, or were you out to punish Mr Dominey?'

'Why would I attend this evening with him if that were the case?' Sophie Cornish asked, and Thomas had no response.

Matilda thought like a single woman. 'Perhaps to meet an eligible new suitor – there is no shame in that, as you must be lonely and, after all, the evening was just for potential buyers of art, a wealthy group indeed.'

'That is true,' Mrs Cornish said, 'but as you can see, I am hardly in need of a wealthy husband. The company, however, would be welcomed,' she said with a look to Thomas, which did not go unnoticed by Matilda or anyone in the small party.

Harry diverted the conversation. 'Are you in hiding from Mr Dominey, Miss Reubens?'

Sapphire Reubens touched her throat. 'I will admit he frightened me. He was without inspiration and angry, and was holding me in passion, and then suddenly my fear and helplessness seemed to excite him. I think I might have fainted and when I awoke, he was so busy painting that I rushed out quickly before he could stop me.'

'Did you see what he was painting?' Harry asked.

'A little of it,' she said without hesitation.

'You must have known how it would appear?' Thomas

continued. 'A missing muse, your shawl and shoes found in the river in the fashion of the painting you saw enough of to emulate, and two dead artists whose murder remains unsolved.'

'Well, now that you put it like that,' Mrs Cornish said, and gave Thomas an endearing smile.

'Were you going to allow us to arrest Mr Dominey and for him to be punished for Miss Reubens' disappearance or death?' Thomas asked of Mrs Cornish, increasingly frustrated by her games.

She sighed. 'Of course not. I love Marlon.' She looked to her cousin and then exhaling said, 'We just wanted to frighten him.'

Miss Reubens nodded.

Mrs Cornish continued: 'I wanted to make him realise he has something beautiful and irreplaceable, and if he wishes to cause Sapphire harm, he too will know what it is like to create something beautiful and lose it.'

Chapter 32

Thomas reined in his anger and Harry rose, tapping him on the shoulder.

'A word,' Harry said, and the two detectives departed the room, leaving the ladies alone. In the hallway, Harry said, 'We've got nothing. I suggest we find out a little more about Mrs Cornish's deceased husband and how he died.'

'Frustrating,' Thomas conceded. 'I want to know more about this doctor too, the mutual friend of Mrs Cornish and the deceased artist.'

They turned as yet again, they could hear a carriage coming at speed up the path. Thomas and Harry went to the doorway. Marlon Dominey jumped down from the cab before it had fully stopped.

'Where is she?' he said angrily and strode by the detectives, who turned and followed in his wake.

'Where have you been?' He demanded of Miss Reubens and then turned to Mrs Cornish. 'All the time you knew where Sapphire was and did not put me out of my misery?'

'Look at my throat!' Sapphire rose and snapped at him.

'You took the life from me to fuel your inspiration with so little regard for my welfare.'

'And I will always protect my cousin over your needs,' Mrs Cornish snapped.

Mr Dominey turned to Matilda.

'Thank you for sending the note to Gideon,' he said.

Thomas was caught by surprise; he had wondered how Mr Dominey knew to come. When he caught her eye, Matilda gave Thomas a small shrug.

And as if the stress of the last few days washed from him, Marlon Dominey took a deep breath and the fight left him. He turned to Miss Reubens. 'Would you have seen me ruined?'

She did not answer.

'You have been my inspiration and my life for all these years, and you would see it end like this.'

Tears welled in Miss Reubens' eyes and the group shuffled uncomfortably. Mr Dominey dropped to his knees in front of Sapphire. 'I captured your light forever on my canvas, my greatest work yet. I am nothing without you. Forgive me, please?'

Miss Reubens softened and touched his face. 'Yes, yes, my love. I forgive you, I did miss you.'

And then he rose and pulled her into his embrace.

Thomas resisted rolling his eyes, but cleared his throat to gain the group's attention.

'Do you wish to charge Mr Dominey with your assault, Miss Reubens?' he asked routinely.

She looked at Marlon and touched his face. 'No, definitely not.'

Thomas turned to Mrs Cornish. 'Consider yourselves lucky that my partner and I don't charge you with wasting police time, Madam.'

'But Detective, we did not know that you were looking for Sapphire,' Mrs Cornish said, her face a mask of innocence. 'We did not report her missing and nor did Marlon, did you?' she asked of him.

'No.' He shook his head. 'Although I was worried.'

'Ladies, shall we?' Thomas asked Matilda and Alice, having had enough of the group for one evening. He intended to see the ladies home or back to the gallery and then head to work despite the hour. The husband and the doctor deserved his immediate consideration, and he would not sleep for thinking how they might fit in the mystery of the two dead artists.

He recognised the look on Matilda's face… she had other ideas.

*****

Matilda accepted Thomas's arm as the four walked down the long driveway to return to the main road and hail their rides. Slightly in front, Harry escorted Alice and they talked about all that had transpired. Matilda studied Thomas – his jaw was locked with frustration and he was a million miles away.

'I guess a quote won't be forthcoming then,' she teased and, distracted, he turned to her and then smiled.

'A deal's a deal, but I'd rather give you a quote when we've solved the case.'

'I am not convinced that Miss Reubens will be safe with Mr Dominey in the future should his creativity disappear again.'

'Nor I,' he agreed.

'Do you think that is the end of Sophie and Miss Reubens' involvement in the murders?' Matilda asked, and added on seeing his expression, 'Strictly between we four, of course.'

Harry and Alice turned slightly to wait for them and partake in the conversation.

'My gut instinct is they are not involved further, and that Mr Dominey's violence towards Miss Reubens was the motivation for the behaviour of the two ladies. What do you think, Harry?' Thomas asked.

'I'm inclined to agree,' Harry said. 'But only regarding the ladies. I am not yet convinced one way or the other if Mr Dominey is capable of killing off fellow artists for his own advantage.'

'Or,' Alice mused, 'because of rivalry and jealousy, since I can't see how he would benefit greatly from the two artists' deaths unless I am missing something.'

'Right you are,' Harry said, 'unless he owns some of their paintings.'

'I guess that is a motive for Mrs Cornish. I must check out her financial situation,' Thomas said, more to himself than anyone else. 'It would cost a considerable sum to maintain that home and staff.' Remembering the company he was in and their inquiring minds, he cleared his throat, announcing: 'We shall drop you back at the gallery, ladies.'

'I am sure Gideon would like to thank you both if you

wanted to come in. No doubt the crowd will be smaller now,' Matilda said.

'I'm not so sure Gids wants to thank me for anything,' Thomas answered. 'But no, I have several things I want to pursue and I'm sure Mrs Dart would like Harry home tonight.'

'What are you pursuing tonight?' Matilda asked boldly, eyebrow raised, hoping for a reply.

Thomas smiled. 'I am not revealing that to you now, but I will honour our agreement, I assure you, and give you a quote. Thank you for your help tonight, ladies.'

'It was our pleasure and quite fun,' Alice said as the two hansom cabs came into sight.

Matilda persisted with Thomas. 'I am guessing that you are going to pursue the doctor friend of Mrs Cornish, Dr Robert Humphries.'

'That's him,' Harry said. 'She did mention his name to us the day we visited the State Gallery I believe.'

Thomas gave Matilda a wry look. 'I'm not confirming my next actions with you, even if you guess correctly.'

Harry smiled. 'But it always worth a try, Miss Hayward.'

Matilda gave Harry a conspiratorial grin. 'It's just that I believe Dr Humphries was at the gallery launch tonight.'

'Was he?' Thomas asked, surprised.

'Well, he is a keen buyer,' Alice said. 'And as Sophie said, he moves in those circles. Only the buyers were invited tonight.'

The two ladies exchanged looks and Thomas caught them in the act.

'What does that mean?' he asked. 'That look between you both?'

'Looks like some scheming to me,' Harry added, getting into the spirit of the discussion.

Matilda laughed. 'I have an idea,' she said, teasing Thomas. 'As you suggested, Alice and I will return to the gallery and update Gideon on all that happened. If the good doctor – Dr Humphries – is still there, we'll get ourselves introduced and tell you our impressions in the morning.'

Alice nodded with enthusiasm. 'An insider point of view; that might be useful should you wish to interview him tomorrow. He's bound to be different with us than how he reacts with the police.'

Thomas' eyes narrowed. 'That would be most helpful,' he said, and Matilda laughed.

Somehow, she was one step ahead of him again.

Chapter 33

Thomas was right, he didn't sleep. He tossed and turned as his mind went over the case, backward and forward, with every door closing in front of him. Then he would think of Matilda in all her beauty, clever and defiant and damn distracting. He gave up at first light, pushed the sheet off himself and rose. He tried to keep the noise down so as not to wake his nephew, Teddy, sleeping in the bedroom down the hallway. An hour later, groomed and dressed, he was in the archives section of the police station requesting the death file for Mr Cornish – Mrs Sophie Cornish's husband.

'Let's just check if that was death by natural causes,' he said to himself, departing for his office.

'What are you muttering to yourself there, Thom?' Harry asked, following him down the corridor. Thomas swung around.

'Ah, Harry, morning. I've just ordered the post-mortem file for Mr Cornish. We should have it shortly.'

'Good, breakfast then while we wait, come on,' Harry said and headed to the police quarters canteen. 'The missus had an early church meeting, so I told her I'd eat at the office. I suspect you haven't eaten?'

'No, I'm starving,' Thomas agreed. It was many hours since his last meal – a bite on the run with Harry before last night's wait-and-watch at the gallery.

'What a night,' he said, thinking aloud.

'Never a dull moment,' Harry agreed.

The canteen was doing a good trade and they grabbed a tray and plate each and helped themselves to a good-sized hot breakfast before hearing a call from the corner of the room.

'Thom, Harry, here,' Burton, a colleague from Thomas's training days, called out. The last time they had seen each other was at the pub after work where a few too many drinks and women were celebrated.

Thomas and Harry joined the small group in the corner who had cleared room for them on the table.

'Caught yourself an artist murderer yet, lads?' Burton asked.

'Not like you to take this long, Thom,' Lou, Burton's partner, ragged him.

'Don't you be stressing my boy out there, you two.' Harry gave them a good-humoured dig, and the men laughed.

'All in good time,' Thomas said. 'We'd hate to arrest the wrong guy,' he said and grinned. Burton and his partner, Lou, had done just that and got their wings clipped along with it.

'Yeah, well, *touché*,' Burton said with a smirk, and passed the salt. They talked a little of the ineptitude of management – a favourite conversation amongst all employees – and then Lou spoke up.

'I knew the husband of that woman who owns the paintings from your dead artists,' he said.

Thomas and Harry looked at him with interest.

'Cornish?' Harry asked.

'That's him,' Lou confirmed. 'Nice bloke, used to play golf at my club. You met him too, Burty, once or twice. Not much of a golfer, mind you, but we were all envious when he hitched up with the younger bride.'

'Yeah, well money will earn you that,' Burton said. 'Meanwhile, Thom and I have to pay for it,' he joked.

'Not these days. I'm courting,' Thomas said.

Burton's eyes widened. 'You finally asked her out and she said yes! Saints preserve us.'

Thomas laughed. 'You'll keep. So, what can you tell us about Mr Cornish, Lou? How was his health?'

Lou shook his head. 'I know where you're going with that. He was never an overly robust bloke. Still, I was surprised on hearing of his death; he appeared in good health and humour just the week before his death when we had a round of golf.'

'He'd be more attractive if he wasn't in good health,' Burton added. 'Old, rich, and as my grandma used to say – God rest her soul – one foot in the grave, the other on a banana peel.'

The men chuckled, and Thomas shook his head at his friend.

'Ordered the post-mortem file?' Lou asked.

Thomas nodded. 'Expecting it any moment and we'll

check with the coroner too, just in case there's something that might have slipped through when suspicion wasn't called for the first time around.'

'The technologies are getting so good now, it's hard for the crims to get away with anything,' Burton said. 'I almost feel sorry for them.'

'But still, someone has got away with killing two artists,' Harry said and sighed. 'No evident suspects, no notable motives and we've only a couple of leads left to follow.'

Thomas nodded. 'If they don't pan out, well, it's back to the starting block.'

'There was one interesting thing about the whole Cornish marriage,' Lou added. 'I mean, if you're desperate, every bit of information helps, doesn't it?'

'Hell yeah,' Harry said. 'What have you got?'

Lou shrugged. 'Gossip. But the marriage caused a bit of a problem between Cornish and his friend. The friend had his eye on Mrs Cornish first but made the mistake of introducing her to the late Mr Cornish.'

Harry and Thomas exchanged looks.

'Mr Cornish's good friend wouldn't be a doctor, by any chance?' Harry asked.

'That rings a bell, I believe he was. Couldn't tell you his name though, but gossip was that it came to blows and put a strain on the friendship for a while. I guess with Cornish gone, the doctor can pursue the widow and try his luck again.'

'Lou, we owe you a drink,' Harry said and tapped Thomas's shoulder as he rose.

Lou looked surprised and Burton said, 'Not finishing that sausage then?'

But the two detectives were gone in moments, a new zest in their step. The doctor was lining up better than they thought as a potential suspect. They were yet to determine what his connection was with the two deceased artists other than being a patron and lover of art. But one piece of the puzzle at a time… at least that's what Harry was always telling Thomas when he ran off too fast in one direction.

Chapter 34

Thomas could hear laughter and female voices as he and Harry returned to their offices from the police canteen. He was intent on seeing if Mr Cornish's post-mortem file had arrived before a visit to the coroner. He glanced at Harry, narrowing his eyes, and Harry chuckled.

'Well, they did say they were going to give you an update on the doctor if he was in the house. The gallery house, that is,' Harry reminded him.

Thomas entered his office to find Matilda and Miss Doran being kept company by the desk sergeant and another handsome young constable who was smiling at something Matilda was saying.

'Ah, here they are now,' the desk sergeant said, and all eyes turned to them. 'We'll leave you with the detectives then.' With the constable in tow, the police officers hurried out.

Thomas gave a small bow. 'Miss Doran, Matilda.'

'Ladies,' Harry said, offering a similar salute.

'How charming your colleagues are,' Matilda said to Thomas.

'Yes, when they choose to be,' he said unenthusiastically. Harry gave the ladies a wink at Thomas's mood.

'We're on our way to the *Women's Journal* and thought you might wish to avail of our observations,' Matilda said.

'We met the doctor,' Alice finished, excited. 'A most interesting character.'

'Would you care to be seated?' Harry asked, remembering his manners even if Thomas didn't. 'Tea perhaps?'

Matilda thanked him. 'Too kind, Detective Dart, but we know how busy you are and how important it is to find this killer,' she said the last word in a hushed toned as if not to cause panic in the police hallways.

'Plus, we can't be late for work. We have a weekly editorial meeting this morning,' Alice said.

'Of course,' Thomas agreed. 'Your observations, then? They will be welcomed.'

Matilda nodded. 'I shall give you my observations first and then the factual comments Dr Humphries made. I will leave Alice to give you her thoughts as she desires.'

The two men nodded. Thomas did his best to look as if he was taking her seriously, even if he thought she was quite adorable with her solemnity. He cleared his throat and Matilda proceeded.

'I found Dr Humphries to be pretentious, as if moving in the right circles was important to him and the right connections gave him prestige, instead of relying on his character to achieve the same.' Matilda glanced at Alice.

'I completely agree, Matilda,' she said. 'He was very British in that respect. I have found since being in Australia that class does not seem so important, but yet it appeared that status seemed very important to Dr Humphries.'

'What did he say or do to make you think that?' Harry asked, drilling down.

Matilda nodded and continued. 'I studied him and he did not seem to take an interest in talking to anyone who he thought would not advance his status. Us, for example.'

'Agreed,' Alice said. 'At first, he was quite dismissive of us and then Gideon introduced Matilda as his sister, and myself as a ward of my uncle, who is known for being an art benefactor. Suddenly Dr Humphries found us much more interesting.'

Matilda laughed. 'Yes indeed.'

Thomas's brow furrowed and his hands clenched. 'And what did you think of him once he regaled you with his attention?'

'I thought he tried too hard. While he was handsome and clearly a clever man, he felt like a chameleon,' Matilda said.

Alice's eyes widened in admiration. 'That's a good description, Matilda. He did seem to change depending on whom he was talking with at that moment.'

Thomas relaxed a little on hearing her views on the good doctor. He was a man secure in himself, but he knew the character of men and that Matilda was a rose that many men would covet.

'Now to our discussion with him, which was brief, mind you,' Matilda said. 'I asked him if he was putting in a silent bid, and he said Mrs Cornish had asked him to bid on her behalf.'

Thomas looked at Harry and said, 'There's that connection again.'

Alice took a turn. 'I said that we had the pleasure of knowing Mrs Cornish as well, hoping to glean more from him, and Dr Humphries said that they were old friends and she was very dear to him.'

Matilda nodded. 'The way he said it was strangely intimate. But as for placing Mrs Cornish's bid, well, he didn't put the bid in,' Matilda said, 'because I asked Gideon at the end of the evening if Mrs Cornish or Dr Humphries had bid on any of the artwork and he said no. Mind you they all sold for a phenomenal amount. Gideon is thrilled.'

'That's brilliant news, Miss Hayward,' Harry agreed.

'Good job, Matilda, Miss Doran,' Thomas said, his eyes narrowing as he thought. 'So, if Dr Humphries did not bid, was he just being a name-dropper and pretentious when he mentioned Mrs Cornish?'

'Or was he being territorial?' Harry asked. 'Who else was privy to your conversation?'

'Oh, several wealthy men, so there is every chance he was staking a claim on Mrs Cornish, Detective Dart,' Matilda said. She caused Thomas to bristle without realising it. The thought of wealthy, influential men spending time with Matilda did not sit well with him. He could not offer her that life. Oblivious, Matilda continued, 'Well, that's the best I could do. Alice?'

'I think we have covered all our observations,' she said. 'Best we are off.'

'That was extremely helpful, ladies, thank you,' Thomas said.

'Indeed,' Harry agreed. 'We are on our way to the morgue, let us see you out.'

Alice grimaced. 'The morgue, what a shame on such a fine day.'

Harry nodded and smiled. 'Such is the life of the detective. I hope your view this morning is much more pleasant than the morgue, Miss Doran.'

*****

The coroner looked at the post-mortem file of Mr Cornish and then turned his attention to the two detectives. He tapped the file.

'Dead as a doornail,' Dr Nevins said and the men chuckled.

'Thanks for the diagnosis, we'll be off then,' Thomas joked.

Dr Nevins grinned, not something he did often in the mortuary. 'But down to business,' he said. 'Yes, it appears that Dr Robert Humphries – your doctor in question – signed the death certificate for Mr Cornish, but that need not be a suspicious matter. If what you say is true, then Dr Humphries knew both Mr and Mrs Maxwell Cornish before they met. He introduced them, did he not?'

'He did,' Harry confirmed.

'Well, he may have been Mr Cornish's regular physician and well versed in his ailments. Thus, death was not unexpected or suspicious and not requiring a post-mortem.'

Thomas nodded. 'Is there anything in the cause of death that might be suspicious if we were to cast a new light on it?'

Dr Nevins placed the file down and pushed his thin steel-rimmed glasses a little further up his nose. 'Yes and no. There is nothing suspicious or overlooked because there is little of anything in this report. The cause of death – heart disease – is a common cause of death for men of Mr Cornish's age. Without seeing Mr Cornish's medical files, I can't tell you if he had been treated for this long term or if any of his existing ailments contributed to it.'

'Other than asking Dr Humphries directly, what would you suggest would be an appropriate course of action if we wanted to question Mr Cornish's medical history?' Harry asked.

'First, I would determine if Dr Humphries was his regular doctor,' Dr Nevins said. 'If not then I'd be getting his medical files quick smart from his usual doctor and determining if his past ailments were consistent with the post-mortem cause of death.'

Thomas continued, 'If Dr Humphries was the medical doctor for Mr Cornish, then we need to cross-check his records with the patient's history.'

'Yes,' Dr Nevins agreed. 'If you still have doubts, then you may need to get the body exhumed and we'll take another look if too much time has not passed.'

'Right then. First, a visit to Dr Robert Humphries. Thank you, Patrick,' Thomas said. 'We'll leave you to the recently dead,' he joked, as the men departed.

Chapter 35

The doctor's office was in a shared room in Wickham Terrace, which was no surprise – it was a prestigious address for the medical fraternity and suites were expensive. If what Matilda and Alice said was true, then the pretentious Dr Humphries would want to be seen in this area. It was also close enough to the Roma Street police precinct for the men to walk the distance. As they made their way there at a good pace, they exchanged thoughts.

'Is it bad to wish the doctor is a murderer?' Thomas asked, and Harry chuckled.

'Let's hope so. Then we can get him off the street and close the case,' Harry agreed. 'He fits the bill in some areas, and if he is a chameleon, let's hope his true character is rougher, capable of murder.'

'We're short on suspects but you are right, he has a motive,' Thomas said. 'If he was in love with Mrs Cornish when she was Miss Sophie Reubens, then he might be the man who fell out with Mr Cornish when he introduced the pair and had her stolen from right under his nose. Jealousy and anger are well-respected motives for murder.'

'Agreed,' Harry said. 'I wonder if he is a member of the golf club, and if that is how he knew Cornish in the first place. If he bumped off the old fellow, then Mrs Cornish becomes a widow and available again. And a wealthy one at that.'

'A much more attractive prospect,' Thomas agreed. 'But connecting the other two artists to him...'

'Well, we know one of the artists, Benjamin Bannon, was a talented man who painted the then Miss Sophie Reubens before she married. She knew Dr Humphries and they both knew the artist,' Harry said, stepping back as a hansom cab came too close to them both.

'Jealousy again? Was Mr Bannon showing an interest in the widow and Dr Humphries removed the competition once more? Quite extreme courting,' Thomas said in jest. 'I wonder if he knew the other artist, Christopher Gill. If it is a small and tight community, I imagine he did.'

'We know that Mrs Cornish knew both of the artists because she or her husband owned two recent paintings by the deceased artists, so there's every chance they all knew of each other,' Harry said. 'Did Mr Gill have intentions too of winning Mrs Cornish's hand, I wonder, and the doctor was knocking off his competitors?'

'It would be a handy option,' Thomas joked. 'I'd like to know the doctor's background. If he owed money or has personal wealth.'

The two men arrived outside of the doctor's chambers within five minutes. Finding the right floor, they took the stairs to his rooms to find three patients seated and a young woman behind a reception desk.

'He'll be finished with a patient shortly if you care to take a seat. He then has a thirty-minute window,' the attractive receptionist informed them. She glanced at the other patients. 'They are waiting to see Dr Rubenstein.'

The men thanked her and declined a seat amongst the patients that looked less than healthy or who sported handkerchiefs near their faces. Within moments, the door open and a female patient departed. The receptionist waved the men into Dr Humphries' office and closed the door behind them. Harry showed his badge and introduced himself and Thomas.

'Gentlemen, please take a seat, I am always happy to assist our fine police constabulary,' he said. 'I hope you weren't waiting for long; I seem to attract many ladies in search of relief for their nerves.'

Harry cleared his throat, uncomfortable with the doctor's indiscretion. 'Barely minutes, thank you,' he responded.

Thomas' first impressions were that Matilda was right, Dr Humphries was full of charm. He guessed his age at early forties, his clothing looked expensive, his hair was groomed and cut in a manner to accentuate a curl, and a small moustache framed what would have been a weak top lip. Thomas's father would have declared Dr Humphries – in an unsavoury tone – a dandy. His demeanour quickly changed once the questioning began about his connection to Mr and Mrs Cornish.

'I'm a good friend and great admirer of Mrs Cornish,' he acknowledged, his eyes narrowing shrewdly and his voice losing a little of its plummy quality. 'In fact, I am a great admirer of both of the beautiful Reubens' cousins – Sophie and Sapphire.'

Thomas embellished the truth. 'We have information from several reliable sources that you intended to make an offer for Mrs Cornish's hand when she was Miss Sophie Reubens. However, a friend – that you introduced to her – availed himself of the opportunity first.'

Dr Humphries sat back and webbed his fingers across his lap. 'Yes. Can I ask what this might be concerning? Has she come to some harm?'

'No, not at all,' Harry assured him. 'Did you and Mr Maxwell Cornish have a falling out over the matter?'

'Well, falling out is a little harsh,' he said, scoffing at the terminology. 'I wasn't pleased, to say the least, and Maxwell knew of my intentions but acted in a moment of passion, or so he said. Miss Reubens, that is, Mrs Cornish accepted his hand, so that was the end of that.'

'Were you Mr Cornish's regular doctor?' Thomas asked.

'Yes, for many years.'

'And how long had he suffered from heart complaint?' Thomas continued. 'He wasn't a big man, how did he come to have this weakness?'

Dr Humphries's lips narrowed as the reason for the line of questioning became more evident. He endeavoured to impress the two gentlemen with his medical prognosis.

'It was a combination, I believe, of aortic stenosis and regurgitation. If Maxwell had abided by my constant warnings to rest more, mind his diet, especially in regard his imbibing, and manage his regimen to ensure his cutaneous circulation continued to be active, he would no doubt still be with us this day,' he pronounced.

Harry frowned. 'I thought he must have suffered from a past illness to the chest or childhood malignancy to have succumbed, when apparently he was quite fit and appeared in good health, or so we were told. He had a cook who, I understood, ensured he ate at home regularly and not at the club, and did not eat to excess.'

Thomas continued, 'And he was a keen golfer, undertaking regular activity. He also had a younger wife who no doubt insisted on his accompanying her frequently to activities,' he said, keeping his thoughts discreet and looking to Dr Humphries for a jealous reaction. He was satisfied with the outcome as Dr Humphries made a huffing sound.

'Being slight of build does not guarantee good health,' he said curtly.

'Could we see his medical records please?' Harry asked.

'I should say not. They are a private matter,' Dr Humphries said, his refined tone slipping and a roughness coming into his speech.

'The patient is dead, Dr Humphries,' Thomas reminded him, and then peppered him with questions. 'What is your relationship with the artist Benjamin Bannon?'

'Bannon? I barely knew him.'

'We were informed that you knew Mr Bannon and knew that he was painting the image of Mrs Cornish – then Miss Sophie Reubens – under the autumn blanket of leaves. You introduced Mr Cornish to Mr Bannon, and Mr Cornish bought the painting featuring Miss Sophie

Reubens promptly, along with the artist in the bath image and then claimed her hand as well,' Thomas said, watching and waiting for a reaction from the doctor.

Dr Humphries jumped to his feet. 'What exactly are you asking me? Any accusations that I had something to do with the death of Mr Cornish or those two artists is preposterous!'

'Your relationship with Mr Bannon?' Harry asked again.

The doctor looked from one detective to the other and took his chair again. He regained his composure and cleared his throat.

'Mr Bannon and I were childhood acquaintances,' he said.

'Really?' Thomas asked, interested, and lowered himself into the seat in front of the doctor's desk. 'And where would this be?'

'Our parents were from the Warwick district, and we were both school boarders at the Toowoomba Boys' College,' he said.

'Same year?' Harry asked, and the doctor nodded.

'So perhaps more than acquaintances,' Harry suggested.

'I did not see him for many years after school. We were at best, acquaintances.'

Thomas exchanged a look with Harry and both men knew it was time to slow down the interview – the answers may prove to be damming. It was turning out just as they hoped.

'When did you reignite your friendship?' Thomas asked.

'I met him at the club, here in Brisbane, and then on the golf course.'

'Were you Mr Bannon's doctor as well?' Thomas pushed.

Dr Humphries swallowed and nodded.

'What is your relationship with the deceased artist, Christopher Gill?' Harry asked.

'I didn't know him,' Dr Humphries said dismissively.

Thomas nodded, rose, and went to the door. Opening it, he asked in a low voice, 'Miss, could we please have the patient records for Christopher Gill, Benjamin Bannon and Maxwell Cornish?'

'Yes, sir,' she said without hesitation, jotting down the names and repeating them. Thomas thanked her and closed the door. He returned to sit opposite Dr Humphries. 'So Mr Gill was also a patient. Perhaps it is time to speak the truth now, Doctor.'

Women's Journal
Tuesday, 26 June 1888
Fortnightly edition Vol.1, No.16.
Price, 3d.

A *Story of Passion and Three Extraordinary Murders*

An exclusive interview with Detectives Thomas Ashdown and Harry Dart, and art benefactor, Mrs Maxwell Cornish.

Report by Matilda Hayward and Alice Doran.

Our fair city has been in the grip of panic with the recent outrageous murder of two pre-eminent artists. The *Women's Journal* can now reveal the extraordinary story of passion that has since been connected to the crime.

Respected doctor, Robert Humphries, recently practising at the Wickham Terrace suites, lost his heart to the beautiful Miss Sophie Reubens before her betrothal to Mr Maxwell Cornish. Dr Humphries assumed his affections would be reciprocated and he intended to make Miss Sophie Reubens his bride.

He introduced Miss Reubens to his schoolboy friend and successful artist, the late Mr Benjamin Bannon. Immediately, Mr Bannon insisted on capturing Miss Reubens' beauty for all time in his painting 'The Lady Sleeps in Season'.

Dr Humphries, who moved within the artistic circles of our city, also introduced the artist and Miss Reubens to his friend and former patient, Mr Maxwell Cornish.

Mrs Cornish recalls: 'We were enamoured from the moment we met,' she said. 'I could not be without Maxwell, nor he without me. He was charming and kind and swept me off my feet. We were married within months.'

Feeling betrayed by the haste in which Mr Cornish had won the heart of Miss Sophie Reubens, thus ruining Dr Humphries own future happiness, the two men had a falling out, and within nine months, Mr Cornish had passed away from heart failure. The bereaved Mrs Cornish described her observed mourning period as a time served with bitterness for a love and shared life cut so short.

Dr Humphries then determined to present himself once again as a suitable amour to the widowed Mrs Cornish, after the appropriate period. To his dismay, other suitors, including his artist friends, Mr Bannon and Mr Christopher Gill, began to call on Mrs Sophie Cornish.

Soon both men were found dead in a manner most peculiar and representing that of a selected work from their famous paintings.

The detectives from the Roma Street Police Station had their work cut out for them when little evidence or motive presented itself. But Detectives Thomas Ashdown and Harry Dart proved themselves again to be the shining lights of the force, with a breakthrough in the case.

'We were fortunate to have the support of fellow officers and the public,' Detective Ashdown said. 'Information provided to us about the long-time friendship of the doctor and the falling out with Mr Cornish, cast the doctor into a new light.'

'We soon discovered that the doctor and the two artists were good friends, but that the doctor felt he had been the subject of their amusement on losing the hand of Mrs Cornish,' Detective Ashdown explained. 'Humiliated, he determined to accelerate Mr Cornish's death.'

The recent exhumation of Mr Cornish's body showed evidence of poisoning, which was not clear in the death certificate signed off on by none other than Dr Humphries himself.

Detective Dart said discord found its way into the Cornish household as Mrs Cornish felt overwhelmed with the doctor's attention at a time when she was mourning the loss of her husband.

'Once the doctor realised his two artistic friends also intended to pay court to the widowed Mrs Cornish, he soon discovered he was not the preferred suitor for her hand,' Detective Dart said.

Detective Ashdown said Dr Robert Humphries felt slighted by his friends and vowed revenge.

Thus, he endeavoured to show them how skilled he was despite not being an artist, and designed their deaths to emulate their paintings.

'If imitation is the sincerest form of flattery, Dr Humphries gave the men the death he thought they deserved,' Detective Ashdown said.

Mrs Cornish bears the heartbreak of her husband's death and the terrible shock that the gentleman that she believed to be a dear friend took the lives of those dearest to her.

In this sad tale, passion transpired as a motive for committing three heinous crimes.

Dr Humphries wrote a note which the detectives have permitted the *Women's Journal* to reprint:

'Have mercy, I beg of you, for I endeavoured to do good in my life. But moments of horrible madness consumed me to commit these crimes. Beauty had robbed me of my heart and mind. It was too much for a man to bear.'

Dr Humphries remains in Boggo Road Gaol. The jury will determine his fate.

Chapter 36

Thomas was feeling intrepid about attending lunch at the Hayward household. He was, and had been, a permanent fixture at the Sunday table for close to twenty years, since he was a young boy, and his presence had always been expected. He knew the house as well as he knew his own childhood home, but after the tension with Gideon and the unfortunate display of fighting in the Hayward hallway last time they met, stepping over the threshold had him concerned. He need not have been, as the matter was resolved early.

'Ah, here he is then,' Gideon said as Thomas entered the drawing-room with Matilda on his arm.

Thomas's eyes narrowed, ready for an assault of some form – words or physical – but Gideon extended his hand.

'Truce. Although it's not the first time I could have whipped your butt had I not been held back,' he said, with the hint of a grin.

Thomas shook Gideon's hand. 'Yet, I can't recall that ever happening,' he joked and gave Gideon a sly smile.

'Nor I, for that matter,' Daniel said, joining them while

Matilda went to talk with Aunt Audrey and Alice, who was a guest of Daniel's for the church service and lunch.

Aunt Audrey was not one to be left out of the conversation and a short time later when they were all seated, she brought the matter to a head again.

'You young men will have to accept that now your life-long friend and soon to be brother-in-law, Thomas, is a respected officer of the law and duty comes first and must come first,' she said.

Matilda sighed. 'A little premature on the wedding bells, Aunt.' But no one else was focussed on that aspect of Aunt Audrey's comment.

'I think the family should come first,' Gideon said, deferring to his father, who sat on his left. 'Pa, do you not agree?'

Thomas shuffled uncomfortably; he knew he was to be outnumbered and the room suddenly felt too small. He felt Matilda's gentle touch and turned to smile at her.

'It is a tricky one,' Mr Hayward said, not immediately siding with his youngest son.

'Nonsense.' Aunt Audrey cut them both off. 'One must have a good moral conscience and a duty to the community. How could you expect Thomas to let your client get away with murder just so that your evening and the artist's sales are not spoiled, Gideon? Saints preserve us!'

'I was only asking for Mr Dominey to get away with murder for one night,' Gideon said. His twin, Elijah, chuckled.

'You need not laugh about that, Elijah,' Aunt Audrey

scolded, as if the men were still young. 'You are usually the most sensible at this table, except for Amos, of course,' she said, looking fondly at her favourite Hayward nephew. 'If the situation was in your workplace, let us imagine an emergency were to happen at the hospital and you were the doctor on shift, would you operate on your brother before patients just as needy?'

Elijah thought about it. 'Most likely yes, Aunt,' he conceded, and Gideon grinned, pulling his twin brother in closer for a one-armed hug.

'Of course, you would,' Gideon said.

'I'm sorry, Aunt. It would be a terrible ethical dilemma, but I would have to save him,' Elijah said with a smile to his twin. 'However, if Thomas and Gideon came in at the same time both needing assistance, then I might need some time to think.'

Gideon pushed him away with a smirk.

'And you, Amos,' Matilda asked, and turned to her eldest brother. 'Would you defend us through your law practice if you knew we were guilty of an atrocity?'

'Well, it is easier for me,' he said, not wishing Aunt Audrey to be without an ally. 'The law says everyone must have a defence whether we perceive them to be innocent or guilty, and the jury determines their guilt. So, I could be legally obliged to defend you bunch of lawbreakers.'

Aunt Audrey sighed. 'Adversaries, all of you. Let me look outside the Hayward family for a sensible response. What do you think, dear Mrs Hayward?' she asked Amos's wife, Minnie.

Minnie sat up straighter, feeling important for being asked. 'I agree with you, Aunt Audrey, we need to take a moral stand.'

Amos was not surprised by her answer; Minnie had come from a strict religious household.

Aunt Audrey nodded her approval. 'And you, Miss Doran?' she asked of Alice.

Alice put her head to the side and thought. 'It is a pickle, Aunt Audrey,' she said in her English accent and addressing Aunt Audrey as if she were a relative, having been invited to do so. 'If I were Thomas, I would follow the letter of the law, but if I were Gideon, I'd do my best to stretch it. If it were my family and I liked them, well I'd probably bend the law, as shocking as that may sound, but I would do the same for you, Aunt Audrey.'

'Goodness, well I guess that is worthy of consideration,' Aunt Audrey said and then gathered herself. 'But I think you have a point, young lady. This is indeed a close family and Thomas has been a member of our family for so long we sometimes forget he is not a Hayward by birth.'

Her words affected Thomas, and he swallowed before speaking.

'I assure you all, I was conscious of Gideon's situation and I wanted to be fair to him. But I was also fearful for the safety and whereabouts of Miss Reubens and, by association, the ladies in Mr Dominey's presence, including Matilda and Miss Doran.'

Mr Hayward senior raised his glass. 'Admirably said, Thomas, well done. I would like to make a toast to the talented and successful young people around our table. Every one of you achieving great things. To the achievers.'

'To the achievers,' the group said and raised their glasses.

After they sipped, Aunt Audrey added, 'I thought your article was very good, Matilda, Miss Doran.'

'Thank you, Aunt!' Matilda exclaimed. 'I didn't think you approved of my writing for the journal, let alone read my work.'

'I too, am thrilled to know you read the *Women's Journal*, Aunt Audrey,' Alice said.

'I purchased a copy when Matilda first told me she was writing for them, and then I decided to subscribe. There have been some excellent articles,' she said.

'You are full of surprises, dear sister,' Mr Hayward said, 'and a good example of how we can all be open to change and support each other.'

Mr Hayward's words delivered his implied and unspoken lesson. Thomas and Gideon exchanged sheepish looks, despite the fact Mr Hayward did not look at them directly.

Thomas cleared his throat. 'So, Gids, did the paintings all sell?' He accepted the plate of potatoes from Amos at the end of the table, and held it as Matilda served them both before Thomas passed it on.

'They not only sold, but sold beyond our wildest expectations,' Gideon said.

'They were exceptional,' Matilda said.

'I would like to see the exhibition before it closes, Gideon, before the paintings are shipped to the buyers,' Aunt Audrey said. She turned to Thomas. 'Perhaps you might accompany me, young man, and we can talk about your intentions for my niece. Unless my brother, Mr Hayward, has already had this discussion?'

Thomas shuffled uncomfortably as Matilda smiled at him, and the brothers did their best to hide their grins.

'I have not discussed Thomas and Matilda's future with either of them, sister,' Mr Hayward said, smiling. 'Please, be my guest.'

'Excellent,' she said, turning to Thomas.

'It would be a pleasure to escort you, Aunt Audrey,' he said, looking somewhat pained.

'I too would like to see Mr Dominey's artwork,' Minnie said with a glance to her husband, Amos. 'Perhaps we can make a party of it.'

'Indeed,' Amos agreed.

'That's a lovely idea, Minnie,' Matilda said. 'There's a wonderful tea house nearby that we could visit after seeing the paintings.' She smiled at Thomas, who did his best not to sigh. The last thing he wanted was more time in the company of art and artists, but for the sake of pleasing Aunt Audrey and Matilda, he would fulfil his duty and admirably.

He felt a kick to the shins and looked up to see Daniel grinning at him from the opposite side of the table. He gave him a smirk.

'Daniel,' Aunt Audrey said on seeing his grin, 'I'd like to join you and Miss Doran at another time for tea as well. I'm sure Miss Doran, being so far from home, would appreciate someone enquiring about your intentions on her behalf too.'

'Thank you, Aunt Audrey,' Alice said, with a blush and smile, while avoiding looking at Daniel.

'Of course, Aunt Audrey, that would be a pleasure,' he said and caught Thomas's amused look and gave him a less than affectionate look.

It was lunch as usual at the Hayward household.

*****

After lunch, Thomas wanted some time alone with Matilda.

'Let's take a walk,' he suggested to her once the family saw Aunt Audrey, Minnie and Amos off. Gideon and Elijah were heading out, and Mr Hayward was off to his study to read.

She enamoured him when she looked up at him, her eyes bright and lips kissable.

'I could do with some exercise after Cook's wonderful efforts and it is a fine afternoon for some fresh air,' she agreed, understanding his motives to have some time alone.

Before he could offer his arm and get Matilda out of the house, Daniel appeared at his side.

'A walk! Excellent idea, Alice, what do you say?' Daniel asked.

'A perfect afternoon for it,' she agreed.

Thomas frowned and Matilda grinned, giving him a playful dig in the side. He refrained from giving his best friend a frustrated look and intended to fall behind Daniel and Alice for a few moments alone with Matilda.

The couples headed down the driveway, out onto the streets and towards the river and parkland. Thomas avoided any of the areas where he might be forced into duty to break up a brawl or send a drunkard on his way. He let Daniel and Alice get a small distance ahead and, as they entered the park, slowed more.

'I have to talk with you about something that I've given some serious thought to recently,' he said, and looked uncomfortable.

Matilda's smile faded as she saw his intensity, and she frowned slightly.

'What is it? Are you upset about my brothers' reaction to the recent case and my loyalty? It won't be like that again, I'm sure. After all, how often will our paths and crime cross?' she said, talking faster now as she sensed the discussion was not going to end well.

Thomas shook his head and took her hand a little tighter as she pulled away.

'It's not that, do not concern yourself. I understand what was going on and if Gideon and I were in opposite roles it probably would have played out the same,' he said. He looked at Matilda, then back to the path in front of them.

'I think you might be best suited to someone else,' he started.

She stopped and turned to face him. 'You think this is a mistake?' Tears welled in her eyes. 'I was worried you might decide you wanted only a friendship with me. It is because I did not defend you appropriately, isn't it?'

'No,' he said, 'it has nothing to do with the recent art gallery incident, I assure you.'

'I… I release you, of course, Thomas.'

'No, no, Matilda, I don't want to be released,' he said,

reaching for her despite the impropriety, his hand touched her face. 'I am convinced that you are, and have always been, the only woman for me. I have loved you since we were youngsters and you used to drive me crazy with your competitiveness. You continue to drive me crazy being so close to me and not realising that I am dying to kiss you.'

She breathed a little easier. 'Then what is going on? You are scaring me, Thomas.'

'I am sorry, I don't mean to, but this week you were in several situations where you were surrounded by men who could provide you with more than I will ever be able to offer you.'

She tilted her head as she studied him, and he wanted to grab and kiss her for being so infuriatingly beautiful.

'I'm not sure I understand,' she said.

'You thought of my situation recently and if I should attempt to woo Mrs Cornish. I must offer you the same consideration, even if it will destroy me.' He cleared his throat. 'At the buyers' evening at the gallery, did you not think once, twice maybe, that you belonged with one of those gentlemen? I am sure you could have anyone you pleased, Matilda, and I must be fair. Would you like to date a gentleman from those ranks with the better expectations they can provide you?'

Thomas held his breath, waiting for her response, but he did not have to wait for long.

'Good grief, no!' she exclaimed in true Matilda style, like it was the most ridiculous idea in the world. 'If I wanted to move in wealthy art circles, Aunt Audrey would have had me there long before now. You have worried yourself about this since the exhibition?'

He looked away and with her arm through his, began walking again. Thomas gave a slight nod of his head.

'Let us not talk of this again,' she said. 'I am the happiest I have ever been. I have a handsome man that I love and trust and have long admired. I have a role at the *Women's Journal* that excites me, and the love and affection of my family and friends, old and new. Without you, Thomas, none of that would look as good. You are my future.'

He smiled and kissed her hand, pleased and relieved. He then became serious again.

'I won't give you this opportunity again, Matilda. Once you commit to me now, at this moment, I will never let you go from my heart and my arms. Be warned.'

He heard her breath hitch and then she sighed.

'Promise me that will be so?' she said.

'I promise. Let us agree we are stuck with each other then,' he said, smiling down on her as she looked up at him, her face beautiful and bright and full of affection.

'With pleasure,' she agreed.

They strode along for a little while in their happiness, both content to share the moment with the lightest of allowed touches.

And then Matilda said, 'I'll race you to catch up with Dan and Alice.'

'Alright… No, what am I saying, no, Matilda, we're in public and we are not twelve.'

She sighed and pouted.

'Besides, I would win anyway,' he said and took off. Hearing her laugh, he slowed down until she passed him and he began his chase. Again.

He was right where he wanted to be, in arm's reach of Matilda and behind her to catch her if she should fall.

THE END.

Mystery at the Asylum

Miss Matilda Hayward has a nose for a story which serves her well as a writer for the Women's Journal newspaper. Her beau, Detective Thomas Ashdown, is not quite as enthusiastic about her role.

When Matilda's brother, Elijah, takes up a doctor's position at the Asylum for the Insane, she volunteers, seeking more life experience to improve her writing. Joined by her illustrator friend, Miss Georgina Urry, the two ladies are thrust into the mystery of several strange asylum deaths as patients believe they can fly. When Thomas is sent to investigate, their worlds collide. Now the race is on to find the sinister threat dwelling inside the dark and gloomy walls of the asylum.

There is secrecy, danger, and love afoot!

*****

You might also enjoy by this author…

The Forgotten House (historical fiction):

"If you've ever been truly in love, you'll identify with Lexie and James." Judy Alter, Story Circle Book Reviews.

Once the grandest of homes, now deserted and ramshackle; Autumn Manor lies in ruins. But when Carrie Howell asks her granddaughter, Rachael, to stop awhile in front of the old mansion, Rachel decides to investigate the house's history. Behind the facade, she finds a love story interrupted by war. Who were these people her grandmother was remembering, and what was her connection?

Jesse Clarke series (cosy mysteries):

Death by Sugar:

"If you are a fan of Kathryn Ledson or Janet Evanovich you will love unravelling the mysteries in the Jesse Clarke series." Carol, Reading, Writing and Riesling

Private investigator, Jesse Clarke, thought sugar was such a friendly substance, until it appeared in two of her cases for all the wrong reasons.

Traces of sugar were connected to a bomb that blew up her client's Mercedes. Was the bomb meant to kill or was it just a warning of what was to come? And could sugar have duped the immune system of a client's mother over thirty years ago, resulting in death? Juggling the two cases—one in the present and one in the past—Jesse finds herself talking to the living and the dead to get results.

Death by Disguise:

"A fantastic read that had me laughing; it thoroughly surprised me!" Christine – Goodreads

The dead are walking and it is not even Halloween! Sassy private investigator Jesse Clarke knew it would not be a normal week when two dead people are spotted alive but their death certificates say otherwise, Spiderman steals a collection of costumes made for the next Comic Con, and Batman drops in to warn her that all is not as it seems. Supported by her own man of steel—the tall, dark and handsome Dominic; business partner Ed; police contact Officer Jason who has more than a professional interest in Jesse; and, best friend Melanie, Jesse finds herself talking to witches, superheroes and morticians to solve her two cases and looking behind the disguises for answers!

Death by Reunion:

Jesse Clarke's 10-year school reunion boasted a few shocks – and that didn't include Jesse running a publicity and private investigator business. Rather, the talk of the reunion was Alex Bryson, the overweight kid who transformed himself thanks to winning a place on the TV reality program, *Lose it!* But a week after the reunion, Alex is dead.

That's not the only reunion that's taking up Jesse's time. At a family reunion and 80th birthday celebration for a family matriarch, a very expensive Titanic relic goes missing – a Titanic Mourning Bear. And now T-Bear, as he is known, is showing up all over the country! With support from her boyfriend, Dominic, along with her grumpy business partner Ed, Police Officer Jason, and Jesse's enthusiastic best friend, Melanie, Jesse is back solving mysteries while juggling publicity clients include Mona and her choir, again.

About the Author:

After studying English Literature, Media, and Communications at universities in Queensland, Australia, and obtaining a Counselling Diploma, Helen Goltz has worked as a journalist, producer and marketer in print, TV, radio and public relations. She was born in Toowoomba and has made her home in Brisbane.

Visit her website at: www.helengoltz.com

Or Facebook at: www.facebook.com/HelenGoltz.Author

Follow on Twitter at: https://twitter.com/HelenGwriter

Sign-up for Helen's newsletter to hear when the next *Miss Hayward & the Detective* adventure is released!